Damian's Conquest is a work of fiction. Names, characters, places, and incidents are the products of the author's imagination and are used fictitiously. Any resemblance to actual events, locales, or persons, living or dead, is entirely coincidental.

Cover design: Leah Kaye Suttle
Cover photo: Shutterstock
Author Photo: © Marti Corn Photography

Printed in the United States of America

Books by Tina Folsom

Samson's Lovely Mortal (Scanguards Vampires, Book 1)
Amaury's Hellion (Scanguards Vampires, Book 2)
Gabriel's Mate (Scanguards Vampires, Book 3)
Yvette's Haven (Scanguards Vampires, Book 4)
Zane's Redemption (Scanguards Vampires, Book 5)
Quinn's Undying Rose (Scanguards Vampires, Book 6)
Oliver's Hunger (Scanguards Vampires, Book 7)
Thomas's Choice (Scanguards Vampires, Book 8)
Silent Bite (Scanguards Vampires, Book 8 1/2)
Cain's Identity (Scanguards Vampires, Book 9)
Luther's Return (Scanguards Vampires, Book 10)
Blake's Pursuit (Scanguards Vampires, Book 11)
Fateful Reunion (Scanguards Vampires, Book 11 1/2)
John's Yearning (Scanguards Vampires, Book 12)
Ryder's Storm (Scanguards Vampires, Book 13)
Damian's Conquest (Scanguards Vampires, Book 14)

Lover Uncloaked (Stealth Guardians, Book 1)
Master Unchained (Stealth Guardians, Book 2)
Warrior Unraveled (Stealth Guardians, Book 3)
Guardian Undone (Stealth Guardians, Book 4)
Immortal Unveiled (Stealth Guardians, Book 5)
Protector Unmatched (Stealth Guardians, Book 6)
Demon Unleashed (Stealth Guardians, Book 7)

Ace on the Run (Code Name Stargate, Book 1)
Fox in plain Sight (Code Name Stargate, Book 2)
Yankee in the Wind (Code Name Stargate, Book 3)
Tiger on the Prowl (Code Name Stargate, Book 4)

A Touch of Greek (Out of Olympus, Book 1)
A Scent of Greek (Out of Olympus, Book 2)
A Taste of Greek (Out of Olympus, Book 3)
A Hush of Greek (Out of Olympus, Book 4)

Venice Vampyr (Novellas 1 – 4)

Teasing (The Hamptons Bachelor Club, Book 1)
Enticing (The Hamptons Bachelor Club, Book 2)
Beguiling (The Hamptons Bachelor Club, Book 3)
Scorching (The Hamptons Bachelor Club, Book 4)
Alluring (The Hamptons Bachelor Club, Book 5)
Sizzling (The Hamptons Bachelor Club, Book 6)

DAMIAN'S CONQUEST

SCANGUARDS VAMPIRES #14

SCANGUARDS HYBRIDS #2

TINA FOLSOM

1

"Do you think I should have breast reduction surgery?" Naomi Sutton asked.

Heather, her best friend since high school, stared at her. They were having lunch in the food court of the Westfield Shopping Center just around the corner from Naomi's office at the San Francisco Chronicle, where she worked as a news reporter. It didn't happen often that they had time for lunch together, because Heather worked in Mission Bay at one of UCSF's new medical research buildings. But today, Heather had to run errands downtown, and they'd gotten together for an impromptu lunch.

"Why would you do that?" Heather asked, her dark-brown eyes boring into her.

"Well, wouldn't you in my shoes?" Naomi gestured to Heather's perfect figure. "You're a size six, and look great, but look at me, I can barely fit into a twelve as is, and with my boobs, I always look like a cupcake with frosting spilling over the top."

Heather laughed. "You don't look like a cupcake. You're just... uh, voluptuous."

"Voluptuous, my ass. People stare at me all the time."

"You mean guys check you out," Heather corrected her.

"I get so self-conscious, you know. I always have the feeling I should cover up."

"Don't do that, Naomi. You look gorgeous. You have beautiful blond hair. I wish I had that, instead of dull brown. And on top of it you've got blue eyes. No wonder guys look at you, you're pretty. So what if you're a little larger than other women? Not everybody can be model-thin. And guys like boobs. I wish I had more up top." She gestured to her breasts, which to Naomi looked perfectly proportioned. "Just because your ex is now dating a skinny bitch doesn't mean that he dumped you because you're...uh..."

"Fat?" Naomi helped.

"You're not fat. Your figure is more like what women used to look like, you know, in the fifties. Besides, Marilyn Monroe wasn't skinny either. There. You're basically like Marilyn Monroe. And nobody ever told her to get a breast reduction or lose weight."

Naomi forced a smile. "You sure? It's just, I haven't been on a date in months… and I figured maybe it's because guys want a slim girlfriend."

Heather chuckled. "The reason you haven't been on a date in a while is because you intimidate guys."

"I don't intimidate guys."

"Yes, you do. You're bossy, opinionated, and you don't take shit from anybody."

"Well, in a guy those characteristics would be positive. He'd be seen as assertive."

Heather shrugged. "Yeah, but that's the world we live in. Guys want women who're easier to handle. Whereas you are Capital-T grade trouble. You'll just need to find the right guy who's up for the challenge."

"Hah!" Naomi blew out a big breath. "Guess I'll be single and dateless for a while then."

Naomi's cell phone chimed. She looked at it and saw a message from her editor, Wei Guo. "I've gotta get back. Wei wants to see me."

She quickly typed a message to let him know that she was on her way.

Heather sighed. "Bad timing. I wanted you to come to the Halloween store with me. I still need a costume for Carrie's party tonight."

"Sorry, no can do."

"Why don't I buy you an outfit, and you'll come to the party with me?"

Naomi rose and grabbed her jacket. "You know how much I hate costume parties. Or parties in general. It's just another excuse for everybody to get shitfaced and behave badly."

"Mr. Right could be at the party, waiting for you," Heather teased.

"More like Mr. Right-Now," Naomi said with a chuckle. "I'll think about it, okay?"

"Just don't wait too long to make a decision. The stores are all pretty much out of decent costumes already."

Despite her claim to think about it, Naomi knew it was doubtful that she would go to the Halloween party with Heather. She would most likely curl up in front of the television and watch a horror flick while eating ice cream.

Naomi rushed back to the office. Her editor immediately called her into his office.

"Hey, Wei, what did you want to speak to me about?"

The short Chinese man with the full black hair pointed to a manila folder on his desk. "I want you to check something out for me. We got reports that there might be something odd going on at one of the nightclubs South of Market."

Naomi raised an eyebrow. "What do you mean by going on? Drug dealing?"

To her surprise, Wei shook his head. He tapped on the folder. "Neighbors are reporting that people are coming out of the back entrance of this club covered in blood."

"Are you saying the neighbors witnessed a crime at the club? Have you asked Katrina what info she can get from SFPD about that? Because I haven't seen anything like that come across my desk." After all, she handled mostly entertainment news.

"That's because the neighbor who saw this, a Mrs. Zhang, says the police dismissed her claims. And she couldn't give them any definite proof that a crime happened there. Apparently, she's previously lodged noise complaints against the club, so the police think she's just stirring up some shit again."

"So why are we looking into it then? I mean she's probably doing just that: complaining about the club because she's annoyed about the noise. And since the police aren't doing enough about it, she's escalating." Naomi shrugged.

Wei rubbed his neck. "That's probably what it is, but what if there's something to the story after all? What if there's some kinky BDSM shit going on down there? Or some satanic rituals? You know, like those fraternity societies. Why would she invent something so outlandish like people with blood all over their clothes and their faces? We could do with a juicy story. Our subscription numbers are down. Find something. Just go there, and look around."

"Why me?" Naomi asked. "That's more a story for Katrina. She works the crime beat."

"Yeah, and she's pushing fifty and not the right demographic for the club. If she goes there, she'll stick out like a sore thumb. You're the right age. You'll blend in." He handed her the folder. "Club's name is Mezzanine."

"The Mezzanine?" Naomi asked. She'd heard of it. Everybody who was anybody went to the Mezzanine. "How am I gonna get in there? They're pretty choosy about whom they let in. I mean the bouncer—"

"Wear something sexy, and they'll let you in. Just like any other nightclub," Wei claimed. Then he pointed to the folder in her hand again. "Mrs. Zhang's contact info is in there, as well as who owns the club. Look into it, and let me know if there's anything to her claims."

Wei Guo turned to his computer, and Naomi left his office.

The large newsroom was half-empty not only because some of the staff had taken off early to go trick-or-treating with their kids, but also because there'd been layoffs. Naomi still had a job, because she was one of the young staff members whose salary was low. Some of the senior and much better paid staff had either been laid off or been lured away by online news blogs or cable news outlets.

In her cubicle, Naomi perused the thin file Wei Guo had given her. There wasn't much: the contact information for Mrs. Zhang, a neighbor living in an apartment building behind the club, a summary of her rantings about bloody clubbers and seemingly clandestine meetings behind the club, as well as information on the ownership of the club.

According to the public records, the club was co-owned by two individuals: Samson Woodford and Amaury LeSang. She couldn't find much about the two men on the internet. They had no social media accounts. The only time she found the two men's names mentioned anywhere was in a report about security companies. It appeared that both men were associated with Scanguards, a nationwide security company providing bodyguards for personal protection. However, their website was bare-bones, only giving an address in the Mission neighborhood of San Francisco and a telephone number. By the looks of it, they didn't advertise their services anywhere Naomi could find, leading her to believe that they relied mostly on word-of-mouth to grow their business.

Luckily, the Mezzanine had a website. According to the *About Us* page, the club was run by two managers, Damian LeSang and Patrick Woodford. The same last names as the owners. She guessed that the two managers were sons of the owners. She knew what that meant: the owners had bought their sons a business to run. Yeah, rich kids who wanted a toy and got it in the form of a successful nightclub. To confirm her assumption, she googled the two managers, but neither of them had a social media presence. Odd. However, she dug a little deeper, and found that Damian was mentioned in several social media posts. She clicked on the first post and saw a photo of a gorgeous redhead with a model figure who fairly clung to a tall hunk with dark hair and blue eyes. According to the post, this was Damian LeSang. He looked like sex personified.

Her heart began to flutter at such perfect maleness. She quickly closed the tab on the browser and went back to the nightclub's homepage. There she looked closer at the colorful banner announcing a Halloween party at the club tonight. She read through it, until she came to the end, where two lines were bolded.

If you're not wearing an awesome or sexy costume, you won't be admitted tonight. Impress us!

Naomi's breath caught. There might as well have been a third sentence: *We mean you, Naomi.*

Well, she wasn't one to back down from a challenge. Maybe checking out the club during a Halloween party would actually be a good thing. She would be disguised, and the club would be so busy that nobody would notice her sniffing around. In fact, the more she thought about it, the more she liked the idea.

She glanced at the clock. She had to hurry to find a suitable costume before everything was sold out. She needed to find one that would guarantee her admittance to the Mezzanine.

2

In the secret room behind the manager's office at the Mezzanine, Damian LeSang put the finishing touches to his costume. He was dressed in black slacks and a white ruffled shirt with poofy sleeves and a necktie befitting a gentleman from the late eighteenth and early nineteenth century. He draped a large black cape with red satin lining over his shoulders and fastened it with a bejeweled clasp in front. He could have gone full *Interview-with-the-Vampire* style, but he found the gold embroidery on the coats the actors had worn a bit too garish. The cape was much more his style.

He'd always loved Halloween, because it was the only night of the entire year where he was allowed to flash his fangs in public, without having to worry about exposing what he was. Everybody would know that the costume he wore identified him as a vampire, and assumed that the fangs that peeked from beneath his lips were fakes made of plastic. If only they knew that those fangs could pierce a vein without effort and suck a human dry. Of course, he'd never go that far. He was civilized.

As a hybrid vampire, a child born to a full-blooded vampire and his blood-bonded human mate, he could sustain himself on human food and human blood alike. While he enjoyed human food, and San Francisco offered some of the best cuisines in the country, he loved drinking human blood. It gave him strength. As a child, he'd grown up on bottled blood, but later as a teenager, he'd developed a taste for blood coming straight from a human's vein. And as a healthy thirty-one-year-old male, he particularly enjoyed drinking from a human woman, while having sex with her. He loved the heightened sexual arousal that the bite brought with it.

His gaze drifted to the double bed in the room. Maybe he'd come back here later tonight, accompanied by a woman before the night was out, because tonight he was in the mood for not just sex, but also a bite. There would be no shortage of women tonight. Just like on other nights, plenty of women would throw themselves at him, attracted by his charm and good looks, not knowing that beneath the surface, a barely-restrained vampire lurked.

Damian grinned. Tonight would be fun. But first, he had to make sure everything was ready for the party. After all, he was one of the two managers of the club, and had responsibilities.

He left the room and closed the door behind him. From inside the manager's office, the door to the secret room wasn't noticeable, unless one knew what to look for. There was no door handle, no obvious grooves, no hinges, nothing that indicated that there was a door. It opened only by pressing at the right spot on the outside.

The office itself overlooked the dance floor, allowing the manager to look down into the club via a two-way mirror. Right now, the club was still empty. Only staff members were rushing around, getting ready for the party. He glanced down to the long bar lining one wall of the club, and saw several bartenders preparing for the onslaught of drink orders.

Damian left the office and let the door fall shut behind him, while he already walked downstairs and crossed the dance floor. At the coat check, he waved at the two female staff members, Beth and Melanie. Beth was dressed as a sexy nurse though she didn't have the boobs to fill out her costume fully, Melanie as a 1920s flapper.

"Ready for tonight?" he asked them.

"We've got it under control," Melanie said.

"Don't worry, Damian," Beth purred. He knew the vampire female had a crush on him, but she just wasn't his type. Too skinny.

"Thanks, both of you for working tonight," he said. "I appreciate it. Keep an eye out for any trouble, will you?"

They both nodded. They knew what he meant. And as vampires they were equipped with the right tools. He wanted no trouble at the club tonight. Damian walked to the entrance door, and opened it a few inches, just wide enough to see the long line that had already formed along the building. Orlando, a vampire who worked as a bouncer, stood there, legs spread wide, arms crossed over his muscled chest, his size and gaze intimidating. He rarely smiled, and Damian had never seen him being taken in by any woman's charm. As if he was impervious to it, though he knew that Orlando was straight. He wasn't just a bouncer. Orlando was a trained bodyguard and employed by Scanguards.

"Orlando," Damian said quietly, knowing that the vampire could hear him without any trouble.

"Yes, Damian?" he answered and turned his head slightly.

"Just a reminder: only hot chicks tonight. And they'd better be wearing something sexy. For the guys the usual standards apply."

"Understood." Then he took a step closer to the door. "And our kind?"

Damian knew what Orlando meant by that: vampires. "Let them in, unless they're known troublemakers. Any Scanguards staff will probably use the back entrance anyway. But if they don't, just usher them in."

"Got it."

Damian nodded before he closed the door again and made his way to the bar. The bartenders were busy stocking the shelves with booze. All bartenders the Mezzanine employed were vampires. Considering the hours the club operated, it was the perfect job for any vampire. While the club belonged in equal parts to Damian's father, Amaury, and Patrick's father, Samson, and not to Scanguards itself, the club operated in many ways with the same principles in mind: to provide vampires with employment opportunities and a good income to keep them on the straight and narrow. And to discourage the vampires working at the Mezzanine from snacking on the patrons, there was a separate breakroom accessible via the storeroom in the basement, where bottled human blood was available free of charge.

"Where's Mick?" Damian asked, when he saw only three bartenders working behind the bar: Sam, Andrew, and Tanja.

Tanja, dressed in a dominatrix suit that fit her like a second skin, turned. "Didn't show. I called him, but he's not picking up his cell."

"Yeah, to leave us hanging on a night like this," Sam interjected, "pisses me off." He growled, which didn't quite fit with his pirate outfit. *Argh* would have been more like it.

"I'll call him." Damian pulled his cell from his pants pocket and scrolled through his contacts, then tapped on Mick Solvang's number. He liked the guy, and so far, he'd always been responsible. He let it ring. After the fourth ring, it went to voicemail.

"It's Mick. You know what to do."

"Where the fuck are you?" Damian barked into the phone, knowing he didn't need to give his name. "We're opening in half an hour, and you're not here. You'd better have a good explanation."

He disconnected the call.

"Voicemail?" Tanja asked.

"Yeah," Damian replied. "Are you gonna be able to handle the bar just between the three of you?"

"No chance," Andrew piped up as he lifted a crate of clean glasses onto the counter. He wore a *Village-People-style* police uniform, though his pants barely covered his ass. But Damian didn't care. The Mezzanine catered to all tastes, and Andrew was popular among the gays in San Francisco. "We need at least one more, and even that's pushing it."

"Let me see what I can do," Damian said and started scrolling through his phone when he picked up a movement from the corner of his eye. He turned his head, and grinned. "You're just what I need right now."

Buffy, John Grant's adopted daughter, approached the bar. She'd entered the club via the back entrance that allowed Scanguards staff and associates to get into the club by using a biometric entrance system, bypassing the front entrance. Buffy was black, human, and only twenty-one years old. At age ten she'd been kidnapped by a child sex trafficking ring, and Savannah, her mother, had hired Scanguards to get her back. John had moved heaven and earth to rescue Buffy, and Savannah had blood-bonded with John shortly after that. Buffy regarded John as her father, and had known about vampires since the night of her rescue.

"Hey, Damian, what's up?" Buffy said and hopped onto the bar, letting her feet dangle in the air.

Damian gestured to her clothing, a short black leather skirt, boots that reached to her knees, a skimpy red tank top, and a belt. Was that a *stake* tucked into it? Around her neck hung a necklace with a large cross.

"Who are you supposed to be?"

"Can't you see?" Sam asked from behind the bar. "She's the slayer, you know, *Buffy the Vampire Slayer*? It's a classic."

Buffy did a high five with Sam, before turning back to Damian. "See, he gets it."

Damian pointed to her belt. "How about you lose the stake. You're gonna make a hell of a lot of people in here nervous."

Buffy rolled her eyes. "It's made of plastic." She pulled it out of her belt, gripping it as if she wanted to attack him.

Damian encircled her wrist before she had a chance to do anything else. "Looks pretty realistic to me."

"You chicken?" She chuckled.

"You have no respect for your elders. That's where your dad got it wrong. He should have raised you better and paddled your ass occasionally."

"Daddy would never hurt me."

She was right about that. John was a total softy when it came to his daughter. "Yeah, 'cause you and your mom got him wrapped around your little fingers so tightly, it's a wonder the guy can breathe."

Buffy winked mischievously. "Let's check back once you have a daughter, and see whether you can raise her better."

From behind the bar, Tanja laughed. "I think she's got you there. Not bad for a human."

Damian turned to look at Tanja. "She's lucky that I can't hurt her, or John would have my hide."

Buffy threw her arms around his neck and squeezed him. "Admit that you love me like a sister."

She wasn't wrong. He was fond of Buffy. "Okay, you wanna play the sister card? Then how about doing your big brother a favor?"

She raised her eyebrows.

"Since you're officially old enough to be allowed around alcohol, can you work behind the bar tonight?"

"Me? I came to party."

"Come on, Buffy, be a good girl and help me out. Mick hasn't shown up, and no matter how good Sam, Andrew, and Tanja are, tonight's gonna be too busy for three bartenders. I need you." He gave her his best puppy-dog-eyes look.

She looked at him, then let out a breath. "Fine. But you owe me, bro."

"Anything you want." Then he gave her a kiss on the cheek. "You're the best."

"Yeah, yeah, where have I heard that before?" Buffy turned on the bar, and Andrew was already there, lifting her off it on the other side. "Thanks, Andrew."

She would be safe with the three of them, because they knew that her father would stake them without hesitation should they harm Buffy.

Damian turned away from the bar and saw the first people entering the club, hurrying to claim the private seating areas on the elevated level overlooking the dance floor, or the high tables around the perimeter of the dance floor, while others headed straight for the bar to get their drink orders in before it got too busy.

Damian walked toward the door leading to the restrooms and the supply rooms, when his identical twin brother entered. They both froze when they saw each other.

"Are you kidding me?" Damian asked. "You stole my idea."

Benjamin shook his head. "No, you stole mine."

Damian chuckled. Benjamin was wearing the exact same outfit that he wore, down to the clasp that held his cape in place. "Guess that's the trouble with being a twin."

Benjamin slapped him on the shoulder. "This is gonna be fun! How about we each fuck a hot chick tonight, and then do a switch on them for seconds and see if they spot the difference? You game?"

Damian laughed. "You're now officially the more debauched of the two of us."

"Come on," Benjamin coaxed, grinning. "It'll be fun. And it's not like we haven't fucked the same girls. I mean, it's not our fault that we have the same taste in women."

Damian rolled his eyes. "Let's clarify this. I have a certain taste in women, and you haven't met a woman yet that you don't like. So, of course, you'll fuck anything you can lay your hands on, while I'm a little more selective."

"Okay then," Benjamin conceded. "So, let's find two women *you* find hot, and then we'll do the switch after—"

Damian gave his brother a light slap over the back of his head. "Go and get whatever woman you want. I'm not in the sharing mood tonight."

Benjamin laughed. "Ahh, looks like my big brother is getting to that possessive age where he wants a woman just for himself."

"You're only an hour younger than I."

"Yeah, but I'm not there yet. I'm still playing the field. Just because Ryder got hitched a year ago, and Scarlet is already pregnant, doesn't mean the rest of us have to follow like sheep."

"Are you calling me a sheep?"

"Baa, baa!" Benjamin mimicked the sounds of a sheep.

Damian boxed his brother in the chest. "Watch it, bro! Or what happened to Ryder will rub off on you too."

"Yeah, not gonna happen for a while for sure," Benjamin claimed and winked. "See you later, bro."

"Have fun."

Damian watched his brother walk to the other side of the club where he could watch everybody who entered, so he could target the hottest women before anybody else could lay claim to them.

Damian shook his head, smiling to himself. As twins, Damian and Benjamin had always been totally in sync with each other, but in the last year their tastes and preferences had started to change, and it looked like they were becoming more individual rather than being one half of a pair. They still lived together, occupying the floor beneath their parents' penthouse in a building their father, Amaury, owned. It was vampire-proof with UV-impenetrable windows and other security features, and located centrally in the Tenderloin, a somewhat seedy part of downtown. And so far, Damian had no reason to move out and get his own place. He liked living with his twin and being close to his parents, but he knew that one day, he'd find a place of his own, maybe even a house. In the meantime, he enjoyed the closeness he and his brother shared.

3

Naomi opened the door to the store and rushed inside, relieved that it was still open, even though it was already past 9 p.m. This was the last store on her list. The other three she'd tried had only had a few Halloween costumes left, and all had been far too small for her. This was her last chance to find something suitable so she would be admitted to tonight's party at the Mezzanine.

"We're closing in a minute," a young man coming toward her from behind a clothes rack said.

"Please, I just need a costume for tonight. It's really important."

He sighed. "I'm on my way to a party. You won't have any time to browse, so unless you know exactly what you want—"

"Something sexy," she interrupted.

He ran his gaze over her body before it landed directly on her boobs. "Oh, dear, I'm not sure we have anything in your size left."

Where had she heard that before? "Please, I need something. There's this guy. I really want him to notice me tonight," she lied.

"Well, why didn't you say so immediately? Come on in the back. I might have something." He already turned toward the fitting rooms. "The lady who ordered it didn't pick it up. You might be able to squeeze into it if you hold your breath."

Naomi followed him, and watched as he went behind a screen, from which he emerged seconds later, a hanger with a costume in his hand. The first thing she saw was red. A long red cape with a hood.

"But that doesn't look sexy." The bouncer at the Mezzanine would send her packing.

The guy smirked, then peeled the cape away from what lay beneath: a strapless short dress in red, black, and white, elaborately detailed with faux lace-up on the tight bustier, with molded red cups and lace detailing. The skirt, which didn't even reach to mid-thigh, sported black lace ruffles and a tiny white apron.

"Little Red Riding Hood," the salesman said. "The sexy version." He handed her the hanger. "Try it on."

The costume looked small, but she didn't have a choice. Quickly, she stepped into the fitting room and drew the privacy curtain closed. She felt hot already from running all over town to find the right costume. Maneuvering in the tiny fitting room didn't help, but she managed to undress, and slipped into the costume. She squeezed her boobs into the entirely too small cups, and reached behind her back to zip up, but she only got the zipper halfway up.

"Fuck!" she hissed.

"Do you need help?"

"I can't get the zipper up."

"May I help you?"

"Yes, please," she said and drew the curtain back.

"Turn around, please." A moment later, she felt his hands on her back. "Okay, now inhale."

She took in a breath, and the salesman pulled the zipper all the way up.

"Let's have a look at you."

She stepped out of the cabin and the man directed her toward a large mirror.

"Perfect," he said. "As if it was made for you."

He had to say that, of course. After all, he was a salesperson. She cast a hesitant look into the mirror and froze, barely recognizing herself. The costume was tight and gave her even more of an hourglass figure than she had. Her wide hips were hidden beneath the skirt that reminded her of a ballerina's tutu. Her waist looked slim in comparison, the tight bustier making the most of her shape. Her boobs were barely contained by the red cups, and had it not been for the black lace trim, her nipples would have popped out.

"If that guy doesn't notice you now, then he's blind, honey," the salesclerk said.

"I'll take it." Then she met his eyes in the mirror. "May I leave it on? I don't think I'll be able to zip it up on my own." How she was gonna get out of the dress when the night was over, was anybody's guess.

"Of course, you may." Then he reached for the cape and draped it around her shoulders. "I'll pack your clothes and ring you up."

She glanced at the mirror again, grateful that the costume came with a cape, so she wouldn't have to walk around town in this skimpy outfit. Her eyes fell on her shoes. She was wearing tennis shoes. Damn, she had to go back home first to slip into her high heels.

After paying for the costume, and returning home to change into black high heels, she called an Uber to drive her to the Mezzanine in SOMA. There was a line outside, but it seemed to move relatively quickly. With the red cape draped around her, Naomi waited patiently. She'd put her cell phone, her house key, a credit card, and some cash into a zipped pocket inside the cape, glad that she didn't have to carry a handbag.

Naomi glanced at the people in the queue. Several of the men were dressed like pirates, one guy behind her had chosen to dress up like a devil, the woman next to him an angel, a *Victoria's Secret* angel. Ahead of her were a couple of nurses, a woman in a catsuit, a gladiator, and a man in a Pharaoh costume.

The gladiator and the woman in the catsuit were let into the club by the big bouncer. He was at least six foot three, and had arms and a chest that looked like he spent twenty-four hours a day in the gym bench pressing two hundred pounds. His facial expression could only be described as stoic and unyielding. Yeah, nobody would mess with somebody like him.

The bouncer waved the Pharaoh inside, then blocked the two nurses. "We've already got enough nurses in there," he claimed.

"What?" one of the girls asked.

"And sexier ones too. You've gotta do better than that," the bouncer added.

"Come on!" the second girl complained. "I don't see you wearing a costume."

The bouncer took a step closer to the girl that had dared complain and glared at her. "This is my costume. I'm a bouncer."

"Orlando. Be civil."

At the female voice, the bouncer's head whirled to a woman walking past Naomi. She was wearing a French maid outfit.

"Isabelle, evening," he greeted her, a smile all of a sudden curling around his lips, his eyes drinking in the young woman's enticing form.

She walked straight past him to the entrance door, bypassing the line. "See you later."

"Enjoy your evening," Orlando said, before he looked back at the two nurses. "Beat it."

As the two nurses walked off cursing, Naomi quickly took her cape off and draped it over her arm, worried now. Would he reject her too?

When she suddenly stood only a few feet in front of Orlando, his earlier smile was gone. He ran his eyes over her, lingering first on her legs, then on her cleavage. Would he find her sexy enough to let her enter? Or did she not measure up? Was she looking vulgar rather than sexy, trashy rather than hot?

"Now that's what I'm talking about." He inhaled deeply. "Go in, enjoy yourself."

Relieved, Naomi entered the club. Cool air blasted toward her, and she realized that the air conditioning was running overtime, clearly to make sure that the clubbers didn't overheat inside their costumes.

The music was loud like she'd expected, a mix of eighties and nineties rock 'n' roll and pop. The place was packed, the dance floor rocking, the bar buzzing like a beehive, four bartenders busy serving drinks. Yes, tonight was the perfect night for snooping around the club. Everybody was so busy with enjoying themselves that they wouldn't take any notice of her.

Game on.

4

Damian spotted Patrick in the crowd and waved to him. Patrick nodded and paved a way through the throng of dancers to reach him. Only now, he noticed that Grayson was following him. The brothers were dressed up like vampires, both of them with their fangs extended.

"Guess everybody is having the same idea," Damian said with a motion to their fangs, when the two joined him near the stairs that led up to the office.

"It's the only night of the year," Patrick said, grinning.

"It's already hopping here," Grayson said. Then he glanced around appreciatively. "Glad you told Orlando to let only hot girls in tonight. I can see a few already that I'm gonna have fun with."

The son of Scanguards' founder and owner, Samson Woodford, was aware of his good looks and charm, and used it to the fullest whenever the occasion presented itself, which was pretty much constantly. His younger brother, Patrick, was just as handsome and charming, but less aggressive when it came to women, though he too got his fair share of action.

"Just be discreet," Damian warned. "Unless you wanna be on camera."

Grayson shook his head. "Don't worry, I know the drill."

"Have you seen Isa?" Patrick asked. "She came in her own car."

Damian motioned to the corner with comfortable seating that overlooked the dance floor. "Isabelle was up there a short while ago, hanging out with Lydia."

"Oh, is Lydia gonna sing tonight?" Grayson asked.

"Yeah, she's gonna do a couple of songs later. I'm setting up the stage right now. There's something wrong with the dry ice machine. Can you give me a hand, Patrick?" Damian asked.

"No can do, bro. It's my night off. We tossed for it. You lost, remember?"

"Come on, it's only gonna take a few minutes. You're better at this than I am."

"What's Patrick better at?"

Damian turned to the familiar voice behind him. "Sebastian."

The twenty-three-year-old half-Asian, who was the only son of Oliver and Ursula, stood behind him dressed in white Judo pants. His chest was bare, and he wore a bandana over his forehead.

Damian pointed to him, then looked at Grayson and Patrick. "See, he's wearing an original costume."

Grayson shrugged. "And who's he supposed to be?"

"Bruce Lee, of course," Damian said and exchanged a look with Sebastian.

"Hey guys," Sebastian said. "Good music. Who's the DJ?"

"One of my friends," Patrick said. "We snatched him away from the Nightowl Club in the Castro." Then he grinned at Damian. "See, I do my part in running this place."

"Yeah, when it comes to the fun stuff. But not everything about running a club is fun. Like fixing a dry ice machine."

"Is that what you need help with?" Sebastian asked.

"You offering?"

"Yeah."

"You're on," Damian said. He knew that Sebastian was handy with technical stuff. Besides, the kid looked up to him, and he enjoyed mentoring him. "Let's go then."

They walked to the area where a small stage sat next to the DJ's station, and Damian ushered Sebastian behind a partition.

"So how's the training at Scanguards going?"

"I like it," Sebastian said. "It's tough, but I can't imagine doing anything else. Dad's happy that I decided to join rather than go to law school."

"Good for you!"

"And you? Don't you like being a bodyguard anymore? I'm surprised you decided to run the club with Patrick."

"Oh, I love it. Don't get me wrong. But I like running the club too."

"Isn't that a bit much, doing both jobs at the same time?"

Damian shrugged. "What else am I gonna do with all my time? I like to be busy." Then he winked. "Besides, where else do you meet a lot of pretty women, huh?"

Sebastian grinned. "Yeah, good point. Do you need an extra bartender or a bouncer?"

Damian chuckled. "I think Orlando is doing a pretty good job screening tonight, don't you think?"

"Yeah, though I heard he can be a bit rude."

"He's not a man of many words." And that was an understatement.

"Ain't that the truth? So, what's his deal? How long ago did he join Scanguards?"

"About a year ago. Just showed up at Samson's doorstep one night and asked for a job. And that's about all anybody knows. I assume Samson knows him from somewhere and trusts him. That's good enough for me." He wasn't one to question Samson's decisions. Besides, Orlando was a great bouncer. Nobody dared cross him for fear he'd beat the living daylights out of them.

"Guess so," Sebastian replied. His cell suddenly chimed, and he pulled it from his pocket. "Oh, Adam just got here." He typed a message and sent it. "Let's have a look at this dry ice machine."

They both crouched down to the machine, and Sebastian started tinkering with it.

"You still hanging out a lot with Zane's sons?"

"Mostly with Adam. We're closer in age. And let's face it, Nicholas is a lot more like his father than he wants to admit."

"Yeah, a barrel of laughs," Damian joked.

"Don't let him hear that," Sebastian warned. "Or he'll go off like a Roman candle. He's got no sense of humor whatsoever."

"Well, one of his sons had to inherit Zane's temperament."

"Is it true what they say about Zane? That he once ripped a man's heart out just for the hell of it?"

"Like you I wasn't around back then, but there's more to that story. Apparently, the guy whose heart he ripped out was raping a young woman. Zane stopped him, and decided to dole out the punishment right there and then."

"Gruesome," Sebastian commented. "But I guess that makes him a hero."

"If you wanna call it that. Still makes him a vigilante. But he's changed. Don't get me wrong. He's no teddy bear, but at least he isn't as volatile as he used to be."

"Nicholas wants to be like him," Sebastian said.

"And you, do you want to be like Oliver?"

"Nah. My dad, he's great, you know. But I wanna be my own man. Forge my own path."

"Just like the rest of us. You're in good company." Damian motioned to the dry ice machine. "Any clue what's wrong with it?"

Sebastian grinned. "Oh, it's fixed."

"Wow, thanks. Anytime you wanna moonlight here, just let me know. We could use somebody with your skills."

They rose to their feet.

"Now go and have fun."

5

Naomi hadn't dropped off her cape at the coat check, wanting to have all her belongings with her, particularly her phone so she could take photos of anything that looked suspicious. She'd draped the cape over her shoulders again to avoid men leering at her. She felt uncomfortable enough in the tight outfit and worried that any moment her boobs could pop out of their cage, and she'd have an embarrassing *wardrobe malfunction*. With her cape she attracted much less attention, since many of the men who were in vampire costumes complete with fake fangs also wore capes.

At first, she familiarized herself with all entrances and exits, then scouted out the restrooms. In the same corridor as the restrooms, she found a door marked *Employees Only*. It wasn't locked, probably because it also led to a fire exit in the back of the building. She walked through the door and found herself in a much quieter area of the club. Several doors lined the corridor. She opened them one after the other. Only the door to the breakroom was unlocked, the other two were locked. She assumed that they were storage rooms, or perhaps one door led into a basement.

When she reached the end of the corridor, she opened the door leading outside. This was the area where the nosy neighbor had claimed to have seen people with blood on their clothing. Naomi glanced around. Apart from three large dumpsters and cigarette butts on the ground, there wasn't much to see. She went back inside, and made her way back into the public area of the club. Somehow, she had to figure out how to find out what was behind the locked doors, because if there was really a satanic cult operating in this nightclub, it would be behind a locked door. There had to be keys somewhere.

Naomi let her gaze roam over the crowd, then to the bar, and suddenly recognized one face: Damian LeSang, one of the club's managers. He stood at the bar, dressed in a vampire costume, and was flirting with a girl with model looks. The young woman threw her head back, sending her long dark hair flying, before placing her hand on Damian's chest. Damian took her hand and clasped it, pulling her closer to him. By the looks of it, he would be busy for a while. This was the perfect time to check out the manager's office. It was easy to find. A set of stairs that was partially hidden behind a mirrored partition led up to the room.

To her surprise, the door wasn't locked but ajar. She peered in through the slit, but the office appeared to be empty. When she pushed the door open wider, she realized why the door wasn't locked. A small piece of cardboard lay on the ground next to the doorframe, preventing the door from closing fully.

Quickly, she entered the room, removed the piece of cardboard and made sure the door closed. She heard it click shut. There was only low lighting in the large room. She understood why: one wall consisted entirely of glass, or rather, a two-way-mirror that allowed the occupants of the office to watch the goings-on in the club below. If the light in the office was too bright, people on the other side of the two-way mirror would actually be able to see into the office. There was a curtain that could be pulled in front of it, if more light was needed in the office, but privacy was required at the same time.

There was a large desk with a computer, a printer on a shelving unit behind it, several filing cabinets along the wall, a seating area with a coffee table close to the two-way-mirror, a refrigerator as well as a coffeemaker and other odds and ends. Naomi headed for the desk. Maybe the manager kept the keys to the storage rooms in there. She started opening a drawer and rifled through it. When she closed the drawer again, her cape got in the way, and she took it off and laid it over the office chair, before continuing.

She went through all the drawers of the desk, but apart from notepads, files, and writing implements, she found nothing that would have helped her to figure out what was hiding behind the locked doors on the first floor.

Naomi turned around and looked through the shelving unit that housed the printer and a few decorative items, then moved on to the coffee machine. It stood on top of a small refrigerator. She bent down to open it, when she heard a sound behind her and whirled around.

The door fell shut behind Damian LeSang, his black cape with red lining flapping as if a draft had caught it. His fangs peeked from between his lips, and even his eyes shimmered golden. She hadn't noticed the color of his eyes when she'd seen him from afar.

"Who are you? And what are you doing here?"

The timbre of his voice reverberated in her chest, and she let out a tiny gasp.

Fuck! What now? He'd caught her snooping around in his office. How was she going to get out of this mess? Why hadn't he continued flirting with that skinny model when she'd looked like she'd wanted to jump his bones right there at the bar?

"I asked who you are and what you're doing in my office," he repeated, his eyes narrowing as he took a few more steps toward her.

"Uhm, uh... I... I'm Naomi," she said, stalling. Fuck, what now?

"That's only a partial answer."

He looked like somebody who had ways of always getting answers to his questions. She had to come up with something, anything.

"I'm here on a dare."

He tilted his head to the side, but didn't say anything.

"My... my girlfriends said I wouldn't have the guts to go up to you and kiss you... And I, uhm, I told them I would," she lied. Her entire body heated, and her palms were sweaty. She wasn't good at this, at making up stories. That's why she was a reporter and not a fiction writer. "But I see now that it was a really stupid idea. I mean, you're clearly somebody who can have any kind of woman, a model, a supermodel even. So I'd better leave. Sorry about that. I shouldn't even have tried."

She tried to walk past him, but he held out his arm, blocking her.

"A kiss? You came here for a kiss?" He raised his eyebrows, while he looked her up and down, before his gaze settled on her cleavage.

"Yeah, but, as I said, it was a really bad idea. I'm just gonna tell my girlfriends that the bet is off."

"Oh, I wouldn't want you to lose a bet."

Naomi took a step away from him, but he put his hand on her waist and shook his head. She could have easily pulled away, and his hand would have slipped from her, but the way he looked at her, his eyes shimmering even more intensely golden than when he'd entered the office, made her hesitate. When her gaze dropped to his mouth, where his plastic fangs peeked from between his parted lips, her heart suddenly beat faster.

She barely noticed that she stepped closer to him, and that Damian put his arms around her waist, drawing her closer. Her breasts touched his chest, and she heard him suck in an audible breath.

"I think we can do better than just a kiss," he murmured and lowered his lips to hers.

She didn't stop him, even though she knew she should. But when she smelled his intoxicating scent, and felt his firm lips capture hers, all inhibitions flew out the proverbial window, and she parted her lips to allow his demanding tongue inside to explore her.

Damian tasted just as good as he smelled and looked. She couldn't believe what was happening. Her lie had been meant for her to throw him out of her office without suspecting that she'd been snooping around. She'd never in a million years expected that he would actually take her up on her supposed dare. Why, when he could have any woman? She knew for certain that the skinny dark-haired model he'd been flirting with five minutes earlier would have never rejected his advances. So why was he kissing her, and kissing her as if he enjoyed this kiss as much as she did?

And it wasn't just a kiss. All of a sudden, she felt the floor under her feet gone, and a moment later, Damian was pressing her against a wall, kissing her passionately, while his hands were roaming her torso, his fingers stroking over the exposed flesh of her breasts.

At the tantalizing touch, she moaned into his mouth, unable to hold back the lust that coursed through her. Nobody had ever gotten her aroused so quickly and so thoroughly. So expertly.

Damian ripped his lips from hers. "Fuck, you're beautiful."

He sank his face to her cleavage and kissed her skin, before he tugged on the bustier and pulled it down. When she felt cool air blow against her nipples, she realized that her boobs had escaped from their prison. She should stop him now, tell him that she wasn't the kind of woman who allowed a stranger to touch her like this, but when he put his lips around one nipple and sucked it into his mouth the reason why she wanted him to stop suddenly eluded her. Only one thought counted now: to feel Damian's lips and hands on her.

6

When Damian had entered his office and found the woman in the Little Red Riding Hood costume bending down, about to open the refrigerator that contained bottles of human blood, he'd seen red, and had been close to attacking her for breaking in. But when she'd turned around, his thoughts had turned in a totally different direction.

He'd never been attracted to a woman on such a primal level as he was to Naomi, whom he knew nothing about, other than that he wanted to drive his fangs into those perfect tits. Had she really come to his office to get a kiss because of a bet with her girlfriends? He wasn't sure about that. But right now, he didn't give a fig about her motives, as long as she allowed him to kiss her and touch her.

Other men might have described Naomi as chubby, even though they would at first be drawn to her pretty face, her blond hair and her blue eyes. But Damian liked her figure, because everything about her was real, the way it was meant to be: Full breasts, wide hips. She was real, because he knew that her breasts were natural, not an ounce of silicone in sight. Not like the skinny models that threw themselves at him. Just by looking at their boobs he could tell that the only reason they looked so firm and large was because they were fake. And he hated fake.

But Naomi's breasts were beautiful, big, and responsive. He loved kneading them with his hands, while he sucked on her nipples and teased the little rosebuds into stiff little peaks. He kept his fangs extended, and brushed them against her skin, feeling bolts of lightning race through him at the contact. It felt as if he was rubbing his hard-on over her tits. And fuck was he hard. His cock was ready to burst, ready to plunge into this hot woman.

Even the costume looked perfect on her. The skirt was so short that when she'd bent down to open the refrigerator, he'd seen that she was wearing a black G-string. As if she needed to look any more enticing than she already did. He could barely hold on to his control. Another five minutes, and she'd be bent over the desk, and he'd be fucking her until she begged him to stop.

He lifted his head from her breasts, and looked into her blue eyes. Her lids were at half-mast, and arousal shone from her eyes.

"Touch me," he demanded and pulled her hand to his groin, making her aware of what she did to him.

Something in her eyes flickered. Surprise? How could she possibly be surprised at how hard he'd gotten so quickly, when surely, any man she touched reacted the same way?

"I love your tits," he said and pulled one hard nipple into his mouth and licked over it.

Naomi released a strangled moan.

He squeezed both breasts with his hands, and suddenly felt her squeeze his cock in the same fashion.

"Oh, fuck, yeah!" he ground out, and rubbed his cock harder against her, demanding she repeat the action.

Then he sank his lips back onto her gorgeous tits and sucked them. He'd always loved big-breasted women, but Naomi was the first one who came in this perfect package. She had beautiful eyes, sensual lips, and the aroma of her blood spoke to the vampire inside him. Both sides of him were drawn to her, and while he'd been with tantalizing women before, none had ever ticked all the boxes.

"I want you, Naomi, I want you now," he murmured against her heated skin, while he reached underneath her short skirt, eager to feel how wet she was for him.

"Damian, I need you—"

Damian froze. The female voice wasn't Naomi's. He spun his head to the left. There, at the door, stood Lydia, dressed in a Steampunk costume.

"Fuck!" he hissed, while simultaneously using his cape to shield Naomi from her view. Not that he could hide what they were doing, since Lydia's hybrid vampire senses would have already picked up on the scent of arousal in the room. "Can't you see I'm busy?"

Already, Naomi was pulling on her dress, trying to squeeze her boobs back into the bustier, with little success.

Lydia had the decency to look sheepish. "Sorry, but the microphone's not working, and I'm supposed to sing in a few minutes."

"Can't you ask Patrick to help you?"

"He's even busier than you."

Damian knew what that meant. "Fuck!" This was the worst timing ever. But he had responsibilities. His own needs would have to be postponed, but not for long. "Just a sec, Lydia."

He turned back to Naomi, and reached behind her to lower the zipper.

"What are you doing?" she ground out under her breath and glared at him.

He lowered his voice though he knew that Lydia could probably hear him anyway. "You're not gonna get your boobs back into your dress like that. Just let me help you. Turn around."

She turned, still shielded from Lydia's view by his cape, and tucked herself into the dress, then he pulled the zipper back up and cupped her shoulders. He pressed a kiss to her neck. "I'll be back in a few minutes. Don't go anywhere, we're not done."

Damian turned back and walked to Lydia.

"Lydia, why don't you keep my guest company while I fix the microphone? Be back in a minute."

At the door, he added so low only a vampire's or hybrid's hearing could pick it up, "Don't leave her alone in the office."

Lydia raised an eyebrow, indicating that she'd heard him, and Damian left the office.

~ ~ ~

Naomi felt as if she were coming out of a daze—or as if somebody had poured a bucket of ice water over her. She'd been about two seconds away from allowing Damian to fuck her against the wall of his office. What had gotten into her? She'd never acted like that with any man. She wasn't the kind of woman who had one-night stands, let alone quickies with strangers. Yet feeling Damian's hands and lips on her had smothered all her inhibitions.

"I'm Lydia. I sing here occasionally. What's your name?" the pretty woman in the Steampunk costume asked. She wore her blond hair braided and artfully draped around her head.

"Uhm, Naomi. I'm Naomi. Nice to meet you."

"Nice to meet you, too, Naomi. I didn't know Damian was dating anyone. Guess I'm out of the loop."

Naomi recognized a fishing expedition when she saw one. She wasn't going to step into that trap. It was bad enough that Lydia had walked in on them. Didn't anybody knock these days?

"So, Lydia, you sing here? That's great. What kind of music?"

Unexpectedly, Lydia chuckled. "I like you. You're not one to kiss and tell."

"Wha—"

Lydia interrupted her by lifting a hand. "Don't take it the wrong way. Some secrets should definitely be kept."

At the cryptic remark, Naomi wondered what Lydia meant by it, but she wasn't going to ask. She didn't want to get drawn into a conversation about secrets. It was a minefield she planned to avoid.

When silence spread between them, Naomi said, "Nothing to tell, really. I'm sure I'm not the first woman Damian has kissed in his office."

She shrugged. There'd probably been hundreds. And most likely he'd made all of them feel like it meant something. Why that bothered her all of a sudden, she didn't want to examine. It didn't matter. Or at least, it *shouldn't* matter. After all, she was only doing this for her job.

Yeah, not even she believed that. She could have easily extricated herself from his arms if she really didn't want him to kiss and touch her. She'd taken self-defense classes, and knew how to stop unwanted attention. She could have kneed him in the balls. Instead, she'd palmed his cock, and boy, he'd felt good. He'd been hard, and thick, and big. Just thinking about it now made her womb clench in response.

If she stayed any longer, she'd probably say something to Lydia that she didn't mean to divulge just because she was nervous.

"I should go down to the bar and get something to drink," Naomi lied, searching for an excuse to leave.

"Damian asked you to stay and wait for him."

"I'll be right back." Then she realized that she had to retrieve her cape, but it would look strange if she wore the cape to simply go down to the bar. She needed an excuse to take her cape, because she couldn't leave without her phone, her keys, or her money. That was it. Money. "Oops, almost forgot my money." She walked to the desk chair to snatch her cape.

"You won't need that. Just tell them at the bar that you're with Damian. They'll comp your drinks," Lydia claimed.

Damn it! "Anybody could say that. How would the bartender know?"

"They'll know."

Another cryptic response by Lydia.

Maybe a half-truth would satisfy Lydia. "Well, if you must know, I feel a little uncomfortable in this outfit. Every guy just stares at my boobs, and it's just a little… unsettling. So I'd rather cover up."

That seemed to have done the trick, because Lydia nodded, "I get it. I'll come with you. I need a drink anyway. Nerves before the performance, you know?"

Naomi forced a smile, put her cape around her and tied it under her chin. Great, now she had to shake off Lydia somehow. Hopefully, it wasn't too difficult. After all, it was a mad crush in the club, and it wouldn't take much to slip away while Lydia ordered a drink at the bar.

On the way down to the bar, Lydia followed her like a shadow. She didn't understand why she was so adamant about not leaving her alone. As if she sensed that Naomi wanted to leave. She had to resort to a ruse to get out of here.

"Ouch," Naomi cried out and turned to Lydia. "Somebody just stepped on my foot."

"It's a hazard in here. Most guys have two left feet."

"Now I really need a drink." She smiled at Lydia. "Do you think you could order me a martini, while I hobble after you?"

"Sure. With olives or a twist?"

"Two olives, thanks." The lie worked.

The moment Lydia turned away and made her way to the bar, Naomi headed in the other direction. She wanted to walk around the dance floor to get to the other side of the club where the exit was located. But she spotted Damian standing only a few yards away from her, talking to another guy dressed as a vampire. Shit! Had he fixed the microphone already and was on his way back?

Naomi quickly turned on her heel and headed onto the dance floor to disappear amidst the crowd. The clubbers danced to a popular eighties pop song, and she tried as best she could to avoid elbows and feet. She was almost at the edge of the dance floor, when somebody to her left gripped her arm.

She spun her head toward him. Damian! How had he gotten to her so quickly when he'd been all the way at the other end?

"You're not leaving already, are you?" he asked and pulled her into his arms. "'Cause, you and I, we're not done." He rocked to the rhythm of the music, his arms snaking underneath her cape to hold her close to him, while the cape hid what he was doing.

"I was just… I thought…" But just like earlier, she couldn't think. Not with his hands on her, one palming her buttocks, the other stroking up the side of her torso toward her breasts.

"Dance with me," he murmured seductively.

"You could dance with any woman here," she protested weakly.

He chuckled and lowered his mouth to her ear. "Why would I do that when I already have what I want in my arms?"

Maybe taking his offer wasn't such a bad idea. After all, it would give her a chance to find out more about him and whatever was going on at the Mezzanine. Or was her reason more personal? Was the reason for staying that she wanted to let herself go in his arms, if only for a night, just to experience being desired by a gorgeous hunk? But did Damian only want her, because whomever he'd flirted with earlier had perhaps rejected him? Was she too easy?

Damian pressed his cheek to hers. "I enjoyed touching you. And I don't want the night to end."

"Damian," she murmured, her hand on his biceps tightening. "I gave you an out. You could have just let me leave. We both know I can't compete with the kind of girl I saw you flirt with earlier."

"You saw me flirt with somebody?"

"Yeah, and why wouldn't you? I'm sure you get plenty of offers every night. So, really, you don't have to follow through with this, just because we kissed earlier and it got a little out of hand."

"So that's what you're calling it when you're a few minutes away from climaxing."

She jerked back, stunned that he'd been able to read her so well. But of course, she couldn't admit that. "I wasn't—"

"You weren't? I apologize. That means I'll have to work harder on making sure you come, because I don't want to be the only one climaxing when we're in bed together."

Naomi gasped, though she liked his directness. He made it very clear what he wanted from her. He was different from other men who claimed they wanted to take it slow, only to steamroll her with their next breath.

"You're very sure of yourself," she said into his ear. "I hope you can deliver."

"Is that a challenge?"

"What if it is?" Because suddenly she was eager to explore what he was capable of. It was as if a little devil was sitting on her shoulder, urging her on to do something naughty and brazen.

Damian laughed softly. "Then I'm very grateful that we're both wearing capes."

All of a sudden, the music changed, and Naomi realized that Lydia was on stage and had started to sing a love song. The lights dimmed over the dance floor.

"You can't just… we're in public," Naomi protested.

Yet she didn't stop him when he started caressing her under the cape. "Nobody can see what I'm doing. All you have to do now is to make sure you hold our capes together. I'll take care of the rest."

"You're wicked," she said, but clutched the fabric and held the capes together. She was certain that anybody looking at them had to suspect that *something* was happening underneath the capes. Why didn't Damian seem to care about that? After all, everybody in the club knew who he was. Wouldn't he ruin his chances with other women by this public show of…

well, she wanted to say *affection*, but that couldn't be it. She searched for a better word. Public show of, uh, *lust*. Right. That's what it was. Had to be.

"Now kiss me," Damian demanded, and she lifted her face and offered her lips to him. "You really do look like Little Red Riding Hood. A very sinful version of her."

7

It had been a stroke of luck that the red cape had caught his attention, or Naomi might have left before he could stop her. And then he would have missed out on caressing her while they danced to the slow rhythm of the music.

Damian felt Naomi's soft lips and captured them, slanting his head to allow for a deeper connection, while beneath the fabric of their capes, his hands weren't idle. He didn't care if any of the vampires or hybrids in the club knew what he was doing. They would never get a chance to see Naomi's naked body or know what it was like to knead her heavy breasts and turn the nipples into hard little pebbles. Nor would they get to touch the place from where her arousal was wafting to his nostrils. With one hand he squeezed her breasts, while he slipped his other one down between her legs and underneath the short skirt.

Her panties were already soaked with her arousal, and even though he'd wanted to take his time, he couldn't wait finding out that she was already wet for him. He slipped his hand underneath the thin fabric and through the curly hair to touch her pussy. At the first contact, Naomi moaned, and he captured the sound in his mouth. Ah, how he loved a responsive woman. There was no shyness in her. Not anymore.

Damian bathed his fingers in her juices and stroked along her warm cleft, before he swept upwards to find her clit. The tiny organ was plump and ripe, ready for his attention.

He released her lips and pressed his cheek to hers, so he could whisper into her ear. "Tell me how you like it. Slower? Faster?"

"Damian," she murmured sounding dazed as if tipsy, though he smelled no alcohol on her. "You can't just, oh, oh…"

"Ah, so that's how you like it." He sucked her earlobe between his lips and bit down very gently, while he drew small circles around her clit, his tempo increasing. "That's the right spot, isn't it?"

He loved teasing her like this. He didn't need her to answer him, because her body was already telling him everything he needed to know.

And fuck, it made him hot. He'd never done this in such a public place, never pleasured a woman right on the dance floor of his club. He'd always liked his privacy, but when Naomi had told him that she'd seen him flirt with another woman earlier, he wanted to make sure she understood that he was sending a signal to all the women in the club that he was taken. That's why he was kissing her in full view of everybody, his fellow vampires too. If they saw them, they could easily guess what was going on beneath the capes.

"You make me so hot," he murmured close to her ear. "I could burst right now."

Naomi breathed hard, and her heartbeat accelerated. He could feel it beneath his palm that was still fondling her breasts.

"It feels so good," she let out on a breathless moan.

"Just let yourself go," he said and brought his hand from her breasts down around her waist to steady her. "I'll catch you, *chérie*."

He turned his face to her again and looked into her lust-drugged eyes. Her lips were parted, and her tongue darted out to lick them. The sight was just too much to resist. He took her mouth again and swept his tongue into the sweet cavern, teasing, exploring, and dueling with her. Farther below, he rubbed over her clit with an ever-increasing tempo in a rhythm her body dictated, when he suddenly felt her gasp into his mouth. As she climaxed, he slipped one dew-covered finger into her slit as deep as he could and felt her muscles spasm around him.

Damian released her lips and lowered his face to her neck, fighting against the urge to free his cock and take her in the middle of the dance floor.

Fuck! He hadn't expected Naomi climaxing in his arms to be such a breathtaking feeling. He couldn't wait to find out what it would feel like with his cock inside her.

Slowly, he felt Naomi's orgasm ebb, and pulled his finger from her tight sheath. She went all soft in his arms.

"How about we go back to my office?" he murmured.

"Yes." Her answer was more breath than word.

He made sure that Naomi's clothing beneath the cape was properly adjusted, before he guided her through the dancers.

"I need water," she said.

"There's water in my office." He didn't want to waste time at the bar, even though his staff would make sure he didn't have to wait long to be served. But waiting even a second was a second too long. Besides, he didn't want to run into a bunch of people who would all see that he was sporting a boner of massive proportions.

The moment they were back in his office, he shut the door behind them and flipped the lock shut.

~ ~ ~

Naomi felt as if in a daze, but she heard Damian lock the door to the office behind them. She turned around to him and noticed the lusting look he raked over her. It made her even hotter than she already felt. She untied her cape and tossed it on the seating arrangement.

"Water, right?" he asked in a hoarse voice and stalked toward the refrigerator, while ridding himself of his cape and tossing it to join hers.

A moment later, he handed her an ice-cold bottle of water, and she gulped half of it down, before she handed it to him.

"Thank you."

He downed the remaining half of the water, then tossed the bottle in the trash bin next to the desk. While he did that, Naomi's gaze fell onto his pants, or rather the bulge hidden behind his zipper. His arousal was undeniable. The fact that he'd just pleasured her on the dance floor where everybody who cared to look could have easily guessed what they were doing, should make her feel ashamed. Instead, it excited her. And made her feel bold.

She'd never been aggressive when it came to sex, but Damian stirred something in her, and she couldn't help but act upon that feeling. She took a step toward him, then placed her hand over the outline of his erection, feeling it pulse hotly against her palm.

Damian put his arm around her waist, and pulled her even closer. "You want to feel me inside you?"

She squeezed his cock, and his eyes were shimmering golden now. His fangs peeked from his lips again like earlier, and she realized something now. She lifted her free hand to his lips.

"When you kissed me, I didn't feel your fangs. I thought you'd taken them out."

"No, I just retracted them," he said.

"How? I thought they're just stick-ons." She slid her finger across one fang, and felt him suck in a breath.

"Fuck!" Then he swallowed visibly.

"They don't feel like plastic." They felt really sharp. "How do you retract them?"

"By touch."

He took her finger and pressed it against one fang. To her surprise the fang slid upward, and was suddenly gone.

"See?"

"Wow, that's genius." She'd never seen props that real.

He chuckled. "I had them made especially." Then he glanced down to where her hand still cupped his erection. "But you didn't answer my question. Do you want to feel my cock inside you?"

Now she was the one who swallowed hard. Damian was direct, and she liked that. "Why are you still dressed?"

"I guess that's a yes."

But instead of opening the button of his pants, he took her hand and led her to the far wall of the office. Was he going to fuck her up against the wall, rather than on the couch? Clearly, Damian wasn't a man of ordinary tastes.

When he pressed his hand against a spot on the wall, a door suddenly opened up toward them, a door that looked exactly like the wall. Stunned, she allowed him to usher her into a secret room, then heard him close and lock the door behind them, while she let her eyes roam. A large bed dominated the room, which was bathed in subdued light coming from several wall sconces. There was a second door, which was ajar and looked like it led into a miniscule bathroom. In one corner of the room was a safe, next to it a clothes rack and a small dresser, a few bottles of alcohol sitting on top of it.

"Do you bring a lot of women here?" she couldn't help but ask.

He pulled her into his arms and slid his fingers under her chin. "Forget about anything that might or might not have happened in here before tonight. Can you do that?"

She nodded.

"Good." He captured her lips, and kissed her deeply, before withdrawing again.

He started unbuttoning his shirt, and she let her eyes roam over him, before she reached behind her back to try to lower the zipper of her dress.

"Wait," he demanded. "I'd like to undress you myself."

She smiled and dropped her hands, while he rid himself of his shirt. She reveled in the way he undressed himself with natural grace and self-confidence. The body he revealed was perfect, like that of a Greek God: strong muscled arms and legs, a ripped stomach, and a nearly hairless chest. When he stood in front of her with only his black boxer briefs, her mouth went dry. She'd never seen such male perfection—other than in a magazine or on TV.

Naomi met his gaze, when he hooked his thumbs into his boxer briefs and rid himself of them. His cock sprang free, hard and heavy, curving up toward his navel.

A breath rushed from her lungs. He was beautiful all over. And she wondered whether she'd passed out somewhere along the way and this was only a dream. A man like Damian wanted to sleep with her? Why?

"Something wrong?" he asked and took a step toward her. "You don't like what you see?"

She ripped her gaze from his cock and met his eyes. "No, I like, I like it very much."

"Then why are you frowning?"

"'Cause this is probably not real. I must be dreaming."

A soft chuckle rolled over Damian's lips. "I'm the one who's dreaming, *chérie*."

She loved the way he said the last word.

Damian put his hands on her shoulders, then turned her and unzipped her dress. As cool air blew against her back, he kissed one shoulder and worked his way toward her neck, planting open-mouthed kisses on her heated skin. She shivered at the sensual contact. Then she felt his hands on her breasts and realized that he'd pushed the dress down and freed her of it. Aware that she was only wearing her high heels and a G-string now, she felt self-conscious. Now he would see that she was chubby around her waist, hips, and stomach, and how truly heavy her boobs really were, how much extra weight she carried around her midsection, which with the right clothing she could sometimes disguise. But in the nude, everything was laid bare. Would he regret this?

"Damian," she murmured. "Can we dim the lights?"

He lifted his head from her neck and turned her to face him. "You don't like looking at me?"

She shook her head. "It's not you. It's, ahm, me. My body… it's not as perfect as yours."

Damian stepped back and ran his eyes over her. "I beg to differ. I love looking at you, so please don't make me make love to you in the dark. You're perfect."

He thought she was perfect?

"I'm not perfect."

"Beauty is in the eyes of the beholder." Then he motioned to the bed. "Now be a good girl, and lie down on the bed."

8

Damian watched as Naomi lay down on the bed, only wearing her G-string and her high heels now. She looked like a pinup girl from the fifties: luscious curves, red lips, and golden locks. With almost innocent eyes, she looked up from under her long lashes. Oh yes, she was perfect for him, even if she didn't want to believe it.

He slowly reached for her feet and freed her of her shoes, before he leaned over her and brought his hands to her hips.

"Let's get rid of this," he said, and pulled on her G-string. She helped him by lifting her backside off the bed for a second, then allowed him to slide it down her legs.

The tiny triangle of hair at the apex of her thighs was blond. From there, the aroma of her arousal drifted to his nostrils, making him even harder than he already was. Slowly, he lowered himself over her, and pushed her legs apart to make space for himself.

"Condom," she said, a panicked look on her face.

"Don't worry, I've got some here. But I'm not quite ready to get inside you."

"You look pretty ready to me," she said with a smirk, and it looked like she was finally starting to relax.

Damian chuckled. "That hard-on isn't going anywhere anytime soon, *chérie*. But I believe I was interrupted earlier when Lydia barged into the office." He dropped a deliberate gaze to her breasts. "And I don't like being interrupted. Particularly not when I'm feasting on something so gorgeous."

"Oh," Naomi said on a breath. "You don't think they're too big?"

He dipped his head to her breasts, soaking in the scent of her warm flesh, feeling her soft skin caress his face as he pressed a kiss into the valley between them.

"They're perfect. And some other time I'd like your tits to cradle my cock." He looked at her face, then licked a wet path between her breasts as if preparing her for his cock, and he noticed something flicker in her eyes. Interest? "And hold me tight between them until I come. But not tonight."

"Then what do you want to do tonight?" she murmured seductively.

"How about I show you?"

Braced above her, Damian put his lips around Naomi's hard nipple and sucked it into his mouth, while he squeezed her ample flesh, massaging it. Ever since he'd been a little kid and had seen his father, Amaury, bite his mother's breast to feed from her, he'd dreamed of doing the same with the woman who would one day become his blood-bonded mate. The thought of such intimacy suddenly flashed in his mind, and though he'd never bitten a human woman in her breast to drink from her there, the thought was more than just a little tempting right now.

He allowed his fangs to descend so he could rub them along her soft skin, and was glad that Naomi had bought his lie about his retracting fake fangs. It allowed him to play with her now, to get an idea of how erotic it would be to bite her while he sucked her stiff nipple into his mouth.

Beneath him, Naomi moaned in obvious enjoyment of his caresses. Her tits were overflowing his palms. They were firm and ripe, like fruits ready for harvest. And they were sensitive. A flick of his tongue, a little sucking, and already, the beautiful woman in his arms was writhing beneath him, asking for more. He switched to her other breast, giving it the same treatment, while farther below, he rubbed his cock over her mound, without entering her. If he wanted to, he could thrust into her at any moment, and he knew he wouldn't meet with any resistance, but he would respect her wish to use a condom, even though it wasn't necessary. Vampires didn't carry disease, and only a blood-bonded vampire could impregnate a female.

Naomi's hands were exploring him now, one stroking over his shoulders and nape, the other roaming his lower back, then sliding onto his ass to press him more firmly against her.

"Easy, easy," he murmured as he let her nipple plop from his mouth. "We've got all night."

"But I want you inside me," she demanded.

He laughed softly. "Well, look at you. First you wanted me to turn down the lights, and now you can't wait to feel my cock inside you. Why the rush, *chérie*? You've got somewhere to be?"

"I just don't want you to change your mind…" She lowered her lids slightly as if trying to hide from him.

"That'll happen, sure…" He paused and noticed disappointment spread on her face. "…when hell freezes over." Then he leaned over to the small bedside table and opened the drawer, which was full of condoms, and took one out. "But just in case you don't believe me, I'd better take your pussy now, so we can put that little insecurity of yours to rest."

Quickly, he ripped the foil packet open, and rolled the condom over his cock. Then he positioned himself at her center. With one quick thrust, he seated himself to the hilt in her wet sheath and shuddered.

"Fuck!" he hissed. This felt even better than he'd expected. And he'd already had high expectations after he'd slipped his finger into her earlier. But the way Naomi's interior muscles gripped his cock, was out of this world amazing. "Naomi," he murmured at her lips. "You feel so good."

Naomi let out a slow, trembling breath. "Oh God, you're… you're so… perfect." She spread her legs wider, then wrapped them around his hips, the action making him slide even deeper into her.

"You trying to kill me?" Damian ground out, barely able to hold on to his control. "Hold still, babe, or I'm gonna come in two seconds flat."

When she smirked, he added, "Wait until I've got you teetering on the edge of an orgasm, minx. Not my fault that your pussy feels better than anything I've ever felt."

"Do you say that to every woman you sleep with?"

He had to chuckle at that. "Maybe I should let you know one thing right now, so you're clear on the rules in my bed. Everything I say in bed I say because I feel it, not because a woman wants me to say it. So, no, I've never been inside a woman's pussy that felt as good as yours. And I've never slept with a woman who's had a more perfect body than yours."

"You mean that?" She looked at him, a look of surprise on her face. "I thought with all the skinny models who clearly like you—"

He put his finger over her lips. "Time for talking is over." He drew his hips back, pulled his cock out of her tight channel, then slammed back into her.

He grinned with satisfaction when he noticed that Naomi let out a breath and pressed her head harder into the pillow, her back arching, her breasts thrust in his direction. They bounced up and down, side to side with every thrust he delivered, and he couldn't get enough of the erotic sight. Yeah, there was no way he'd ever switch the lights off. He wanted to feast his eyes on her delectable beauty, and see her react to him fucking her.

"You're so fucking sexy," he said, pinning her with his gaze, while he rammed his cock deep and hard into her to underscore his words. There was only one thing that would make this experience even better: tasting her blood.

He dipped his head to her neck and kissed her there, feeling her plump vein drum against his lips.

"Can I interest you in a little roleplaying?" he murmured into her ear.

"Like what?" she asked, her voice sounding eager and receptive.

He drove in and out of her, shifting his angle slightly so his pelvic bone brushed over her clit with every thrust. Then he lifted his head to look at her. "How about I play vampire and bite you, and you play my willing victim?"

His heart beat excitedly, while he waited for her response.

"I won't hurt you," he added.

"You're gonna give me a hickey," she said, but simultaneously she turned her head to the side to offer her neck to him. She brushed her long hair aside. "Will that turn you on?"

"More than you can know," Damian admitted. "I'll make sure you enjoy it too." He knew she would, because a vampire's bite was pleasurable not only for the vampire, but also for the human host. And when performed during sex, it guaranteed sexual ecstasy.

"Okay."

"Thank you," he murmured and lowered his lips to her neck. He licked over the spot where her vein pulsed, preparing her for the bite, his saliva assuring that there would be no pain.

His fangs extended fully. Slowing his thrusts, he rubbed his fangs over her skin, then set their sharp tips to her skin, before driving them into her.

A gasp burst from Naomi's lips, then her hands were on his ass, shoving him deeper into her slick pussy. "Oh, God, yes!"

Relieved that Naomi was responding positively to him, Damian began to suck on the plump vein. Her rich blood tasted of vanilla and oranges, and it coated his throat and made his tastebuds explode the way fireworks exploded. The vampire inside him took over now, and his hips moved faster, driving his cock deeper and harder into her.

Beneath him, Naomi spasmed, and he realized that the effect of the bite was making her climax. He let himself go, and felt his semen rush through his cock and burst from the tip, while he continued thrusting in and out of her, his cock still hard and relentless. Naomi moaned and writhed beneath him, her hands still on his ass, still holding onto him as if she didn't want him to leave her warm channel. He had no intention of stopping now, though he knew that he would have to stop drinking from her, so as not to weaken her.

He swallowed the last drops of her delicious essence, and withdrew his fangs, then licked over the incisions so that there would be no evidence of his bite. The two small holes healed instantly. With Naomi's blood inside him now, his cock filled with more blood despite his orgasm, and he continued riding her, feeling her muscles contract around him a second time.

He lifted his head from her neck, and looked into her eyes. She looked well-loved. Her eyes had a dreamy quality to them, and a thin sheen of perspiration covered her skin. Looking deep into her eyes and seeing her look at him with wonder, he let himself go once more, and climaxed a second time.

This time, he slowly rolled off her. "Fuck!" He'd never felt anything so breathtaking. Quickly, he rid himself of the used condom, and turned back to Naomi to pull her into his arms. "You okay? I didn't take you too hard, did I?"

"You kidding?" She breathed hard. "That was amazing."

Damian let out a contented laugh. "Good. So I guess that means I met your challenge."

"And then some," she admitted.

He pulled her onto him, and her legs fell open to either side of his hips, while her heavy breasts flattened against his chest, and she nuzzled her face in his neck.

"You liked that bite?"

9

Naomi contemplated Damian's question. "It didn't feel like a bite." She put her hand to the spot where she'd felt his teeth only minutes earlier, but her skin seemed unbroken. "It doesn't even feel sore."

"Tell me what it felt like for you," he demanded.

She didn't even know how to describe it. "I can't compare it to anything else I've ever felt. All I could feel was your cock inside me, and a sensation as if you were licking my clit at the same time. I know it makes no sense, and it's not possible, but it's—"

"It doesn't have to make sense. I'm happy to hear that you enjoyed it. I did too. You made me come twice."

Naomi sat up and looked down at him. She'd sensed him spasming twice inside her, but had thought she was wrong. "I thought men don't have multiple orgasms."

Damian smirked, and his eyes sparkled in a beautiful blue. "Guess you allowing me this little roleplaying turned me on so much that I just had to come twice."

Then she suddenly noticed something. "Your eyes."

"What about them?"

"Earlier tonight they were golden and then red. When did you take out your colored contact lenses?"

"I didn't."

"But now your eyes are blue."

"It's special lenses that change color depending on which way the light hits them."

He sat up and put his arm around her back then turned his head slightly, and suddenly there was a golden hue in his irises.

"Wow. You really went all out with your costume."

"So did you." He pressed a sweet kiss to her lips. "Your Little Red Riding Hood costume made me wanna be the big bad wolf."

"I thought you were playing vampire."

"Same thing: creatures with sharp teeth."

She dropped her gaze to the spot between their bodies, where Damian's cock stood erect again. "And apparently rampant cocks."

He winked at her, and suddenly looked even younger than she guessed him to be. "Care to help alleviate that condition?"

She cocked her head, becoming more confident by the second. "How?"

"By riding me like Lady Godiva," he suggested. "So I can get my fill of your pretty tits."

She noticed the way he looked at her, and not just at her breasts. At all of her. As if he really meant what he'd said: that he thought she was perfect. As if she were his equal in beauty. And now he was suggesting that she ride him. It had never been her favorite position, because it meant that she couldn't hide her body. Everything would be on display, every ounce of her. But the lusting look Damian now raked over her made her forget about all her body's imperfections.

"What do you say?" he prompted her, and she realized that she'd been silent for too long.

"Hand me a condom please."

As he bent toward the bedside table, Naomi's gaze was drawn to the mirror on the wall. She saw herself, and pushed back the hair from her neck to examine the spot where Damian had bitten her. But all she saw was unblemished skin. Had he bitten her on the other side? She pulled back the hair from that side of her neck too, but there was no sign of a bite either. Not even a reddening of the skin.

When she stared back at Damian, he held her gaze. "I thought you bit me. But my skin looks fine. It's not even red."

He put his hand on her nape and pulled her to him, so his mouth was only an inch from hers. "I told you I wouldn't hurt you."

"I was expecting to have a hickey. At least. You're a magician."

"Hardly." He pressed a soft kiss to her lips, and released her again. "But I *am* insatiable, so how about you put that condom on me, and ride me before I change my mind and toss you on your belly and ride you instead?"

At the image of Damian impaling her from behind, her entire body flushed.

He smiled. "I see, that's apparently not a threat at all. I'll keep that in mind for the future."

Delighted at how eager Damian was to continue their night of passion rather than get her to leave now that he'd gotten what he wanted, Naomi rolled the condom over his erection.

"You're so big," she marveled.

"I'm the right size for you," he said and lay back on the sheets, his eyes on her, the golden shimmer back in his irises. "Ride me as slow or as fast as you want."

She lifted herself on her knees and adjusted her position so Damian's cock was poised at her pussy. She was still wet from earlier, and completely baffled how he could be hard again so soon. When she bore down on him and impaled herself, she caught him looking at her, his lips parted, and his skin glistened.

She'd never had sex with a man who hadn't once closed his eyes, but was instead looking at her all the time. The other men, she suspected had probably thought of other women while they were having sex with her, sexier ones, slimmer ones. Yet Damian looked at her with such hunger in his eyes that she knew with certainty that he wasn't thinking of anyone or anything else other than her at this moment.

"God, you're beautiful," he murmured. "How come I've never seen you before?"

It didn't look like he needed an answer from her. Instead, she began to ride him in a slow but steady tempo, enjoying the feeling of his cock filling her on every descent. When Damian reached for her, she thought at first that he wanted to urge her to go faster, but instead, he caressed her breasts almost as if worshipping them. She bent over him, bringing them to his face.

"Suck them," she demanded.

Heat charged through her when he put his lips around one nipple, and licked his hot tongue over it, while he squeezed both breasts with his hands. She'd always loved it when a man licked and caressed her breasts, always known that they were very sensitive. But tonight, they seemed to be even more sensitive than before, because when Damian gently pressed his teeth against her soft flesh without biting down, a spear of electricity charged into her clit and ignited her.

"Damian, oh God, yes!"

He switched to the other nipple, dropped one hand to her pussy, and combed his fingers through her thatch of hair. When he touched her clit and rubbed over it, she increased her tempo, riding him faster now, impaling herself with more force.

Damian sucked her other nipple into his mouth and licked over it, before he pressed his teeth to her flesh, eliciting the same reaction from her as before. Fire seemed to charge through her entire body. Only thinking of the pleasure Damian was giving her, she let herself go and felt the waves of her orgasm crash over her.

Inside her, she suddenly felt waves of a different kind. Damian's cock was spasming as he climaxed too. He let her nipple slip from his mouth when she collapsed on top of him, and put his arm around her back to hold her closely.

"Fuck, you're hot." His hot breath was at her ear.

"I can't believe how good you make me feel." And how much it had turned her on to feel his teeth scrape against the sensitive skin of her breasts.

He stroked over her hair, then brought his hand to her nape and pulled her face to him. "You didn't mind my teeth on your tits?"

"You made me come by doing that," she admitted.

"Good." He pulled her face to his for a kiss. When he released her, he smiled at her. "And now, I think I do need a short nap."

She got the message. It was time for her to leave. She tried to sit up, but his arms around her held her back.

"Where're you going?"

"Leaving. You said you wanted to sleep."

"Yeah, but not alone. Or don't you like to share a bed with the man you just made love to?"

She hesitated. Did he really mean for her to stay? "You want me to stay?"

"I do." He pushed a strand of hair out of her face. "'Cause I'll enjoy falling asleep with you in my arms."

She smiled and snuggled against him.

"I hope that means yes."

"Yes," she murmured into his ear. "But what if I wake up and want more?"

He chuckled. "Then you'll just have to take what you want. I won't complain."

"I might just do that." Because she was getting slowly but surely addicted to Damian and the way he made her feel.

10

Damian stirred and reached his arm out to pull Naomi closer to him, but she wasn't next to him anymore. His eyes shot open. He was alone in the secret room behind the manager's office in the Mezzanine. He looked toward the open door to the bathroom, but it was empty too. When he looked at the door leading into the office, he noticed that it was unlocked, but closed. He looked at the clock: it was shortly past five a.m.

He jumped out of bed, pulled on his boxer briefs, and went into the office, hoping that Naomi had gotten up to get something to drink from the fridge, but the office was empty too. Her red cape was gone. Naomi had left, and from what he could see, she hadn't left him a note with her phone number. Why would she leave without giving him a means to contact her? Surely, she'd enjoyed their night together just as much as he. Didn't she want a repeat of the same? He did.

Fuck!

Disappointed, he went back into the secret room. In the shower, he recalled how compatible they'd been in bed, how perfect their lovemaking had been. He'd been insatiable, and as a result, he'd fucked her again when he'd woken sometime after two a.m., and Naomi had been a more than willing participant. But despite his vampire stamina and endurance, even he needed a little sleep after the marathon sex they'd had, and he'd slept so deeply that he hadn't heard Naomi leave the bed.

But he wasn't giving up that easily. He'd find her.

Damian finished his shower and got dressed, then went back to the office and took his cell phone from his pants pocket. He sat down behind the desk and dialed his uncle's number. Since it was still dark, Eddie would be at Scanguards HQ in the Mission.

"Hey, Damian, what's up?" Eddie answered cheerfully.

"Hey, Eddie, you have a minute to make an inquiry for me?"

"Sure, what do you need?"

"I need you to find a girl for me."

Eddie chuckled, and Damian could hear a second voice in the background. Apparently, Thomas, Eddie's blood-bonded mate, was with him. Not a surprise. The two were inseparable.

"I don't think you need me to find a girl for you. I wouldn't know where to start."

Damian let out a frustrated sigh. He loved his uncle, but right now he wasn't in the mood for his jokes. "What I meant to say is that I met a woman last night, and now she's gone, and all I have is her first name. Naomi."

"Why didn't you say so in the first place?" Eddie asked, his voice still laced with humor.

"Can you hack into the DMV and see if you can find her?"

"You know we don't need to hack the DMV anymore, right? The governor gave us access."

"Well, good, then can you please do it now. It's important."

Damian heard the clacking of a keyboard. "Okay, first name: Naomi. Can you describe her?"

"She's beautiful, a size 12 and 36DD, and—"

"I meant height, weight, hair color, eye color, not her bra size," Eddie interrupted.

Fuck! What was he thinking? Clearly, he wasn't. "Sorry, uhm, blond hair, blue eyes, about five foot five, between 160 and 170 pounds."

"Ah, a chubby one," Eddie commented.

"She's not chubby!" Damian protested. "She's curvaceous."

"You want my help or not?"

"I do," Damian ground out, swallowing his annoyance. Why did everybody call a woman with curves chubby? She was perfect.

"Okay then, there aren't a lot of women named Naomi, so that helps. Let's see," Eddie replied.

Impatiently, Damian drummed his fingers on the desk.

"There, I think that's her. Naomi Sutton. I'll text you the photo. Let me know if that's her."

A moment later, Damian's cell pinged, and he looked at his messages. Eddie had sent the photo. "That's her!"

"Great. I'll send you a picture of her license with her address. Let me see if we have anything else on her." There was more tapping on a keyboard, then Eddie added, "She works for the Chronicle."

"The newspaper?"

"Yep, San Francisco Chronicle. She must be a reporter or something, 'cause it says here that she has a BA in Journalism."

"Thanks, Eddie, appreciate it."

"You bet."

Damian disconnected the call. For a moment, he just sat there, stunned. Was it just a coincidence that Naomi worked as a journalist, or did her job have anything to do with why she'd been in his office? Had she really been there on a dare by her girlfriends, or was something else going on? After he'd kissed Naomi, and Lydia had interrupted them, he'd dismissed his initial suspicions about finding her in his office, but now, knowing that she was working for the San Francisco Chronicle, the same suspicions reawakened. Had she been snooping around? And if yes, then why?

Fuck! In general, he had no trouble reading a person, and was able to tell whether somebody lied to him or not, but when it came to Naomi, his judgment was clouded. Yeah, clouded with lust. Because that's all he could think of when he thought of her: of her beneath him, his cock in her hot pussy, her nipples in his mouth, his face crushed against her breasts, his fingers on her clit, his hands kneading her heavy tits.

Damian shoved a hand through his thick hair. What now? He couldn't just show up at her place. No, he had to figure out first, why she'd been at the club, why she'd targeted him. But how? He'd have to think on it. And he couldn't very well tell any of his friends, not even his twin, or everybody would know that he'd stepped into a trap. A trap set by a sensual and utterly alluring temptress who knew just how to use her body to get what she wanted. He'd even bought her innocent act, her demure behavior when she'd asked if he could dim the lights because she believed her body wasn't perfect. And it must have been an act, because minutes later, she'd allowed him to bite her. And when she'd ridden him, she'd proved to him how experienced she was, and that a little rough sex wasn't new to her.

She'd enjoyed the things they'd done together. There was no doubt about it.

Was that what she did? Seduce a man for a story she was writing? But what story? He looked around the office. Had she searched the place? Nothing seemed to be out of order. Besides, there wasn't much of interest to anybody, certainly not to a newspaper. A few financial records, orders for booze and other supplies, wage records for the staff, cash receipts, nothing out of the ordinary.

He got up to open the fridge. There were several bottles of water in it, and behind them were several bottles of blood. It didn't look like Naomi had opened the fridge and moved any of the water bottles to give her a view of the bottles of blood in the row behind. But it was probably better from now on to lock the fridge in case another human was somehow able to enter the office. He took out one of the bottles of blood, and unscrewed the top. He was about to set the bottle to his lips, when he heard the door open behind him. He looked over his shoulder.

"Morning, Damian," Patrick said, still dressed in his vampire costume.

Damian turned to him and greeted him before gulping down half the bottle.

Patrick pointed to the bottle. "You have another one?"

"Help yourself."

Patrick marched to the fridge and took a bottle out of it. "The last crate of the blood in the basement is gone. Did you bring it up? We'll have to reorder pronto."

"It was there last night before the party. I checked it myself."

"Yeah, it's not there anymore."

"That can't be. Are you sure?"

"Yep. The entire crate is gone, not just the bottles."

Damian exchanged a look with Patrick, and realized that they were having the same suspicion. "You think somebody stole it?"

Patrick nodded. "It's one thing for a few bottles to be gone, because the staff last night would have had some during their breaks, but why would the entire crate be gone?"

"Let's check the security tapes," Damian suggested. "I checked on the storeroom just before nine o'clock." He let himself fall into the office chair and woke up the computer, logged in, and navigated to the security system. It took only moments to find the right camera and get to the point of the recording where Damian could see himself leaving the storeroom and locking the door behind him.

"That was me checking just before nine p.m.," he said to Patrick.

"Okay, let's speed through it."

As they sped through the recording, they slowed it only when somebody stopped in front of the storeroom. At first it was Tanja, who at shortly before eleven o'clock entered the storeroom, using her key. About ten minutes later, she came back out, and she didn't carry anything with her when she exited and locked the door.

"Probably took her break and drank a bottle," Patrick guessed and pointed to the screen. "With her dominatrix outfit, she can't even hide a single bottle on her let alone a crate."

"True." Damian let the tape run, when suddenly a person in a red cape with a hood entered the corridor. Her cape was drawn deep over her head, so the camera couldn't capture her face, but he knew who this was: Naomi. What the hell was she doing in a corridor that could only be reached through a door marked *Employees Only*?

"Who's that?" Patrick asked.

"No idea," Damian lied, and continued watching as Naomi tested the handle to the storeroom, then disappeared back in the same direction she'd come from.

"Odd," Patrick said. "Particularly since I saw you making out with a woman in a red cape. So you don't know who that is?"

Fuck! Damian scrambled for an explanation. "Listen, she was so drunk, she probably couldn't find her way to the restroom." He hated to lie to his friend and co-manager, but until he knew what Naomi had really been doing at the club the previous night, he wouldn't give anything away.

"Oh, yeah?" Patrick shook his head. "Is that why she practically let you fuck her on the dance floor?"

"I didn't fuck her on—"

Patrick's laughter interrupted him. "Oh my God, you're so easy to rile up today. Didn't get any last night, huh? Did she pass out before you could get down to business?"

"No woman passes out when I fuck her. Believe me, she was fully awake for the entire performance," Damian shot back. The words were out before he knew what he was saying.

"So why not say so right away?"

"Because it's none of your fucking business." Then he pointed back to the screen. "Shall we continue, or shall we discuss your sexual exploits from last night, if there were any?"

"Ouch, I'm wounded," Patrick said in a mocking tone. "But contrary to you, I don't keep my exploits a secret." He gestured to the monitor. "Let's see who took the blood, so I can go home and get some rest. After all, I was busy taking care of *two* women last night."

Damian rolled his eyes. He wasn't going to start a contest who'd had more sex, he or Patrick. Instead, he sped through the tape again. This time, Andrew in his police uniform shorts appeared at the door to the storeroom. But he wasn't alone. A handsome man dressed as a sexy pharaoh was with him. They disappeared in the storeroom together.

"Maybe we should tell Andrew that his breaks aren't there for him to have sex in the storeroom," Patrick suggested.

"Do you really care whom he fucks and where, as long as it's not out in the open?"

Patrick shrugged. "I thought you cared."

Right now, Damian cared only about two things: to find out who'd taken the crate of human blood, and why Naomi had really come to the club.

The time stamp on the recording showed 3:17 a.m. when a figure dressed in a black-and-white Harlequin costume with a Venetian facemask showed up in front of the storeroom and unlocked it. Moments later, the person came back out, this time carrying a large crate, and disappeared via the back exit.

"Fuck! There's our thief," Patrick said.

"Were any of the staff wearing that costume last night?" Damian asked, even though he already knew the answer.

"Not that I saw. Though I didn't see what Orlando was wearing, since I entered via the back."

"He didn't wear a costume. And this person"—he pointed to the screen—"is way too small to be Orlando anyway. More like the size of a woman, now that I'm looking more closely."

Patrick nodded. "You're right. The coat check girls?"

Damian shook his head. "Beth was dressed as a nurse, and Melanie as a flapper. Though either one of them could have slipped the Harlequin outfit over her costume. But at that time, the two of them would have been so busy at the coat check with lots of people leaving between three and four. If one of the girls had left, it would have been noticed."

"Good point. We should talk to them. Separately. I volunteer."

"Sure you do." But Damian was glad for it, because he knew that Beth liked him a little too much, and he didn't want to be alone with her. "I'll talk to Orlando, see if he noticed anything. And the bartenders. Are they still here, cleaning up?"

"No. They left a half hour ago. I just let the daytime cleaning crew in."

"Okay, I'll stop by at Sam's and at Andrew's, but Tanja lives all the way out in the Richmond, near Beth's. Why don't you check in with Tanja too?" Damian asked.

"No problem, but I've gotta leave now, or I won't get a wink of sleep before I have to be back here tonight. Unless you want to work tonight?"

"No chance." He had more important things to do. "But I'll go through the rest of the security tapes to see if the thief was captured by any other cameras."

"Sounds good. Keep me posted," Patrick said. He turned to the door. "Oh, and do you think we need to tell Amaury or my dad?"

"I'm afraid so. A case of human blood bottled by Scanguards disappearing is a security risk. But let me handle it. I'll speak to my dad tonight. Maybe by that time, we'll already know who took the crate." And why.

"Thanks, appreciate it."

Patrick left, and the door snapped shut behind him, leaving Damian alone with his thoughts.

Something felt off. Why would anybody steal the blood that was provided to the vampire employees of the Mezzanine? The blood that Scanguards procured via a blood bank and then bottled was provided free of charge to discourage the staff from feeding directly from humans, minimizing the risk of exposure. The blood was only of value to a vampire—unless a human wanted to use it as evidence for something. Or to back up a story.

11

It was already midday, when Naomi arrived at the apartment building that bordered on the lot occupied by the Mezzanine nightclub. Mrs. Zhang, an Asian woman in her late sixties, had buzzed her into the building, and was now ushering her into the neat two-bedroom flat. And the place was very neat—obsessively so.

"So the paper sent you," Mrs. Zhang said in flawless English. "I'd already given up on anybody listening to me. The police certainly didn't. But then, I'm used to the police not taking me seriously. They have it in for me. Ever since I made a complaint about one of their officers. They never fired him. Instead, they all stood behind him, claiming I made everything up. I think it gives them pleasure to see me suffer."

Naomi forced a friendly expression onto her face, when she wanted to roll her eyes. Already now she realized whom she was dealing with, and she hadn't even spent a full minute in Mrs. Zhang's presence yet. The woman was a complainer, a person who could find fault with anything. On top of it she felt persecuted for whatever reason. And she was a busybody who stuck her nose into everybody's business. Naomi wasn't surprised that the police had dismissed her claim of a satanic blood ritual going down at the Mezzanine.

From everything Naomi had seen the night before, there was no indication that anything odd was going on in the club. Well, maybe a secret room off the manager's office was a little odd, but the room clearly wasn't meant for any satanic rituals, but for something much more enjoyable.

Just thinking of Damian and how he'd made her feel sent a wave of heat through her core, scorching her from inside. She pushed the thoughts away to concentrate on the woman who was now offering her to sit on the sofa.

"Thank you, Mrs. Zhang. Could you please tell me a little more about what you saw happening at the club and when?" Naomi pulled a small notepad and a pen from her handbag.

"That club is a bad influence, a sore in the neighborhood. A bad influence for the young. The things that happen there… And what I saw didn't just happen once. It's been going on for a few weeks now. Most nights, well, at least four or five times a week, I see them. You know, with blood on them."

"Who do you see?"

"Men, young ones. They're well-dressed, you know like rich kids. Still, even with their money they can't disguise that they're not decent people. I could tell immediately. They were bad. I saw the blood on their clothing, and their faces too. You know, blood splatter. I watch *Forensic Files*, I know what it looks like. As if they slaughtered somebody."

Her claim sounded far-fetched, but Naomi had promised her editor to look into this, so she would give it her best effort. "And from where could you see that much detail?"

"Oh, you don't believe me?" She rose. "Come. You can see very well from my bedroom."

Naomi followed her as she walked into the bedroom, which looked just as neat as the rest of the flat, almost as if nobody ever slept in the bed. There wasn't a single wrinkle in the sheets.

"Here," Mrs. Zhang said and pulled the net curtain back.

Naomi stepped closer. She had to admit that from this window, there was indeed a direct view of the back entrance of the club, and the dumpsters lining the alley next to it. "I see. And at what time of the day did you see these, uh, men with blood on them?"

"Always at night. It's always dark."

Naomi raised an eyebrow.

"There are lights over the back exit. I see very well at night."

The words sounded like a reprimand. It appeared that Naomi's raised eyebrow hadn't escaped Mrs. Zhang's notice.

"And you said this didn't just happen once?"

She nodded. "Several times now I've seen them with blood."

"How many men?"

"Two."

"Only two? Always the same men?"

"At least one was always the same, the other one I'm not sure. I couldn't see his face clearly."

Naomi looked down to the club again, wondering if there was anything to the woman's claims. "Did you ever record the men on your cell phone so you could show the police what was happening?"

"I don't have a cell phone. It fries the brain. You know, microwaves."

"Okay, and did you ever see anything else that looked suspicious? Like did you see any drugs being exchanged? Any cash? Or anything else that seemed odd?"

"Hmm. I remember that one of them always gave the other one something. But it was too small to see what it was."

"And when did you last see these two men?"

"Not last night, and not the night before either. But the night before that I saw one of them, but not the other."

"And that was the last time you saw either one of them?"

"Yes, and—" She stopped herself, and started again, "Last night there was something else that was strange."

"During the Halloween party at the club?"

She frowned. "It was even louder last night than normal. I woke up several times. A man came out, well at least I think it was a man. He was wearing a mask, you know, one of those they wear at the carnival in Venice?"

"I know what you're talking about."

"And he was wearing some sort of black and white costume. He was carrying something. He was looking over his shoulder and stumbled. Something made a noise, like glass breaking. I saw him toss something in the dumpster, but he missed. It made an awful noise."

"Which dumpster?"

Mrs. Zhang pointed out of the window. "The one in the middle."

"And why did you find the person strange?"

"Well, it was around 3 o'clock, and he looked like he didn't belong there."

"But there was a costume party there last night."

"I know. But the way he looked around. It was as if he was scared that somebody would see him."

"You said he wore a mask. You couldn't see his face."

"I could tell by the way he moved."

"Hmm." Naomi took that statement with a grain of salt. "And did you see where the person went afterwards?"

"He hurried down the alley and got into a car."

"Do you remember the make and model of the car?"

"I'm not good with cars. Some American car I think."

"Did you note down the license plate?"

"No, why? That's not why I made the complaint. You asked if I saw anything else. So I told you. But it's about those men with blood on them. That's who you should go after."

"Of course, but I'd like to be thorough, just in case it's connected."

Mrs. Zhang nodded. "So you'll look into it?"

"I will. Thank you, Mrs. Zhang."

The information Mrs. Zhang had given her wasn't much to go by. For all she knew, she'd seen a guy taking advantage of the fact that the club was busy because of the party, and had stolen a bottle of booze from the club and then promptly broken it in his haste to get away. The two people meeting at the back entrance and exchanging something could easily be a small-time drug deal. Perhaps one of the employees of the club was taking drugs, and the other person was his dealer. Nothing odd about that. And the blood? Naomi doubted that Mrs. Zhang could see that whatever was on the men's clothing and face was truly blood. It could have been make-up, or wine stains.

"Thank you, Mrs. Zhang. You've given me a lot of pointers to investigate. And if there's something to find, I'll find it," she promised.

Not that she would get her hopes up of stumbling over a juicy story. And if it was true that Mrs. Zhang had always only seen two men, it was doubtful that satanic rituals were performed in the basement of the club. A secret BDSM club didn't make sense either, because there would be more people involved in it, just like in a satanic cult.

After leaving Mrs. Zhang's flat, Naomi looked across the alley to the back entrance of the club. It was quiet there. The door leading into the building was closed. There were no windows on this side of the building that overlooked a small parking lot for no more than four cars. It was empty. To the left were three large dumpsters. Naomi looked over her shoulder, then crossed the alley and walked to the spot where according to Mrs. Zhang the person in the Harlequin costume had stumbled.

There were cracks all over the parking lot, and it looked like several attempts had been made to fill them with asphalt which had resulted in an uneven surface. In the dark, it was easy to stumble here. As she walked to the dumpster in the middle, she noticed different stains on the ground, most likely caused by leaking trash bags or liquor bottles. She smelled the scent of old beer and the sickly-sweet smell of sodas and stale wine. Nothing unusual for a nightclub.

At the large dumpster in the middle, she crouched down and searched the ground. There were glass chards, consistent with Mrs. Zhang's claim that the person she'd seen had tossed a bottle toward the trash but missed. Bending farther down, she peered underneath the container and saw a bottle of transparent glass, its neck broken, but the remainder of it intact. She reached for it, careful not to touch the broken neck and pulled it out, when she noticed a small glass vial that had been hidden behind the broken bottle. She took the glass vial too, then examined both items.

The bottle with the broken neck could hold approximately sixteen ounces of liquid, a residue of which was still inside it. She tilted the bottle. The red liquid was viscous, much thicker than water or wine. She brought it to her nose to smell it. It had a distinct metallic scent. This was no ordinary drink. She turned the bottle to look at the white label.

A+ bottled by Scanguards, it said in black lettering. There was no other information on the label, no nutritional information like calories or alcohol content. She suspected why: this had to be blood. It smelled like it. It was labeled as if it was blood type A positive. But it was bottled by Scanguards, a security company, and two of their directors owned the nightclub. Maybe Mrs. Zhang wasn't wrong with her accusation after all. Maybe something nefarious was going on here, and it involved Scanguards—and blood. But first things first. She had to confirm whether the red residue was really human blood, and not something else like the kind of stuff they used in the movies to give the illusion of blood.

When she examined the small vial she'd found behind the broken bottle, she realized that inside the vial was the same kind of red sticky residue. She sniffed. It too had a metallic scent. But why would they use such a small vial, when there was a sixteen-ounce bottle filled with it? Maybe this was something different. It was definitely worth checking out.

The broken bottle and the small vial in hand, Naomi walked back to where she'd parked her blue Mini Cooper at the entrance to the alley. She opened the trunk, where she kept a small overnight bag with a change of clothes and some toiletries in case she was called to report on a story and had no time to go home to change. She opened the bag now, and took out her toiletry kit. She emptied the small Ziploc bags in which she kept Q-tips, cotton-pads, and tampons, and used a Q-tip to swab the inside of the broken bottle until she had enough of a sample so a test could be performed. She locked the Q-tip in the Ziploc bag, then did the same with the small vial, and put a sample of the contents of the vial into a separate plastic bag. Then she pulled out a Sharpie from her bag and labeled the first Ziploc bag with a B for bottle and the second with V for vial.

She pulled out her cell phone and took photos of the glass bottle and the glass vial, before she put both into an old plastic shopping bag and stuffed it into a side pocket in the trunk. She closed her overnight bag, grabbed the two Ziploc bags with the samples, and shut the trunk.

Naomi jumped into the driver's seat and drove off. Traffic was busy, but she didn't have far to go. The lab her friend Heather worked in was just half a mile south of the 3rd Street bridge that led into Mission Bay, where new luxury housing developments had sprung up in previous years, and UCSF had built a new hospital as well as several new research facilities for their faculty.

Naomi parked in one of the visitor parking spots, and pulled out her cell phone. She texted Heather to meet her in the lobby of the building, but didn't wait for her response. Instead, she grabbed her handbag with the two Ziploc bags and got out of the car. By the time she reached the entrance to the research facility, her cell phone chirped with a reply from Heather.

Down in a sec.

Naomi entered the lobby, and waited impatiently. Finally, the elevator doors opened, and Heather stepped out.

"Hey, what's up?" Heather asked. "You know, I can't have lunch today. I got in late this morning, and I'm behind already—"

"No, no, I'm not here for lunch. But I need a favor." Naomi pulled the two plastic bags from her handbag.

"What's that?"

"Blood, I think. I need to know whether these samples are human or animal."

Heather furrowed her forehead. "Why on earth—"

"It's for a story. I can't really tell you more than that right now. Do you think you could run a quick test today?"

Heather took the two plastic bags. "I can run a precipitin test later this afternoon. You just need to know if it's human or animal blood, but don't need DNA, right?"

"Right."

"That's easy enough. But I've gotta wait until my boss goes to his meeting later. He's already pissed that I got in two hours late." Heather leaned in. "Cool party last night. You could have totally scored. The place was crawling with hot guys."

"Glad you had fun," Naomi said.

"You really should have been there. I wish you'd get out more. Next time, I swear, I'm gonna drag you to the party. No more staying at home when there's fun to be had."

"I wasn't at home last night," Naomi said with a smirk.

"What?"

She winked. "I had to do some work on a story."

"That doesn't count as fun."

"It does when it means that I had to go to a costume party at the Mezzanine." Naomi enjoyed seeing the flash of surprise on Heather's face.

"Oh my God! You went to the Mezzanine? That's the hottest club in the city right now. You have to tell me everything about that."

"I will, but not now. I've gotta chase a few things on this story. So, maybe on the weekend?"

"Can't wait that long. At least tell me if you met someone."

"I did."

"And? Come on, don't make me pull it out of your nose."

"I thought you were busy in the lab and your boss is pissed."

Heather made a dismissive hand movement. "Who cares? So, who is he, and did you sleep with him?"

Naomi felt heat shoot into her cheeks. Her friend always came to the point immediately. "He's one of the club's managers, and yes, I did."

Heather almost squealed in excitement and pulled her into an embrace. "I want details!"

"On the weekend, okay?"

"Tease," she said and sighed. "I'll call you with the results of the tests later."

"Thanks, I owe you one."

Knowing that she could rely on her friend, Naomi went back to her car and drove to her office to see if she could dig up anything else about Scanguards and the Mezzanine.

12

Damian had scoured the security recordings inside and outside the club to search for any indication as to the identity of the thief, but had come up empty. The person in the Harlequin costume and Venetian mask hadn't shown up anywhere else in the club other than in the corridor that led to the storage room. It suggested that he—or she—had either entered through the back exit which required a key or the fingerprint of an authorized person, or gotten changed into the costume in the restrooms, which weren't covered by cameras.

After striking out on the security recordings, Damian made calls to Sam, Andrew, and Orlando, but Orlando wasn't answering his phone. He would check in with him later. Orlando was scheduled to work tonight. Frustrated, he returned home to eat and sleep for a few hours. He would talk to his father, who lived in the penthouse above the flat Damian shared with Benjamin, before Amaury went to Scanguards HQ. But it turned out that Damian's body was more exhausted than he thought, because by the time he was awake again, the sun had already set and his father had left for the office.

Damian jumped into his black Porsche and drove to Scanguards HQ in the Mission. He was grateful that Scanguards had its own parking garage underneath the building, because there was never any parking available in the popular neighborhood known for its diverse restaurants and bars. He parked in his assigned spot, then rode the elevator to the top floor, where the offices of the directors were located.

The place was busy. During the day, mostly humans and hybrids worked in the building, while at night, the full-blooded vampires who had to avoid sunlight took over. The building was vampire-proof and equipped with shatterproof glass that was covered with a special coating that filtered out the dangerous UV-rays that could kill a vampire.

Damian marched to Amaury's office, dreading the conversation he had to have, but the theft of human blood by an unknown perpetrator constituted a security risk and had to be addressed.

Damian knocked, and entered when he heard his father's invitation. "Hey, Dad."

"Hey, Damian, how's it going? Nice party at the club last night? Hope you've got some energy left for the housewarming party tonight."

"That's tonight?" He'd almost forgotten.

"Yeah, Ryder and Scarlet are excited to finally show off their home. It's taken long enough to rebuild it. Just about time, too." Amaury smiled. "You're coming right? 'Cause Benjamin is on assignment, and he won't be able to make it."

"Yeah, sure, won't miss it."

"I'll be there probably around two o'clock. I doubt anybody will be able to make it earlier. See you there, son."

When Amaury looked down at the file in front of him, Damian cleared his throat. He looked up again. "Something wrong?"

"Yeah, I think so."

Damian ran a hand through his thick hair. "Last night somebody stole a crate of human blood from the storeroom at the Mezzanine."

"Fuck!" Amaury hissed. "Did you get the bastard? Where is he?"

"No, we don't have him." Or her. "We got him on security footage though."

"Then let's bring him in and deal with him."

"He wore a costume with a Venetian facemask. Can't tell who it is. I already went through the entire footage from last night to see if he takes the mask off at any time, but he must have gotten in through the back."

"How? Did you check the fingerprint scanner? Was it tampered with?"

"I checked. But it works fine, and nobody entered around the time the theft happened. He must have used a key, because I can't find any evidence of a break-in. Same at the storeroom. It didn't look like he used a lockpick. He was too fast for that. Had to be a key."

"Only the employees have keys."

"I know. Patrick talked to the coat check girls and Tanja, and I already spoke to Sam and Andrew. They all had their keys on them at all times. Nobody could have swiped them. I haven't reached Orlando yet. But all the staff on duty last night was accounted for at all times."

He left himself out of the discussion. His keys hadn't always been on him. In fact, when he'd fallen asleep after having sex with Naomi, she could have easily taken his keys, put on a disguise, stolen the blood, then returned to put his keys back. But he couldn't tell his father that he'd been so careless. He would have his hide.

"You think that one of the staff could have stolen the case?" Amaury asked. "They would have known about the cameras, and been prepared to disguise themselves."

"It makes no sense," Damian said, shrugging. "Why steal a crate when they can get all the blood they need for free? And another thing: the thief wasn't very big. Could have easily been a woman." He could at least acknowledge that.

Amaury grunted in displeasure. "You only had three bartenders there last night?"

"Mick didn't show up for his shift. I had to talk Buffy into filling in last minute. I'll speak to her, but she wouldn't have had keys to the storeroom. I mean, you don't think that Buffy... No, that's not even possible."

Amaury shook his head. "Buffy would never compromise our security. But you should look into Mick. I mean, I like the guy, and I thought he was reliable, so why didn't he show up for his shift?"

"I tried calling him numerous times. It just goes straight to voicemail. I'll check at his home next, see if he's there. But just like with all the other staff, I don't see why anyone would bother stealing a crate of blood knowing we'd notice *and* record the theft on camera. And what would they do with it anyway, other than drink it?"

Of course, there was the other possibility. The possibility that Naomi had somehow figured out their secret, and was planning to expose them, but she needed proof and had therefore stolen the crate of blood. Still, it didn't make sense entirely either. Why would she need an entire crate of blood? Wouldn't one bottle suffice? A bottle that would lead back to Scanguards?

"What are you thinking, son?"

Damian shook his head. "Nothing, just trying to make sense of it. I'll keep you posted. I'll check up on Mick."

"Yeah, let me know as soon as possible."

Damian nodded and left his father's office. Outside in the corridor, he stopped. Was it his fault that somebody had stolen the blood? If the thief was Naomi, then the answer was an unequivocal yes. Shit! What if he had put his entire family and everybody at Scanguards at risk because he'd been so lust-drugged by Naomi that he'd thrown all caution to the wind? If that was the case, then he was the one who had to make it right. He had to fix this.

13

Naomi was in the car, when Heather finally called her with the results of the lab tests.

"So, you were right. The sample you marked with a B is human blood. Blood type is A positive."

Fuck! That meant that the label on the bottle was correct. It had said A+.

"And the other one?" Naomi asked eagerly, while stopping at a red light.

"Hmm. Not sure. I know it's blood. But it's neither human nor animal," Heather said sounding baffled.

"How is that possible? Are you saying it's synthetic?"

"No, definitely not. It's… uh, strange. Maybe the sample was contaminated. I can run it again. Do you have another sample of the same source?"

"Yeah, I should have enough left for a second test. Can I drop it off with you sometime tomorrow?"

"Yeah, sure. So, can you tell me anything yet what this is about?"

"Not yet. I'm still trying to puzzle things together," Naomi said evasively. She didn't want to worry her friend. And if there really were blood sacrifices taking place at the Mezzanine, then where did that leave Damian? Was he complicit in it? Suddenly, she recalled his request to playact during sex. He'd pretended to bite her with his fake fangs, and later he'd even bitten her breasts—though very tenderly without leaving a mark. Was this his fetish? And if it was, was it getting out of hand? Was he doing this to other women too? Was he hurting people?

Oh God, what was she getting into? Finally, she'd met a man who actually seemed to like the fact that she wasn't rail-skinny, and who looked at her as if she was the most beautiful woman in the world, and that man could be involved in a satanic blood cult? She sure knew how to pick them. No wonder she was still single at age thirty.

"Naomi?"

"Oh, uh, sorry, Heather, heavy traffic in the Mission. We'll talk tomorrow. And thanks so much," she said.

"Night," Heather said, and the call disconnected.

Honking behind her reminded her that she was still at the light, which had now turned green. She quickly crossed the intersection, then continued on her way to the Scanguards headquarters building.

She didn't really know what she could glean from visiting Scanguards' headquarters, but she wanted to be thorough. It was too early to go back to the Mezzanine. While the club was probably already open, this early it wouldn't be busy yet, and somebody might recognize her.

Arriving at the block where Scanguards' offices were located, she stopped the car. The building with a glass-enclosed lobby facing busy Mission Street took over most of the city block. The two-story-high lobby was lit up and teeming with people coming and going. Naomi looked at her watch. It was already almost 9 p.m. Yet the office was still open and busy. Two security guards flanked the entrance, checking IDs and directing visitors to a reception desk inside. There was no way she'd make it past the lobby. She had to come up with another idea of how to find out more about the company and why they would be bottling human blood.

Not wanting to look suspicious, she turned at the next corner, and stopped on the side street flanking the Scanguards building, when she noticed a black Porsche drive out from a garage beneath it. For an instant, her headlights illuminated the face of the driver: Damian.

This was a stroke of luck she didn't want to waste. She could follow Damian and see where he was going. Perhaps she could catch him doing something that would shine a light on the goings-on in the club and Scanguards' involvement in a satanic blood cult.

Naomi put the car in gear and followed Damian's Porsche. She had expected his license plate to be a vanity plate saying something like *STUD*, or *DAMIAN*, or *HOT*, but to her surprise, it was a regular plate without any obvious meaning.

She'd never taken a class in how to tail another car, but she'd seen plenty of movies where it was done, and knew not to drive too closely to Damian's Porsche. Unfortunately, that also made it hard not to lose him in the heavy evening traffic. How did professionals do that? Luckily, her Mini Cooper was small enough to squeeze past other cars so she could keep tailing Damian, who seemed to drive around the city as if he had no goal. Was he cruising just for the heck of it? Or was he looking for someone or something?

When Damian took a right turn, the car in front of her suddenly stopped, blocking her, while the driver gestured to an old lady with two shopping bags to get into the car. Naomi tried to pass the car on the left, but right then, a bus drove up and blocked her in.

"Move it!" she ground out.

By the time the woman had gotten in the car in front of Naomi's Mini, and she could finally turn into the street that Damian had turned into moments earlier, there was no sign of the black Porsche.

She slammed her hands on the steering wheel. "Fuck!"

So much for following Damian as if she were an undercover police officer.

~ ~ ~

A few minutes after he'd left Scanguards HQ behind, Damian had noticed that a blue Mini Cooper was following him. He'd been on his way to Mick Solvang's flat to find out why he wasn't answering his phone and hadn't shown up at the club—and if he'd had anything to do with the theft of the crate of blood. But he couldn't risk having somebody follow him to Mick's place. To be sure that he wasn't just paranoid, he'd taken a few turns, switching back and forth, and the car kept following him. It took him a few more minutes to discover who the driver of the other car was: Naomi.

This fact only enforced his suspicion of her motive of why she'd shown up in his office. On a dare! Yeah, right! She'd manipulated him from the moment he'd first laid eyes on her. And she'd gone as far as to sleep with him. And for what? To spy on him and his vampire friends and family. To expose Scanguards. And he'd been stupid enough to fall for it. But no longer. Now he'd turn the tables on her.

It wasn't hard to lose her in the heavy evening traffic. And thanks to his training at Scanguards, he had no trouble following Naomi's car as she zigzagged through downtown, clearly trying to see if she could pick up his trail again. But she was out of luck, because he knew how to tail her without her noticing that who she was looking for was behind her.

Let's see how you like being manipulated.

After twenty minutes of driving around downtown, Naomi seemed to have given up. She suddenly headed in one direction, and it wasn't hard to guess what her destination was: the Mezzanine. He stayed a few cars behind her with his Porsche. When they reached the block on which the Mezzanine was located, she started looking around for a parking spot.

Damian pulled into the alley next to the club and killed the engine. He pulled out his cell phone and made a call.

"Orlando?"

"Hey, Damian."

"Do me a favor. In a few minutes, a busty blonde woman, about five foot five will show up at the door to the Mezzanine. She'll want to get in. Tell her there's a private party tonight, and send her away."

"As you wish."

"Thanks."

Damian shoved his cell phone into his pocket and got out of the car. He headed out of the alley. He looked down the street and saw that Naomi had found a parking spot only a block farther. Her Mini Cooper was easy to spot. He looked toward the entrance of the club, and saw that Naomi was talking to Orlando. Damian timed it so that when she started walking back toward her car, he was walking toward her as if he was on his way to the club.

When their gazes met, Damian smiled, "Hey, what are you doing here?"

She looked stunned, then caught herself. "Actually, I was going to see if you were at the club."

Damian stopped only a foot away from her, and slid his hand to her waist. "You snuck out on me this morning."

To his surprise, she blushed. "I wasn't sure if you wanted me there when you woke up."

That was a weak excuse. Clearly, she was making shit up on the fly. "And why not?"

"Isn't that what you expect from one-night stands?"

Oh, she was gonna blame him? *Yeah, not so fast.* "So that's how you see me? As one of your one-night stands? Does that mean you're not interested in a repeat?" He pulled her flush against his body and could feel her breasts touch his chest, and her heartbeat echo against his. He wasn't above exploiting the sexual attraction between them to find out what she was really after.

"Oh, I didn't think you would be…uhm, interested in more." Her voice trembled.

Good. She had no idea that he was already on to her.

"If you'd stayed until this morning, you would have realized that I wanted a lot more." He pressed his groin to hers, and realized that he was already getting hard. Just holding her close and inhaling her enticing scent had that effect on him.

"Oh." Her lips formed a perfect circle as she gasped.

"How about we go for a drink?" he suggested.

"Sure. There's a bar on the next block," she replied.

"I was thinking of something a little more private," he said, employing a deliberately husky tone as he dipped his mouth to her ear. "Unless you want a repeat of what happened on the dance floor last night."

Naomi sucked in an audible breath, and for a moment he thought that she would reject his suggestion. "Okay, how about your place?"

He drew his head back to look at her. "Sorry, I just had my flat painted today. It stinks of fresh paint. How about your place instead?"

She hesitated, and he could see the little wheels in her mind working overtime. Did she have anything in her place that might incriminate her? Something that would give away that she was working on exposing him and Scanguards as vampires?

"Sure. I'm parked right over there." She pointed past him.

"I'll follow you with my car." He looked over his shoulder. "Which is your car?"

"The blue Mini Cooper."

"I'm parked in the alley over there. Give me a moment to get my car, and I'll be right behind you." Then he pressed a chaste kiss on her lips, before he walked back to the alley and hopped into his Porsche.

Moments later, he was following Naomi's Mini Cooper toward the Mission. He'd memorized her address, and knew she wasn't just leading him around the city trying to ditch him. When she stopped in front of an apartment building, he pulled up alongside her, and lowered the window.

"What's your apartment number?"

"3B, top floor," she replied.

"I'll just find parking and see you up there."

"Okay."

He watched as she drove into the garage beneath the building, and drove around the corner.

First, he would use his charm to make her talk, but if that didn't work, he'd confront her. But either way, he'd get the truth out of her tonight.

Showtime.

14

Naomi parked in her assigned spot underneath her apartment building, and wanted to slap herself. Why the hell had she let herself be talked into taking Damian back to her flat? Was she suicidal? If Damian was behind the satanic blood cult that she now had every reason to believe existed, then wasn't she putting herself in danger? But the moment he'd put his arms around her and pressed her to his sinful body, she'd lost the ability to think clearly.

Annoyed at herself, she locked the car and went upstairs to the lobby. She'd have to make the best of this situation. Perhaps she could get information out of him after all. There was such a thing as pillow talk. As long as she acted normally, he wouldn't find out that she suspected that there was something evil going on at the Mezzanine. And there was always a chance that he wasn't involved, that maybe one of his employees was doing something nefarious behind Damian's back. But if she was honest with herself, she'd admit that it was unrealistic that Damian had no idea what was going on in the club. It was just wishful thinking so that she didn't have to admit to herself that she had the hots for a depraved criminal.

In the lobby of her building, she took a deep breath, then let Damian in. There was no elevator, so they walked up to the third floor.

"How long have you lived here?" he asked casually.

"Seven years. It's rent-controlled. I can't really afford to give it up. I'll never find anything that cheap again." She hoped he couldn't sense how nervous she was.

"I get it." When they entered the flat, Naomi switched on the light, and Damian let his eyes roam. "It's cozy."

She forced a chuckle, trying to pretend that she didn't feel the tension between them, and closed the door. "It's tiny."

It was a rather small one-bedroom flat with a bathroom from the fifties, and a kitchen that was in dire need of updating.

"So, what would you like to drink?" she asked.

"What do you have?"

"Beer, wine, and there might be some vodka left."

"Wine is fine."

Naomi went into the kitchen and opened the fridge to pull out a bottle of white wine, when she felt Damian behind her, his hot breath at her ear. She shivered involuntarily. Was it fear she felt? Or something else?

"So, what do you do when you don't seduce nightclub managers?" he asked in a far too seductive tone.

She closed the refrigerator door and set the bottle onto the counter, trying to buy herself some time to answer. She knew she couldn't lie outright, and had to stick to the truth as closely as possible.

"I work for the Chronicle."

"You're a reporter?" he asked, surprise coloring his voice.

"I'm basically a glorified copy editor," she lied. "It's nothing exciting. But it pays the bills. And the hours are good." She reached for two wine glasses and poured the white wine, before handing Damian one glass.

"I see," he said with an odd expression on his face.

In the living room, Naomi took a seat on the couch, expecting Damian to take the armchair, but instead, he joined her on the sofa. She sipped from her drink, and watched Damian do the same. Then he took her glass from her hand and put both hers and his on the coffee table.

A moment later, he scooted closer and turned to her, one hand behind her on the backrest of the sofa, the other on her thigh. The contact sent a scorching flame through her core. His blue eyes were piercing when he pinned her with them. What was he up to now?

"So what were you really doing in my office last night?"

Her heartbeat kicked up. "I told you already. It was a dare."

"So you weren't snooping around in there?"

Shit! Hadn't she dispelled his suspicions last night? Why was he bringing this up now? She had to counter boldly, or he would steamroll her. She narrowed her eyes. "Are you accusing all the women you sleep with of spying on you?" She pushed his hand off her leg.

"No, only the ones who try to seduce me as a means to an end."

"Excuse me? You think I seduced you?" She shook her head, letting outrage color her voice. "That's laughable. May I remind you that you were the one who practically... uhm... who touched me on the dance floor? And you think I seduced you? And why would I do that?"

"To steal my keys."

She jumped up from the sofa. "What the fuck would I do with your keys?" she asked, this time truly stunned. She hadn't touched his keys though she had to admit she'd looked for them, but that was before they'd kissed.

Damian rose slowly. In that moment he reminded her of a tiger who was stalking his prey.

"Somebody broke into the storeroom early this morning using a key, shortly after I fell asleep after we had sex the second time."

"You're accusing me of breaking in? How dare you?"

"I know you tried the door earlier. I saw it on the surveillance camera. Your red cape was hard to miss."

Shocked, she gasped. Yes, she'd tried several doors in the *Employees-only* area, but except for the breakroom they'd all been locked. She hadn't broken in, and if he had her on camera, then he knew that already. "I got lost, okay? I was looking for the restrooms, and yeah, so I was a little tipsy. But I didn't break into a storeroom or anything else." Which was technically the truth, because the door to Damian's office hadn't been locked. "And if you really have me on camera then you would also have seen that I didn't break in later after we had sex. So if you saw somebody with a red cape on your surveillance video, that wasn't me."

"The person breaking in wore a different costume during the break-in, black and white and a Venetian facemask."

At the description, Naomi realized that Mrs. Zhang had seen the person who'd presumably broken into the storeroom as he'd made his getaway. But she couldn't tell Damian about that, because it would give away that she was investigating the club.

"You probably realized at that point that you were on camera, and that I would recognize your outfit, so you disguised yourself."

Naomi narrowed her eyes at him. She had to defend herself, without giving away what she knew. In fact, Damian was giving her the perfect excuse to extricate herself from him. "I didn't steal anything from you. Not your keys, and not whatever was in the storeroom of your fucking club. Go ahead, search my place. You'll find nothing. And then I want you to leave. And to think that I actually enjoyed sleeping with you! How stupid of me! I should get my head examined!"

Yes, she realized, it was best this way. This was the perfect pretense to get him out of her flat and out of her life. She'd find another way of trying to figure out what was going on at the Mezzanine. It was safer not to be in his presence anyway.

She crossed her arms over her chest and turned her back to him. "You know where the door is."

There was silence behind her. She heard only Damian's breathing and her own heartbeat. What was he waiting for?

"Tell me one more thing. Why did you follow me tonight?"

Fuck! He'd noticed her tailing him. What now? How could she explain why she'd followed him? She had to stick as closely to the truth—or a version of it—as she could.

"Okay, I followed you!" She spun around and glared at him. "I was on my way home, and I saw you in your car when you were stopped at a light in the Mission. I followed you, okay? It was impulsive, I admit that. And yeah, a bit stalkerish. But I wasn't doing any harm. I… I…ahm, I wanted to see you again, but I didn't want to be too obvious, so I thought I could just accidentally run into you. But then I lost you in traffic, so I drove around a bit, trying to find you. When I couldn't, I drove to the Mezzanine. Now you know how pathetic I am. You never asked me for my phone number last night. That's why I left. I didn't want that awkwardness in the morning where you would promise to call me when you really had no intention of doing so."

Oh God, she was waffling. Did he buy it?

"I should have never stalked you. It was stupid." She gestured to the door. "I didn't steal anything from the club, and I didn't touch your keys. But you clearly don't trust me. And you're not interested in anything else anyway. So, what are you still doing here? Just leave."

Naomi turned away, not because she didn't want to be caught in a lie, but because she suddenly realized that part of what she'd said was the truth: she had been afraid that the morning after would be awkward, and that Damian would realize that she wasn't as sexy and desirable in the light of day as under the dim lights of the club, despite everything he'd said during their passionate encounter. She'd been afraid of him rejecting her and regretting having slept with her. That's why she'd left without saying goodbye. To preserve the memory of their night of passion. Yeah, she *was* pathetic.

15

Damian let Naomi's words sink in. Had he been wrong about her after all? Did she really have nothing to do with the theft of the bottles of blood? Her claim that she'd followed him to initiate a coincidental meeting wasn't too far-fetched. Other women had done it before: figured out his habits, so they could run into him and make it look random. And Naomi lived in the Mission. It was entirely possible that she'd seen him in his car after he'd left Scanguards. After all, there were only so many main roads leading from her office at the San Francisco Chronicle to her home in the Mission, and one of those streets passed right by Scanguards' headquarters.

Even Naomi's explanation why she'd left while he was still sleeping was conceivable. He'd noticed during their night together that she wasn't as confident about her body as she should be. Most likely, men and women had told her often enough that she looked fat, though he couldn't fathom why. Her curves were perfect, and any man not seeing that was blind.

Damian ran a hand through his hair. His night with Naomi had been too good to be true, and maybe that was the reason why he questioned her motives. He'd been looking for a woman like her ever since he'd started dating, and now that he'd found exactly what he wanted, he was scared that it was a fluke, a mirage, or a trick somebody was playing on him. Add to that the theft of the bottled blood and the resulting risk of exposure, could anybody really blame him for going off the rails? Still, it didn't excuse how he'd treated her.

"I don't want to leave," he finally said and stepped closer to her. "I'm sorry, Naomi. I didn't mean to lash out at you like that. It's just..." He sighed. "When women come on to me, they always have an ulterior motive, be it that they think I'm rich, or that I have the right connections, or that they want a trophy boyfriend, but they never really want me."

"I don't quite believe that," Naomi said, but still didn't look at him.

"Don't get me wrong: I've always liked the attention. I'm not gonna lie about that. But I never seem to attract the kind of woman that truly appeals to me. A woman like you."

She scoffed. "Please don't."

"It's true. But I do owe you an explanation."

Naomi finally looked at him.

"The break-in has rattled me and my team. And when I saw at what time the break-in had happened, and that the person looked to be about your height, I started doubting why you went to bed with me."

"Please, a little break-in gets you all flustered? What did the person steal? Some booze?" She shook her head.

He knew he couldn't tell her the truth of what had disappeared from the storeroom, but he had to make her understand that it was important. "I was storing something valuable for my father there. And my head's pretty much on the chopping block if I can't get it back."

She hesitated, then took a breath. "Are you saying you were keeping drugs down there?"

Stunned, Damian shook his head. "Drugs? God, no! Why would you think that?"

"I mean, that's what's going on in many nightclubs. People are dealing drugs."

"Not in mine, they're not," Damian protested. He made sure of that. All his staff were instructed to report any suspected drug dealing and drug usage by patrons or staff directly to him or Patrick. "I'm very strict about drugs in the club. If a guest has drugs on them, they get 86'd right away. The club is clean. We don't tolerate drugs. They only bring violence and trouble."

"Sorry, I didn't mean to offend you."

"You didn't." He reached for her hand. "Naomi, can you forgive me for the things I said? I want to trust you, but it might just take me a while to get there."

He saw her hesitate. "Please, Naomi. I think we have a good thing going here." He pulled her hand to his lips and kissed her palm. "I enjoyed being with you last night. I've never felt so good than when you were climaxing with my cock inside you."

Naomi inhaled visibly, and her lips parted. He could hear her heartbeat accelerate, and the aroma of her arousal suddenly drifted to his nostrils.

"Please, say you forgive me," he murmured, pouring all his seductive charm into his voice.

Damn it, he wanted this woman more than anything he'd ever wanted. And he didn't care what he had to do to get her. Even if that meant groveling.

Their gazes suddenly collided, and Naomi's lips moved. "I forgive you."

"May I make it up to you?" he asked, his mouth now hovering over hers.

Her breath teased his skin. "How?"

"By making love to you."

Their lips met, and Damian kissed her tenderly, knowing he had to tread lightly with her, not behave like a bull in a China shop and destroy what he'd just mended. When Naomi put her arms around him and slid one hand up to his nape, he pressed her closer to him and delved deeper into her mouth, exploring her and dueling with her tongue.

For a moment, he interrupted the kiss. "Please tell me you have condoms in the house."

"In my bedroom."

"Good."

He sank his lips on hers again, and lifted her into his arms to carry her to the bedroom. The door was only ajar, and he kicked it open. He placed Naomi on the Queen-size bed and reached for the bedside lamp, flipping the switch. Instantly, the room was bathed in a warm light. This time, Naomi didn't ask him to switch off the light.

Slowly, he started undressing her, peeling away layer after layer until she lay in front of him in only her bra and panties. Both were pink and gave her an innocent look, even though he knew that nothing about her body was innocent. She was pure sin. And he intended to sin plenty tonight.

Damian rose to stand next to the bed. "Watch me undress."

He took his time to rid himself of his jacket and shirt, then his shoes and socks, before he opened his pants and dropped them. When he stepped out of them, he noticed Naomi look at him with passion-clouded eyes. Fuck, how he loved that look. Her gaze dropped to his boxer briefs, and even though he'd planned to keep them on for a little while longer while he pleasured her, he couldn't resist ridding himself of them just so Naomi would look at him as if she wanted to devour his cock.

His shaft was hard and heavy. And while as a vampire this was no surprise, he nevertheless knew that the speed with which Naomi could turn him on, was testament of the attraction that prickled between them. Just a look at her, and he was close to climaxing. And looking at her now, dressed in her pink bra and panties that barely covered the treasure beneath, made his heart race in anticipation of the passion they would share shortly, and the pleasure they would give each other.

Her eyes on his erection, Naomi suddenly sat up and crawled toward him on her hands and knees until her head was only inches from his cock.

"I wanna lick you," she murmured, lifting her eyes toward his face.

"If you do that, I won't last long," he warned her.

"I don't care."

Damn it! The way she pouted, she looked sexier than ever. The thought of those lips around his hard-on got him hotter than hell, and though he'd planned on licking her delectable pussy, he couldn't resist her offer.

"Then what are you waiting for?" he asked with a hoarse voice, and gripped his erection at the base.

A sinful smile curled around her lips, and her tongue darted out to lick them. She moved her face closer, and Damian felt his heartbeat accelerate. A moment later, Naomi licked the tip of his cock with her pink tongue, and his entire body was on fire.

"Fuck!"

Naomi opened her lips wider and took him into her mouth, sliding down on him as far as she could. Damian panted uncontrollably. He wasn't a novice when it came to blowjobs. In fact, many women liked to please him in that fashion, but feeling Naomi's sexy red lips around his cock, her tongue licking him as she moved up and down on him, got him hotter than anything else. He couldn't help but give into the temptation to move his hips back and forth, and slowly began to pump into her willing mouth. Descending and withdrawing. He put his hands on her shoulders, and Naomi lifted her lids and looked up at him. Her blue eyes were pure sin, and when his gaze dropped to her breasts—still held in by her bra, but not any less erotic as if they were bouncing freely from side to side and up and down—the sight nearly undid him.

With a harsh breath he pulled himself out of her mouth. "Enough!"

"You didn't like it?" she asked innocently, tilting her head to the side.

"As if you didn't know what you were doing to me. Trying to make me lose control?" He shook his head, then pulled her up so he could feel her breasts press against his chest. "I loved every second of it. Maybe next time, I'll let you suck me longer, but right now, I have other plans."

She lifted her eyebrows. "What plans?"

"I want to lick your pussy. Unless you don't like that."

A soft smile curled her lips upward. "I'm sure I'll like it."

She lay down on her back again and reached for her panties, but he put his hand on hers. "Let me."

He joined her on the bed and gripped her panties, then slowly pulled them down her legs, and tossed them on the ground. He drank in the tantalizing sight of her beautiful pussy, before his gaze swept up to her breasts.

"It's a front clasp," Naomi said.

Damian reached for it and opened the clasp. Almost immediately, her breasts escaped from their inadequate cage. Round and beautiful, topped with dark, hard nipples, and he hadn't even touched them yet. Naomi wiggled out of the bra and tossed it to the floor.

"I love the way your nipples respond," he said and leaned over them. With both hands he squeezed the ample flesh, before dipping his head and licking first over one nipple, then the other.

A strangled moan rolled over Naomi's lips.

"Easy, *chérie*," he murmured against her heated skin. "I haven't even started yet."

Damian scooted down her body, until he was lying between her spread thighs, his face hovering over her pussy. He rubbed his fingers over her slit and felt the warm juices that were already dripping from her.

"And Naomi? If there's anything you don't like, you'll tell me right away, won't you?"

"Yes."

Damian dipped his face to her pussy and licked over her cleft, tasting her juices on his tongue and feeling a corresponding bolt of lust shoot through his body and into his balls. He loved her taste and the way she rubbed herself against his tongue, while her hands gripped the sheets beneath her. Moan after moan bounced against the walls of the small room, while Damian explored her nether lips with his tongue and stroked upward until he met with her clit. The tiny organ was swollen, and he couldn't resist, and licked over it with his tongue, spreading her juices over it, before he increased the pressure with which he caressed her.

"Oh, oh!" Naomi cried out, her breath uneven now, her heart beating like a runaway train, while tiny droplets of perspiration built on her skin, intensifying her body's scent, drugging him with her aroma.

With one hand, he pushed her thighs farther apart, with his other, he caressed her slit, while he licked her clit relentlessly. She rocked against his mouth, and he adjusted to her rhythm and tempo at the same time as he thrust his middle finger into her tight channel.

A gasp burst over her lips. "Oh, yes, Damian, please, please."

He would have assured her that he would take care of her, but he didn't want to take his lips from her. Instead, he doubled his efforts, and licked her clit harder and faster, while plunging in and out of her pussy, now adding a second finger to the first.

He felt her stiffen beneath him, and a moment later, her interior muscles spasmed around his fingers as she climaxed. When her orgasm ebbed, he pulled his fingers from her and lifted his head.

"Damian," she whispered breathlessly, "that was... wow."

He smiled, and scooted up her body. "I wanted to do that this morning, but you left too early."

"That'll teach me." She chuckled softly.

"It'd better. But I'm always available for a repeat lesson." He pressed a kiss to her lips. "Condoms?"

Naomi pointed to the nightstand, and he opened the drawer and pulled one out. As fast as he could, he opened the foil package and slipped the latex over his erection.

A moment later he was poised above her, his erection lined up with her pussy. He gazed into her eyes, then plunged into her silken depth in one long, continuous thrust, until he was inside her to the hilt.

"Damn it, that feels good," he said and began to move inside her. Her sheath was tight and warm, and her plentiful juices welcomed him.

He rode her slowly, trying to take his time, while he dipped his head to kiss her breasts, loving their fullness. He loved pressing his face into her cleavage, taking in her scent. He understood now why Amaury liked to drink from Nina by biting her breasts. He wanted the same intimacy of feeding from a woman's breasts, and he wanted it with Naomi. The revelation hit him like a sledgehammer to the gut. He wanted this woman, not just in his bed, but in his life, in his immortal life.

When he'd been witness to how fast his friend Ryder had fallen for Scarlet, the woman he'd been assigned to as a bodyguard, he'd secretly chuckled to himself, thinking it was impossible to know that they were meant for each other after such a short time. But he didn't doubt it any longer. His own parents had bonded after knowing each other for only a few days. And they were still as much in love as ever.

But could he trust his intuition now? Already once, he'd been wrong and accused Naomi of being a thief. What if he was wrong now too? What if she wasn't meant to be his? He had to take it slow. He shouldn't rush this, no matter how much he longed to drink her blood again. However, tonight, he couldn't suggest a pretend-bite. Last night, she'd bought the illusion because of his costume, and she'd liked it, but tonight, he couldn't risk it. He had to wait until he was sure of her.

Damian looked at Naomi and reveled in the passion that shone from her eyes. "You're so beautiful." He took her lips and kissed her hard, unable to hold back now. He was close, too close to slow down. He needed to come inside her. He needed her to feel what she did to him, how she affected him, how much he wanted her.

With his last ounce of control, he shifted his angle so the next time he slammed into her, his pelvic bone rubbed against her clitoris. On the third thrust, he felt Naomi moan into his mouth, and a second later, her muscles contracted around his cock. He let himself go and orgasmed, and all the air rushed from his lungs.

"Fuck!"

He felt his fangs extend, hungering for a bite, and ripped his lips from hers to hide his face in the pillow. As they both came down from their high, Damian breathed hard and willed his fangs to recede back into their sockets, before he lifted his head and looked at Naomi.

"You slayed me."

She let out a breath. "Ditto."

16

Naomi lay on her back, breathing hard, while Damian disposed of the condom and cleaned up, before rejoining her in bed. He pulled her halfway on top of him, her head resting on his chest, one leg draped over his thighs, while he wrapped one arm around her shoulders, and stroked her thigh with his other hand.

"I could do this a million times with you, and I wouldn't get tired of it," he murmured into her hair.

Did he mean that? She didn't even know what to say. Instead, she snuggled against him, and caressed his muscled chest.

"You're a very passionate man," Naomi said. "And a very talented one."

He chuckled. "I'm glad you think so. Because I intend to do this again, just as soon as I've recovered a bit. Give me about twenty minutes."

She lifted her head to look at him. "You don't have to prove your prowess to me. I'm aware of it."

"Yet you thought you could escape from my bed without repercussions."

"Repercussions?"

"Hmm hmm," he hummed, his eyes closed. Then he slapped her gently on her ass.

"What was that for?"

"That's part of your punishment for leaving my bed without giving me a means to contact you." He opened his eyes and pinned her with his intense gaze. "Luckily, now I know where you live."

"Let me guess: your place wasn't painted recently."

He had the decency to look sheepish. "Little white lie to find out where you live. You can punish me for it later."

"How?"

"I leave that up to you. I'm game for anything. You wanna tie me up?"

Realizing that he was in a playful mood, she decided to ask him a few questions that might shed a light on whether he was involved in a satanic blood cult. At the same time, a feeling of guilt surged in her. Damian had made love to her, and was opening up to her, and she was using the opportunity to extract information from him. How low could she go? She should be ashamed of herself.

"Something wrong?" he asked.

"No, no, nothing."

"If you're not into light bondage, I'll oblige with anything else." He brought his hand to her breast and squeezed the heavy globe. "I enjoyed biting you here last night."

She shivered at the recollection of the sensual bite on her breasts. "Is that what you're into? Biting your sex partners?"

"Partners? Plural?" He laughed softly. "*Chérie*, I'm a one-woman man."

His confession warmed her heart while her conscience reared its ugly head. She should tell him the truth now. Tell him why she'd gone to his office in the first place, and then confess that things had changed, that she didn't believe that he was involved in a satanic cult. But there was still the bottle and the vial she'd found just outside the club. She couldn't just ignore evidence.

And how would he take her confession anyway? Would he feel betrayed? Would he leave her never to speak to her again? Fuck! What had she gotten herself into? She wasn't good at subterfuge. She liked Damian, hell, *like* didn't exactly describe it. She was crazy about him, even though she knew virtually nothing about him. But whenever she was in his arms, she felt whole, she felt like a real woman, she felt desired and adored. And she'd never felt like that before. But what if it all collapsed the moment she told him the truth, told him that she was looking into allegations of a satanic cult operating in the Mezzanine?

Damn it! She had to tell him. She couldn't just lie in bed with him, snuggling as if they were a couple in love, when she knew that it was all built on deception. Maybe it was better if she fessed up now, before she developed even more serious feelings for him. She had to come clean, or all this meant nothing. She couldn't live a lie. Not when she wanted something real, something lasting with Damian.

"Damian, I need to tell you something…"

"What is it?"

Suddenly a cell phone rang.

"Hold that thought. I've gotta get that," Damian said and got out of bed. He rummaged through his pants on the floor and pulled out his cell phone. "Patrick? What's up?"

Naomi watched him as he listened intently. His facial expression turned to one of concern.

"Fuck! Is she sure?" There was a brief pause, then he said, "Okay, I'll be there in twenty minutes."

He disconnected the call and reached for his boxer briefs. "Sorry, Naomi, I've gotta leave."

She sat up. "What's going on?"

"One of our bartenders has disappeared."

"What do you mean by disappeared?"

Damian continued dressing. "Mick was supposed to work the Halloween party, but he didn't show up, and he didn't call in sick either. And just now his girlfriend showed up at the club and told Patrick that she hasn't heard from him in over two days. I've gotta speak to her."

Naomi jumped out of bed. "I'm coming with you."

"I don't think that's a good idea."

But Naomi was already getting dressed. She didn't want to stay here and wait for him. It would only make her more anxious, because she knew she had to tell him the truth about what she was doing at the Mezzanine, and sitting around with that kind of burden weighing her down would do her no good.

"I can help," she insisted. "Please. I can't sleep right now anyway."

Damian sighed. "All right. We'll go in my car."

Relieved, she finished dressing, and grabbed her handbag. Together they left her flat, and Damian ushered her to his Porsche, which he'd parked a block away.

When they drove off, Damian put his hand on her thigh. "I'm sorry about this interruption. Trust me, I would much rather be back in bed with you." He slid his hand to the inside of her thigh, and the intimate contact made her hot.

"Me too," she confessed, which made it even more urgent that she tell him the truth. But she had to wait until after he'd dealt with the disappearance of his bartender. "Has your bartender's girlfriend reported him missing to the police yet?"

Damian shook his head. "We'd rather handle this ourselves."

She furrowed her forehead. "What do you mean? The police are much better suited for finding a missing person."

"This is different. Anybody associated with Scanguards gets special treatment. We look after our own."

She shivered. Wasn't that what the mafia said about their people? "How is Scanguards involved in this?"

He cast her a sideways look and hesitated for a moment, before answering, "My father and his best friend own the Mezzanine. They're both directors at Scanguards, in fact, Samson is the owner and founder of Scanguards. It's a security company, you know, providing bodyguards. But it's more than that. We have our own investigators, our own patrolling units, our own medical service, our own emergency services. We can handle this."

Surprised, Naomi contemplated his words. "Are you saying the police aren't getting involved in this?" Was that the reason why the police had dismissed Mrs. Zhang's allegations?

"The mayor trusts us to handle any issues concerning Scanguards ourselves. And that includes the welfare of our employees. Think of it like a large university having its own police force."

When he put it that way it sounded almost reasonable. *Almost.* "Interesting. But you don't work for Scanguards, you work for the Mezzanine, right?"

"Actually, I work for both. That's why I share the management with Patrick, so I can work part-time at Scanguards."

"Oh! And what do you do at Scanguards?"

"I'm a bodyguard."

"You are?"

He nodded. "I went through rigorous training." He winked at her, just as he stopped at a red light. "But I've never guarded such a beautiful body as yours."

Before she could react to his words, he leaned over and kissed her on the lips. Slowly, she was getting used to the idea that Damian really liked every bit of her. It made the need to come clean even more urgent. If she told him the truth tonight, then maybe it wasn't too late yet to save their blooming relationship.

Impatient honking behind them made Damian sever the kiss and continue driving. Moments later, he pulled into the parking lot in the back of the Mezzanine, and got out of the car. She followed him, and he took her hand and led her to the back entrance of the club. There was a lock that could be operated with a key, but also a scanner. When Damian put his thumb over it, Naomi realized that it was a biometric scanner.

"That's quite some security," she commented.

"It's handy."

Inside the club it was loud. Damian led her directly up to his office, where a young man, whom Naomi assumed to be Patrick Woodford, was already waiting with a pretty woman with long red hair.

When Patrick's eyes fell on her, he shot an annoyed look at Damian.

"Hey Patrick, evening, Angelica," Damian said and walked straight to his co-manager, and whispered something into his ear.

"All right then," Patrick replied, before casting Naomi another look. "I'm Patrick. I think I saw you at the Halloween party. Little Red Riding Hood costume?"

"Yeah, that was me." The way Patrick looked at her now made her suspect that he'd seen her and Damian make out on the dance floor. "Nice to meet you, Patrick." Then she looked at the young woman. "Hi, Angelica, I'm Naomi."

"Hi," she said, then looked at Damian. "Damian, you need to help me find Mick. Something must have happened to him."

Damian motioned to the seating arrangement for her to sit, and sat down opposite her. "Tell me what's going on. When did you last see him?"

"Mick was at my place two nights before Halloween," Angelica started. "Everything was fine. I knew that he had to work the night before Halloween and the Halloween party, so I'd made arrangements to go to a private party at a friend's house. Mick was supposed to head over to my place after the party at the Mezzanine, but he never showed." She sniffled. "I figured maybe it had gotten so late that he crashed somewhere else and wasn't worried at first. But when he didn't call me back, I went to his house. You know, I have a key. So I went inside, but he wasn't there. It looked like he hadn't been there in a couple of days."

Damian nodded. "We have his cell number. I'll have Eddie triangulate his phone, see where he is. Should be easy."

Angelica shook her head. "He doesn't have his cell with him." She dug into her handbag and pulled a cell phone from it. "I found it in his kitchen. And he never goes anywhere without that phone."

"May I?" Damian asked and reached for it.

Angelica handed it to him.

"Do you know his passcode?"

She shook her head. "Mick's really private about that."

Naomi watched Damian exchange a look with Patrick.

"Eddie or Thomas can probably hack it," Patrick said with a shrug. "See who he's been in contact with before he disappeared."

"Yeah, let's do that. I'll bring it to them," Damian agreed. Then he looked back at the clearly distraught Angelica. "Is there anything else that was different about Mick in the few days and weeks before he went missing?"

Angelica shrugged. "No, he was just like always. In fact, he was in an even better mood lately." She looked straight at Damian and then at Patrick. "I mean, ever since you guys gave him such a great pay raise last month, he's had a lot more money to spend, and I think that put him in a good mood."

"Pay raise?" Damian asked and looked at Patrick. "Did you—"

Patrick instantly shook his head. "The last pay raises for any of the staff was in February."

Angelica looked perplexed. "But he said he got a pay raise. And I saw the cash. I'm sure of it."

"Cash?" Damian asked. "We pay our employees by direct deposit into their bank accounts."

Naomi noticed a frown on Damian's face. Could it be that Mick was the guy Mrs. Zhang had seen meeting with another person behind the club? Had he been dealing drugs after all? Clearly, Damian knew nothing about it, and from what he'd told her earlier, he wouldn't approve of it either.

"Thanks, Angelica, we'll look for him," Damian promised. "Hopefully we can find something on his phone that'll help us figure out where he is. We'll be in touch soon." He rose, and Angelica did the same.

"Thanks, Damian, and Patrick. I know I can count on you." Then she went to the door and left.

The moment the door closed behind her, Damian and Patrick exchanged concerned looks.

"I'll bring the phone to Eddie," Damian said. "Can you talk to the staff tonight? See if they noticed anything odd about Mick lately?"

Patrick nodded. "Yep, will do." He went to the door and opened it, then looked over his shoulder, casting a quick glance at Naomi, before looking at Damian again. It looked like he wanted to say something, but then he simply left the office.

Damian sighed. "Fuck." He shoved the cell phone into his pocket. "Let's go, I need to drop the phone off with our IT department."

Her heart beating into her throat, Naomi took a deep breath. She had to tell him the truth now, because not only could she not continue lying to him, keeping information from him that might have something to do with Mick's disappearance was irresponsible.

"I have to tell you something," she started.

"You can tell me on the way."

"No," she said firmly. "It's something you might want to sit down for. Because you're not gonna like it. And I'd rather you not sit behind the wheel of a car when you get angry."

Damian whipped his head to her, his gaze pinning her. At that moment, she was scared, but she couldn't back down now. She had to tell him the truth.

"I lied to you."

17

Naomi's words sent a shockwave through his body. Damian froze, unable to do anything else but stare at her. He felt his breathing accelerate, and his vampire body harden, preparing itself for the worst.

"I should have told you earlier, but I wasn't sure whether I could trust you or whether you were involved…" Her voice trailed off, and she took another breath, before continuing, "But with everything that's happened, I can't keep this to myself any longer. I came to your club to investigate for a story for the San Francisco Chronicle."

Disappointment charged through him. "You used me." His words sounded flat in his own ears, devoid of emotion. In the same instant, one thing became crystal-clear: he was in love with Naomi. In the span of twenty-four hours, he'd fallen in love without knowing how it had happened. Or when. Naomi had stolen his heart, and now she was stomping all over it.

"It wasn't intentional. I didn't mean for all this to happen."

She sniffled as if she was about to break down in tears. Was that another act?

"My editor told me that there've been allegations of a satanic cult or of blood sacrifices taking place at the club."

Blood sacrifices? Satanic cult? Fuck! He knew that no such thing was going on in the club, but he also suspected that somebody might have seen one of the vampires frequenting the club biting a human and assumed it had something to do with a satanic cult. This wasn't good.

"That's a ludicrous idea," he protested, knowing he had to say something.

"I thought so too, but my editor wanted me to look into it, so I came to the Halloween party to look around. But I didn't go into the storeroom, and I didn't steal anything. I found the door to this office ajar. That's the truth. I went inside to look around to see if I could find anything incriminating."

He narrowed his eyes. "And did you?"

Naomi shook her head. "Not in your office."

At least that meant she hadn't seen the bottles of blood in the refrigerator.

"But outside," she added quickly.

He raised an eyebrow. "What do you mean?"

"I found a broken bottle in the trash. It was labeled *A+ bottled by Scanguards.*"

Fuck! The staff knew never to toss any used bottles of blood in the trash. They were recycled and returned directly to Scanguards.

"I had the residue inside it analyzed. It was human blood."

"That's impossible," he lied. "Can I see the bottle?"

She pulled out her cell phone. "It's still in the trunk of my car, but I took a photo." She scrolled to her photo app and he stepped closer, now in full damage control mode. "Here. That's what I found."

He took the phone from her hand and looked at the photo. There was no doubt about it. It was one of the bottles Scanguards filled with human blood from a blood bank. This was incriminating evidence.

"You said you had the residue tested?"

"Yes, my friend Heather works in a lab at UCSF. She tested the samples for me."

"Samples? There is more than one?"

She swiped to the next photo. "I also found this vial, which had some sticky red residue. Heather tested it, but she said it must have been contaminated, because she couldn't figure out if it was human or animal blood, but she was pretty sure it was blood."

Crap! He knew what it had to be: vampire blood. He would be able to recognize it by its smell. No lab test, at least none available in human labs, would be able to pinpoint what it was.

"Do you still have the vial?"

"Yes, it's with the other bottle in my car."

Good. At least that meant he could get the evidence and dispose of it. But that still left a few other loose ends. And even more questions.

"But that's not all," Naomi said.

"What else?"

"I spoke to the neighbor who made the allegations about a satanic cult. Well, she didn't actually say that... that was my editor's guess. But she did tell me that she saw two men meet near the back entrance of the club several nights a week, and that they exchanged something. I was guessing it was some small-time drug dealing, like at any club. But Mrs. Zhang insisted that she saw blood on them, like on their clothing and their faces."

That confirmed it. Somebody had been careless and probably fed from a human, not realizing that there was a witness to his actions.

"Perhaps there was a fight out back?"

"No, she never mentioned a fight. But she said that on the night of the Halloween party she saw a person leaving through the back entrance, carrying something."

"Did she say what?"

"She couldn't see it. And the person wore a Harlequin costume with a Venetian facemask." She met his eyes. "You said that the thief who stole something you kept for your father wore a Venetian facemask. What if that was him?"

That was the first good news he'd heard in the last half hour.

"Did she say what time it happened?" he asked eagerly.

"Sometime around three in the morning."

It was consistent with the time of the break-in.

"She said he stumbled and something fell, and then he tossed something in the trash container, but missed. And that's where I found the bottle and the vial. At first, I thought maybe he just stole a bottle of booze."

Slowly, Damian nodded. He now had a few leads to follow up on. He should be happy about that. But the fact that Naomi had slept with him only so she could snoop around for her story hurt. But he had to respect the fact that she'd come clean now. Still, it didn't make the ache in his heart go away. He'd fallen for a woman who'd only slept with him to use him. A woman who didn't feel the same for him that he felt for her.

"Thanks for the information, I appreciate it." Then he took a deep breath and said what he had to say. "Guess that's it between us then. You weren't really interested in me after all. I should have known that when something is too good to be true, it's not true."

He turned toward the door. "I'll get one of my staff to drive you home." Because being in the confined space of his car with her, inhaling her tantalizing scent, would make things even worse.

"Damian, please."

He felt her hand on his forearm, and stopped.

"I'm so sorry for hurting you. I didn't mean to. But when you kissed me last night, I couldn't stop you, because—"

"Are you implying that I forced myself on you?" he snapped, and whipped his head to her, furious now, because he needed to channel the pain in his heart into something else. Anger was the perfect vessel for it.

"No, no! What I'm trying to say is that I couldn't stop you because I didn't *want* you to stop. I wanted you. I still want you. Now even more than last night. That's why I had to tell you the truth. Because I care about you. When I'm in your arms, I feel happy and whole, and better than I have ever felt. I didn't want to lose that. To lose you."

Tears were suddenly brimming in her eyes, and she lowered her gaze to the floor.

"I see now that you can't forgive me for deceiving you. But I wanted you to know that I didn't sleep with you because I wanted information. I slept with you because I wanted you. And that part, I don't regret. I would do it again."

Her words sank deep into him. He didn't know why, but he believed her. He saw the truth in her tears, and heard it in her voice. Who was he to judge somebody who'd had to lie to protect a secret, when he wasn't any better? He was still keeping his biggest secret from her. But he knew he couldn't keep it for much longer, because if he forgave her now for her deception, then he had to come clean too. But not here. They needed to be alone, where nobody would disturb them when he confessed that he was a vampire.

"Naomi, you still want me?"

"Yes, but—"

"No buts." He put his fingers underneath her chin and tipped her face up so she had to look at him. "I want you too, *chérie.*" He pressed a soft kiss to her lips and saw her face light up. "We need to talk in private, because there are things you need to know about me."

"What things?"

"Important things." He clasped her hand. "Come, we'll go to my place, where we can talk. But first, we need to retrieve the bottle and the vial you have. I need to get it looked at. And I have to give Mick's cell phone to our IT guys. And then we'll talk, just you and I, okay?"

And he prayed that Naomi wouldn't reject him once she found out that he was a vampire who craved her blood.

18

During the drive back to Naomi's apartment building in the Mission, Damian held Naomi's hand. In the last twenty-four hours he'd been through a rollercoaster of emotions. But right now, he felt relieved. Naomi cared about him, enough to confess having deceived him. And he hoped enough to accept the vampire in him.

They didn't speak much on the drive. Instead, a companionable silence spread between them, only interrupted by loving glances and stolen kisses at red lights.

In the garage of Naomi's building, she opened the trunk of her Mini Cooper and pulled out a small plastic shopping bag from a side pocket.

"Here they are," she said and handed him the bag.

Damian looked inside und pulled the broken bottle out first, though he knew it was authentic. He sniffed. Yes, A positive blood just like the bottle said. He placed it back in the bag, then retrieved the small vial. When he lifted it to his nose and smelled, his suspicion was confirmed: somebody had put vampire blood in this vial. To what end, he didn't know yet, but he'd find out.

"I'll take those with me." Then he pointed to the travel bag in the trunk. "Is that an overnight bag?"

"Yes, I always keep the essentials in the car," she replied.

"Let's take it with us," Damian said, and reached for it. "You'll be sleeping at my place." Though if everything went well, she wouldn't be sleeping much, because he'd be too busy making love to her.

Naomi smiled at him and shut the trunk. "I like it when you say exactly what you want."

"Then you'll appreciate this." He leaned toward her and brought his mouth to her ear. "I want you naked and panting beneath me with my cock inside you until neither of us can move a limb."

"You're making me all hot," she murmured.

He pulled his head back to look at her. "Get used to it."

When he noticed her cheeks flush prettily, he grinned. She was receptive to his charm, and tonight, he'd have to use every ounce of it to convince her that being loved by a vampire was what she needed.

Back in his Porsche, he looked at the dashboard clock. It was already well past 2 a.m., and the people he wanted to speak to at Scanguards would already have left for Ryder and Scarlet's housewarming party.

"I have to stop by a friend's place in Pacific Heights quickly," he said to Naomi. "My uncle will be there, and he'll be the one trying to get information off of Mick's phone."

"Your uncle is the IT guy you were talking about?" she asked with interest.

"Yes, Eddie and his husband, Thomas, run the IT department at Scanguards. They can get into pretty much any system they set their minds to. If there's anything on Mick's phone that might help us figure out where he disappeared to, they'll find it."

"I'm impressed. But isn't that illegal? I mean, hacking?"

He cast her a sideways look and shrugged. "Whatever works to rescue Mick."

"So you don't think that he just disappeared voluntarily. You think he was taken."

"Yeah, I'm pretty sure about it. He's a reliable guy. And I'm not aware of him and his girlfriend having any relationship issues, so he wouldn't just leave without telling her where he was going. Somebody kidnapped him."

Or killed him, though he hoped that the former was the case. Mick wouldn't be the first kidnap victim Scanguards had rescued. However, the question was: why would somebody want to kidnap a bartender?

"Still, there has to be a reason why somebody would kidnap him," Naomi mused.

"We'll figure it out."

Damian stopped the car outside the garage to the brand-new Victorian that Scarlet and Ryder had rebuilt after it had become victim to arson. He blocked the entrance to the garage.

"I'll only be twenty minutes."

"I can come with you," Naomi said and already undid her seatbelt.

Damian put his hand on her forearm. "I think it's best if you stay. If I go in there and introduce you as my girlfriend, they'll bombard you with questions, and we'll never get outta there tonight. And we really need to be alone to talk."

Naomi's blue eyes sparkled. "Did you say girlfriend?"

He leaned over to her. "Well, isn't that what you are? My girlfriend? Or would you rather I tell everybody you're just a woman I have sex with? 'Cause that would be a lie."

Her lips parted and she moved closer. "How about a girlfriend you have lots of sex with?"

"Exclusively?" he teased.

"Yes, exclusively."

"That works for me." Damian put his lips on hers and kissed her. Naomi immediately melted into his arms, and if he didn't stop this now, they'd be steaming up the windows of his Porsche in no time.

He ripped his lips from hers and took a deep breath. "Make that fifteen minutes," he promised. He snatched the plastic bag with the broken bottle and vial from behind his seat and got out of the car.

The door to the house was unlocked, and Damian let himself in. He'd been to the house many times during construction and had helped Ryder and Scarlet move in a month earlier, just like some of the other hybrids had done, even though a Scanguards-approved moving company had done the heavy lifting.

The large living room in the front and the dining room that was connected to it by large pocket doors, which were open, were full of Scanguards personnel and their wives, husbands, and partners. Scarlet was talking to Maya, her mother-in-law, while her hand rested on her belly. Two more months, and she'd make Ryder a father. Who would have thought that the two who'd only met a year earlier would start a family so soon? But there was no denying how happy Ryder was. Damian spotted him talking to Samson and Brandon, Scarlet's father. Despite the animated conversation the three men were engaged in, Ryder's gaze drifted to Scarlet every so often, his eyes shimmering golden, a sign that he was thinking of his blood-bonded mate, and not the conversation with Samson and Brandon.

Damian grinned. Yeah, finding one's mate could do that to a vampire. He tore his gaze from the picture of domestic bliss and let his eyes roam over the crowd, until he spotted his father. Amaury was talking to Blake, a full-blooded vampire, who was holding his two-year-old hybrid son Harry in his arms. As chief of hybrid security, Blake had a special connection to all hybrid vampires born into the Scanguards family.

Damian paved his way through the crowd, greeting his friends and colleagues casually. Before he reached his father, he was rammed from the side and nearly lifted off his feet. He reacted quickly, and snatched the kid who'd plowed into him. It was Dean, John and Savannah's ten-year-old hybrid son.

"Hey, Dean, what's going on? You trying to escape, or what?"

Dean looked over his shoulder, then rolled his eyes as if he was double his age. "My sister really can't take a joke."

Buffy was already rushing toward them. "Give it back, Dean, or I'm gonna make sure Daddy grounds you."

"I didn't take it!" Dean protested.

Damian set the boy back on his feet, shaking his head. "I'm not gonna get into the middle of a sibling rivalry." While Buffy chased after Dean, Damian walked up to Amaury. "Hey, Dad, Blake."

Both greeted him, and little Harry stretched his arms out toward Damian. Damian ruffled the boy's dark hair, and the boy let out a gurgling laugh, his tiny fangs extended. "Wish I had time to play, Harry, but I've gotta talk to my dad."

"Watch out," Blake warned. "Or he's gonna bite you. It's the terrible twos, and he's just discovered the taste of blood."

Amaury chuckled. "At least you only have one at a time. It was harder watching two little ones getting a taste for biting at the same time."

Damian smirked. "I'm sure we weren't *that* bad."

"You were adorable." Damian looked over his shoulder and saw his mother, Nina, join them. "But they grow up so fast."

"Thank God," Amaury replied and pulled Nina to his side. "It took long enough for them to move out and leave us alone."

Nina boxed him in his side. Then she looked at Damian. "Don't mind your father. He loves you and Benjamin. And he still worries about you. Or why else do you think he gave you and your brother the flat right below ours?"

Amaury growled. "Woman, are you trying to make me look like a big softy?"

Nina giggled, and whispered something into his ear. Damian tried to tune it out, but heard it nevertheless.

"You're never soft, baby, you're always hard, just how I like it."

As a result of Nina's words, Amaury's eyes suddenly changed to a golden hue, a sure sign that her words were arousing him.

"I'd say, guys, get a room," Damian said, "but I need to steal Dad for a few minutes."

Amaury nodded. "Let's go into the study, it's quieter there."

"Have you seen Eddie?" Damian asked as they were making their way to the study.

"He's here, probably in the kitchen."

"I'll get him. I have something for him to look into."

While Amaury opened the door to the study, Damian continued to the kitchen and waved at Eddie, who was chatting with Isabelle, Samson's daughter.

"Do you have a minute?" Damian asked.

"Sure. Excuse me, Isabelle," Eddie replied and walked toward him.

"In the study."

When they entered the wood-paneled office with the floor-to-ceiling bookcases and the soft lighting, Amaury wasn't alone anymore. Samson had joined him.

Damian raised an eyebrow, but entered with Eddie and shut the door behind them.

"Did you fill Samson in?" Damian asked his father.

"Only the little I know: that somebody stole a case of bottled blood from the Mezzanine. I assume you found out more in the meantime?" Amaury asked.

"Yeah. Let me bring you up to speed."

He opened the plastic shopping bag and pulled out the evidence Naomi had found, and started to tell his three fellow vampires what had transpired, but left out any mention of Naomi. He didn't want Scanguards to worry that she would divulge their secrets, because once he came clean with her tonight, and she accepted him for what he was, things would be under control.

19

Naomi looked at the clock on her cell phone. After twenty minutes, Damian still hadn't returned. Normally, she wouldn't mind waiting a few more minutes, but she had to pee rather urgently. Perhaps she could just quickly sneak in, use the bathroom, and then leave just as quickly. Through the windows in the front room, she could see that the party was still going strong, even though it was almost three o'clock, however, she couldn't hear any loud noise coming from the house, which was a good thing. Or the neighbors would surely complain.

Not being able to wait any longer, Naomi got out of the car and walked up the steps to the entrance. She turned the knob, and the door opened. She stepped into the foyer from which she could see down the long hallway. A wooden stairway led to the second floor. If this house was like so many other Victorians in San Francisco, then she would find a powder room along the corridor underneath the staircase. Several people were coming in and out of the kitchen at the end of the hallway, and to her left, an open arch led into the living room, where most of the guests were congregating.

Not wanting to attract attention, Naomi quickly walked along the corridor, and tested the first door to her right. It opened, and she'd been right. It was a powder room. She quickly went inside and locked the door. She could tell immediately that everything in this well-appointed half bath was brand-new. Her own bathroom was a far cry from this luxury. She could only dream of something so beautiful and elegant.

Despite wanting to linger in the powder room to enjoy the lavender-scented hand soap and lotion, she hurried, not wanting Damian to think she'd left when he got back to the car. When she unlocked the door and stepped back into the hallway, she nearly collided with a man.

"Oops," she said and jerked back.

He was young, had raven-black hair, and piercing green eyes. Though he was dressed casually in low-riding black pants and a linen shirt with the top two buttons open, there was something commanding about him. The way he looked at her, his gaze roaming over her as if measuring her, made her uneasy.

"Who are you?" he asked bluntly, behaving almost like the bouncer at the Mezzanine. Just more arrogant.

"Uh, I'm Naomi."

"Who let you in?"

She figured that her reply that the front door wasn't locked probably wouldn't satisfy him, so she decided for a different answer. "I came with Damian."

That seemed to surprise him. "Damian? You sure?" He ran his eyes over her body once more. "You don't look like you came with him."

That was downright rude, but she wasn't going to start a confrontation with this arrogant prick. "I'll wait outside for him."

She tried to brush past him, but he didn't budge. She was about to raise her voice to tell him to get out of her way, when a toddler came barreling her way and crashed into her legs. Instinctively, she leaned down, catching the little guy. The little boy couldn't be older than two years.

"What are you still doing up so late?" she cooed. "Isn't it past your bedtime?"

The little boy stretched his arms out toward her, and she was about to lift him up, when a young black woman with an athletic figure came running.

"Harry! You're not supposed to run away," she chastised the boy, before glancing at Naomi. "Thanks." Then she addressed the man who'd finally taken a few steps away from her to give her space. "Grayson, do you know where Lilo is? I think Harry is getting antsy."

"Try the kitchen." Grayson turned around and went down the hallway.

"Is he yours?" Naomi asked the girl and pointed to the boy who was still stretching his arms up toward her.

"God, no! He's Blake and Lilo's little devil. Blake just handed him off to me as if I'm the designated babysitter around here." The woman who couldn't be older than twenty smiled at her, then stretched her hand out. "I'm Buffy. I don't think I've ever seen you here."

Naomi shook her hand. "I'm Naomi. I came with Damian."

Suddenly Buffy's face lit up in recognition. "Oh, you're Little Red Riding Hood."

Naomi felt her face flush with embarrassment. Did everybody know that she and Damian had made out on the dance floor like world champions in oral gymnastics? Was that why he'd told her to stay in the car, to spare her the embarrassing looks and questions? And was that why Grayson had scrutinized her like she was some sort of zoo animal?

When the little boy started wailing, Naomi took it as her opportunity to change the subject and simply picked up the boy and lifted him into her arms. "He's probably tired. It's really late for a child this age."

Buffy shrugged. "Harry is up at all hours."

Naomi rocked him in her arms, and he finally stopped crying.

~ ~ ~

Grayson cast another look at the human woman who was now talking to Buffy. As he walked down the corridor, he saw Cooper, and pulled him aside. Cooper was Haven and Yvette's hybrid son, and had ultra-short dark hair and a muscled physique. He was easy-going, fun to be around, and he was a well-trained bodyguard who didn't mind following orders.

"See the blond human talking to Buffy?"

"Yeah, what about her?"

"Watch her. I think she's a party crasher. Make sure she doesn't go near the kitchen or anywhere else where she could see blood."

"And what are you gonna do?"

"Find Damian. She claims she came with him. Not likely."

"I saw Damian go into the study earlier."

"Thanks, Coop. I'll be right back."

He slapped his hand on Cooper's shoulder, then headed for the study. Grayson knocked briefly, then opened the door and looked inside. Damian was indeed in the room, but he wasn't alone. Amaury, Eddie, and his own father, Samson, were there. And they looked like they were talking business. Without him. Fuck, how he hated that. He didn't like it when they excluded him from business discussions. After all, he was the heir to the Scanguards empire. But sometimes they treated him as if he wasn't ready to lead.

But he'd prove to them, and particularly to his father, that he always looked out for Scanguards, and only had their kind's best interest in mind, particularly when it came to protecting them from outsiders—like the blond woman who'd snuck into the house without anybody noticing.

"We have a problem," he announced. "A party crasher. That fat chick claims she's here with Damian, but that's obviously a lie—"

"Naomi isn't fat!" Damian snapped and lunged for him, his fist connecting with Grayson's chin before he could even comprehend what was happening.

Grayson's head whipped to the side, and instantly his fangs extended to their full length, and he was ready for a fight. He drew his fist back for a counter punch, but his father blocked him, catching his fist in his palm and holding it tightly.

"Stop it! Both of you!" Samson commanded. Then he looked at Damian. "This Naomi, does she know what you are?"

Damian shook his head. "No. Not yet. I was planning to tell her later tonight."

Grayson stared at his fellow hybrid. "Why tell her?"

"Why do you think, you idiot? Because I want her to be mine."

Damian's declaration silenced everybody in the room. Only their breathing could be heard, together with their heartbeats.

"You're not kidding, are you?" Grayson felt his chin drop. "I had no idea you liked—"

"You say the word fat one more time," Damian warned, "and you can pick up your brains from the floor."

"Hotheads," Samson said in a casual tone, addressing his oldest friend, Amaury.

"Yeah, both of them," Amaury replied.

"I think we need to talk," Samson said.

"You know, guys," Eddie interrupted. "I don't need to be part of this. Why don't I go and make sure the girl doesn't stumble on our secrets?"

"Good idea," Samson agreed, "take Grayson with you."

"But Cooper is already watching her," Grayson protested.

Samson tossed a glare at Grayson. "Out, now. What I have to discuss with Damian is none of your business."

Grayson grunted in displeasure. Eddie already opened the door, then looked over his shoulder, lifting his hand that held a cell phone. "I'll get right on this. Will let you know what I can find."

Grayson followed Eddie out of the room, and pulled the door shut behind him, annoyed that he hadn't gotten a chance to punch Damian in return, though he understood now why Damian had lashed out like that. Damian was in love.

20

The moment the door fell shut behind Eddie and Grayson, Samson turned his gaze back to Damian and looked at him with different eyes. Amaury's son had grown up. Where had the time gone? It felt like yesterday, when he and Amaury had fought side by side to rescue the women they loved. And now the second generation was ready to forge their own path, have families of their own. Ryder had been the first to set out on that path, and it appeared that Damian would be the second.

But before congratulations were in order, several things had to be cleared up, because Samson now realized that Damian had conveniently left a few things out of his report about the goings-on at the nightclub.

"This Naomi wouldn't be the person who alerted you to the fact that Mrs. Zhang saw the thief leave the Mezzanine?"

Damian nodded. He'd been very vague about how he'd come by the information that a neighbor had seen the thief, which had led to him finding the broken bottle of blood and the vial that had undoubtedly been filled with vampire blood. They'd all recognized the distinctive smell.

"And you didn't find it necessary to mention that?"

"No, I didn't."

The stubborn lifting of Damian's chin didn't escape Samson's notice. Nor apparently Amaury's.

"And why not?" Samson added.

"Because of this." Damian gestured to him and Amaury. "Because you'd both be giving me the third degree. And by the end of the night, it'll be a moot point anyway."

"Who is she, son?" Amaury asked.

Damian hesitated, and Samson realized that whatever the answer was, he wouldn't like it.

"She's the journalist I told you about. The one following up on allegations of a satanic cult or blood sacrifices at the Mezzanine."

Samson pushed out a breath, while Amaury ran a hand through his long hair.

"And you want to tell her what you are? What we all are?" Samson asked, shaking his head. "For once I have to agree with Grayson. I advise against it. You don't know her. You have no idea how she'll react. And all you're doing is giving her evidence for her story."

Damian let out a bitter laugh. "As if either one of you knew your mates for more than a few days before they found out what you are. How is that any different than this situation? Explain that to me."

When Samson wanted to reply, Amaury stopped him. "Don't, Samson. He's right. It doesn't matter that she's a journalist, or that he's only known her for a few days. He could do worse. After all, the first time I met Nina, she wanted to kill me. And look, it turned out well in the end."

Amaury grinned.

"Yeah, Mom liked to tell that story to Benjamin and me when we were younger." Damian smiled just like his father now, and the resemblance between them was uncanny, except for the hair.

"And what if she uses what you tell her, and publishes her story?" Samson asked.

"She won't," Damian claimed. "She's the one."

"What if she doesn't feel the same?"

"It's not possible."

Samson had to chuckle at the hybrid's stoic declaration. "It's not all about sex." Though he knew from his own experience that being compatible in bed was a fantastic foundation for a happy marriage. And considering that a vampire's sex drive didn't wane with age, he was happy that he and Delilah were as crazy about each other as on the day they'd met. And equally insatiable when it came to their carnal pleasures. Just thinking about her now made him want to drag her from the living room and find a dark corner to make love to her, preferably with his fangs lodged deep in her neck.

Samson cleared his throat. "Well, if you really think that she's the one, then I guess you have to do what you have to do. But I warn you: if she doesn't accept you, you'll have to wipe her memory of everything she knows about you or the Mezzanine. We can't afford the press sticking their noses into our business."

"I understand," Damian said. Then he gestured to the door. "I'd better look for her and take her home."

"Don't make it look rushed," Amaury advised him. "You don't want her to suspect that you're hiding your family. Besides, I think your mother would love to meet her. As would I."

Damian raised an eyebrow. "Let's not overwhelm her. She'll find out soon enough that if she accepts me, she'll also get a whole new family."

"We'll be on our best behavior," Amaury promised.

Damian rolled his eyes as if he didn't believe his father, then left the room and closed the door behind him.

"I didn't see that one coming," Amaury said.

"Just like I didn't see it coming, when you bonded with Nina," Samson replied, chuckling. "When it hits us, it hits us hard and fast."

"No wonder he punched Grayson," Amaury said.

"Don't worry, it'll do Grayson good. I wish he would finally come down from his high horse, and behave better. I sure didn't raise him to be a jerk."

Amaury chuckled. "No, but you spoiled him. Both of you. Now he's used to getting his way, and he doesn't believe that being nice to people is necessary."

"I wish he'd find a woman who'll cut him down to size."

Amaury slapped him on the shoulder. "I'm afraid that woman has to be born first. And she'd better not be shy or weak, because your son needs a strong hand."

"Don't I know it? The problem is finding a woman like that."

"There must be somebody. The world is full of headstrong women."

"I'm sure, but the women Grayson normally goes out with can't keep him in check. No wonder he gets bored with them quickly. If only we could put somebody in his path who has a chance…"

Amaury shook his head and laughed. "Don't even try to play matchmaker. He's gonna smell it from a mile away, and he'll reject her just to spite you."

Samson grinned. "Then I'll just have to make sure that he doesn't know he's being set up."

"Yeah, good luck with that."

21

"He seems to like you," Buffy said with a smile at the toddler in Naomi's arms.

"He's a cutie."

"He's a handful," Buffy corrected her with a wink. "Do you mind holding him for a moment while I grab him a snack from the kitchen? Just in case he starts crying again."

"No problem," Naomi replied, while Buffy already walked down the hallway toward the back of the house.

Grayson had brushed past them only moments earlier, but another young guy stood near the entrance to the dining room, and cast her furtive looks. Did he, too, know that she was the infamous Little Red Riding Hood who'd made out with Damian on the dance floor of the Mezzanine? Was that why he was looking at her? Perhaps she should try to find Damian so that they could leave the party before even more people figured out who she was.

She would go back to the car, but since Buffy had asked her to look after Harry for a moment, she couldn't leave. Besides, the boy really seemed to feel comfortable with her. Harry grabbed one of her blond locks and pulled. For such a small child, he was rather strong.

"Ouch!"

She tried to pry the strands of hair from his little fist, but he held on tightly.

"Harry, you've gotta let go," Naomi said gently.

But the boy suddenly laughed, and she could see his sharp canines. They reminded her of the fangs that Damian had worn with his costume at the Halloween party. They looked just as sharp and realistic. Harry suddenly dipped his head and bit down on her finger, just as she made another attempt at prying her hair from his clenched fist.

"Ouch!" The little devil was biting her. And it hurt.

A man came rushing from the living room and suddenly called out in a scolding tone. "Harry!" He reached for the toddler. "No biting!" He snatched the boy, and cast her an apologetic look. "Sorry, my son is—"

"Naomi!"

She whipped her head toward the back of the house, and Damian was suddenly next to her. "You okay?"

"Harry bit her."

Damian took her hand and pulled it to his lips. "Let me kiss it and make it better."

"It's okay," she said, but Damian kissed over the spot where the toddler had bitten down, before she could even inspect the damage.

"I'm so sorry. I'm Blake, Harry's dad. And this little boy"—he shot a scolding look at his son, who actually lowered his lids sheepishly—"is grounded for the foreseeable future." Blake shook his head. "He's at that terrible age where he just wants to check everything out by putting it in his mouth."

"It's fine. It was just a little bite," she said, not wanting to make him even more embarrassed for his son. "I barely felt it."

She looked at Damian and then at her finger. There was no bitemark despite the force with which Harry had latched onto her finger.

"Looks like he didn't do any damage after all," Damian said with a smile at her. Then he shook his finger at Harry. "No more biting. It's not polite."

"So, uhm," Blake started, "you wanna introduce your date, Damian?"

"Sorry," Damian said. "This is Naomi. We weren't really planning on staying."

Naomi cast him a regretful look. "I was waiting outside in the car, but I had to use the restroom. And then Buffy handed me Harry, and I couldn't really leave before she—"

Damian squeezed her arm. "It's okay."

"Well, now that you're here, you might as well stay a little," Blake said. "And I promise I'll keep this little guy away from you."

Damian looked at her. "If you want to stay, we can stay."

"Uhm, I don't want to intrude," she said, not sure if Damian really wanted them to stay.

"You're not intruding," Buffy suddenly said from behind her and reached past her with a small plastic bag with crackers. "Here, to keep Harry in line."

Blake smirked and took the bag. "Thanks, Buffy. Have you seen Lilo?"

"Nope." Buffy walked past them, and headed into the living room.

"I'd better find her. And you guys should definitely stay for a while. Ryder and Scarlet have a little announcement," Blake said and marched into the dining room with his son in his arms.

"Guess we can't leave right away," Damian said. "You okay with that?"

Naomi shrugged. "It's fine by me. I just hope that not everybody knows who I am."

"What do you mean?"

She looked around to make sure nobody was close enough to listen in on their conversation. "Buffy knew that I was Little Red Riding Hood last night, and judging by the way she said it, she knew what we did on the dance floor. What if everybody here knows?"

Damian chuckled unexpectedly. "Buffy knows, because she was bartending at the Mezzanine last night. Doesn't mean that everybody else knows. She's not a gossip. Well, not a big one anyway."

"You say that as if it doesn't mean anything, but what if she tells your friends and your family? I don't want to make a bad impression."

Damian dipped his head to her ear. "You could never make a bad impression on anybody. Everybody will like you."

"Not everybody. When I came in, this guy gave me the third degree. Buffy called him Grayson."

Damian grunted. "Yeah, he can be a pompous ass. Don't worry, he's not gonna give you any more trouble."

"Who is he?"

"Patrick's older brother."

"I would have never guessed. Patrick seems a lot nicer than him. Not that I've spoken much with him either."

Suddenly, somebody called for silence from the living room, and the voices died down. The people who'd been in the kitchen and in other rooms, made their way toward the living room. Damian put his hand around her waist and ushered her to the arch that led into the front room.

~ ~ ~

Damian had intervened just in time, because Blake's baby son had actually drawn blood. It wasn't unusual for a young vampire hybrid: they were drawn to human blood. And he knew from his own experience how sweet Naomi's blood tasted. Luckily, he'd been able to seal the puncture wounds on her finger with his saliva before she realized that Harry's sharp fangs had actually pierced her skin.

The conversations had died down, and everybody was now looking at Ryder and his blood-bonded mate Scarlet. Scarlet wore a long red dress that accentuated her belly and made her look radiant. Ryder had one arm around her waist and smiled like a Cheshire cat. Scarlet's hand rested on her belly. She was seven months along, but looked much bigger already.

"Scarlet and I have an announcement to make," Ryder started.

"Let me guess: Scarlet is pregnant," Ethan, Ryder's brother, called out, and the entire room erupted in laughter.

Ryder chuckled. "Smartass. You'll be called to task soon, because as the uncle of two boys, you'll be on permanent babysitting duty."

"Two?" The surprised gasp came from Brandon King, Scarlet's father. "Two boys?" The fifty-something man, who'd become a vampire a year earlier after he'd nearly died in the fire that had destroyed his Victorian home, spread his arms out and hugged Scarlet and his son-in-law to him. "I'm so happy for you both. And for me too. I'll have two grandsons to spoil."

Gabriel and Maya, Ryder's parents beamed proudly, and well-wishes echoed in the room, as they all talked to each other.

When Brandon released Scarlet and Ryder from his embrace, Scarlet sniffled. "Don't make me cry now, Dad. And we're not the only ones who have something to announce." She craned her neck. "Katie?"

Katie and Luther came to the front of the room. Luther was practically related to Damian. He was Eddie's sire, the man who'd turned him into a vampire.

"I know I always said I didn't want children," Katie started, "but after seeing all of you hybrids grow up…"

Fuck! Had Grayson and Cooper not managed to tell everybody at the party that there was a human among them who didn't know about vampires? He cast a quick look at Naomi, whose forehead furrowed.

"… Luther and I decided it was finally time for us too." She looked up at Luther, the muscular vampire who towered over her.

"Katie is pregnant, and I couldn't be happier." Luther's gaze strayed to Samson, who now walked up to his old friend, and hugged him.

"I'm so happy for you," Samson said.

Everybody joined in congratulating the couple, and Naomi turned to him.

"What did she mean by hybrid?"

Damian made a dismissive hand movement. "Katie was an actress before she married Luther, and sometimes she just uses words from her time in the movie business."

Naomi seemed to buy the lie.

"Time to dance," Ryder announced, and a moment later, dance music filled every room of the house.

Immediately, several couples started dancing. Perhaps it hadn't been such a bad idea to come to this housewarming party after all. Showing Naomi how normal his friends and his family were, before he told her that they were vampires, might actually make her accepting him easier. Maybe she wouldn't see him as a monster if she realized vampires behaved just like humans.

"Wanna dance?" he asked and already pulled Naomi into his arms, before she could even answer.

"But don't—"

"Of course not," he whispered into her ear, immediately realizing that she was afraid he'd be as intimate as at the Mezzanine. "I don't wanna compete with my parents."

Naomi looked up at him. "What do you mean?"

He maneuvered her farther into the room, then pointed at a couple dancing as if they were auditioning for a revival of the movie *Dirty Dancing*. "Those are my parents."

Naomi gasped.

"Shocking, isn't it?" Damian asked, chuckling. "Now you see why I behaved the way I did at the Mezzanine. Like father like son."

"But they can't be your parents," she said, shaking her head. "They are far too young."

He'd expected that. "Fifty is the new thirty. And they both have good genes."

"Fantastic genes from what I can see." Naomi smiled at him. "They look like they're newlyweds."

"I'll tell you sometime how they met. It was love at first sight. They were a couple within a week, and have never been apart since." And he wanted the same for himself. To find a mate who looked at him the way Nina looked at Amaury. If Naomi would have him, he would worship her the way Amaury worshipped Nina for the rest of his life.

"Wow. You rarely hear about married couples like that. It's unusual."

"You think so?" It wasn't unusual in his circles. Blood-bonded couples were devoted to each other. And the power dynamics within those couples were interesting too. "Wanna know a secret?"

"Hmm?"

"My mother wears the pants in the relationship. My father is absolute putty in her hands."

"You're kidding. He's huge, and... somewhat intimidating."

"He's a big teddy bear. And I know of many couples like that." He gestured to Samson who now danced with Delilah, who wore a form-fitting azure-blue dress. "Those are Patrick's parents, Samson and Delilah."

"That's the owner of Scanguards? The way he looks at his wife... it's as if... as if she's the only woman in here." Naomi looked at him.

"To him, she is." Damian smiled. "I could go on."

"It must be nice to have such role models, to know all these married couples who're still happy after decades of being married. When I look at friends of my family, all I see are a lot of divorces. When I was in high school, most of my friends' parents were on their second marriage. It's uplifting to see that some people can really make it work."

He noticed her glance back at Nina and Amaury and smile. Yes, it had been a good idea to show her what his family was like before she knew what they were. Right now, she saw them without prejudice, and with some luck, she'd recall those impressions once he told her the truth about his family and himself.

"Shall we get out of here, and go to my place? I'd like to be alone with you so we can talk, just you and me. And then I want to make love to you."

"Won't they wonder why we're leaving so early?"

He chuckled at her ear. "Do you really think that anyone will notice that we're leaving? Look around. They're all too busy making eyes at each other."

"Then let's go."

22

Naomi was surprised when she realized that Damian's flat was in the middle of the Tenderloin, a rather seedy neighborhood in downtown San Francisco. But the moment he led her into the full-floor apartment, she was surprised in a positive way: the place was pure luxury, something she'd not expected from the outside. Clearly, even the Tenderloin was gentrifying.

"Do you own this flat?" she asked turning to Damian.

"No. My parents own the building. They live in the flat above."

Surprised, she asked, "You don't mind living so close to your parents?"

"We have a good relationship." He came closer and put his hands on her waist. "But let's talk about us."

All of a sudden, Damian's cell phone rang. He sighed and looked at the display. "That's Patrick. I'd better take that." He answered the call. "Yeah, what is it?" There was a short pause, then Damian put his hand over the phone, and said to her, "Make yourself at home, I'll be just a minute."

He walked toward the balcony and opened the sliding glass door, before stepping outside to continue his conversation with Patrick.

Naomi took the opportunity to let her eyes roam. The elevator they'd ridden up from the garage had opened directly into the flat. The living area was large and open, with a small balcony, a massive TV on one wall, an open-plan kitchen at one end of the room, and several doors to the left and the right of it, which she assumed led to the bedrooms and bathrooms. Since this was the only flat on this floor, she assumed that there were at least two or three bedrooms, and just as many bathrooms. Her own flat could fit three times into the space.

Damian was still out on the balcony, talking to Patrick. Naomi dropped her jacket and her handbag next to her overnight bag that Damian had carried up for her, and walked to the kitchen. She was thirsty, and a little nervous. Normally when a guy said that they needed to talk, it was bad news and involved a break-up. However, Damian had asked her to stay the night, and he'd told her at the party that he wanted to make love to her. So whatever he wanted to talk to her about was probably good. Nevertheless, she was nervous, because she had no clue what he wanted to talk to her about that he couldn't have said earlier in the car.

Naomi opened the refrigerator and looked inside. It was surprisingly well-stocked for a bachelor: orange juice, cream, fresh fruits and vegetables, dips, cheeses, cold cuts, and white wine. She scanned the shelves for bottles of water, and finally found them on the lowest shelf. She pulled one out, and was about to close the fridge, when her eyes fell on two bottles of red liquid that were stashed in the back of the fridge, behind the water bottles. She'd seen those bottles before.

Her heart skipped a beat. The clear bottles were labeled in the same manner as the broken bottle she'd found under the dumpster behind the Mezzanine. There was only one difference. They said *O+ bottled by Scanguards* instead of *A+ bottled by Scanguards*. She dropped the plastic water bottle, and reached for the bottle with the red liquid. Were her eyes deceiving her? Was she hallucinating?

Her pulse drummed faster now. Damian had claimed that he'd never seen a bottle like this before. Yet there were two identical bottles in his refrigerator. She unscrewed the cap and sniffed the liquid. The metallic scent stung her nostrils, and she recoiled involuntarily. This was blood, no doubt. Human blood.

"Naomi, Patrick said—"

At the sound of Damian's voice behind her she whirled around so fast that she tripped over the water bottle she'd dropped so carelessly on the floor, and stumbled. Damian reached for her to steady her, but the damage was done. Her hand jerked upward, and the contents of the open bottle spilled over her chest, splattering on her top and running down her cleavage. She was soaked in blood.

"Fuck!"

It was Damian who'd cursed, but it might as well have been her, because what she now saw, scared the living daylights out of her.

Damian's eyes had lost all of their blue color and glowed red. And between his parted lips she saw sharp, brilliant-white fangs peek out. The same kind of fangs he'd worn at the Halloween party as part of his vampire costume. But she knew that he wasn't wearing plastic fangs or colored lenses right now, just like he hadn't worn any during the night at the Mezzanine. She realized that now, because there was nothing fake about either of them. This was Damian, the real Damian. The vampire. She knew that now. And it explained so much. In fact, it explained everything.

"You tricked me." She pressed out the words, while her mind was working overtime. How would she get past him? How could she escape his flat now?

"Naomi, please, I was gonna tell you. Tonight."

She backed away from him and felt the cool air from the open refrigerator blast at her back. "You're a real vampire."

"Technically I'm a hybrid, half vampire, half human."

His voice sounded calm, but she wasn't fooled. His fangs were extended, and she could see his nostrils flare and his gaze drop to her chest, to the blood that covered her. He wanted blood. She could see that. And something else was evident now too.

"It wasn't just roleplaying last night, was it?"

He shook his head, and appeared to look guilty. How was that possible?

"I'm sorry, Naomi, I got carried away. I wanted you so badly, I couldn't stop myself."

That confirmed it. He'd bitten her. And judging by the look in his eyes, which were now shimmering golden rather than red, he was about to do it again. But she couldn't allow that. Couldn't let herself be at the mercy of a monster.

"Let me go, and I'll never breathe a word of this," she begged, knowing she had to do something to get away from him.

"I can't do that, Naomi."

He took a step toward her, and suddenly his fangs receded and looked like normal teeth again, as if she'd just imagined it.

"Please, let me go."

"Naomi, I'm in love with you."

The words shook her to her core. No, a vampire couldn't love. A vampire was a bloodthirsty creature. Hell, vampires shouldn't even exist.

"I'm sorry for biting you last night without your permission. I promise next time I'll wait until you give me permission."

"Next time?" She shook her head, panicked. "Why would I give you permission? Do you think I'm crazy?"

"No, but why do you think you climaxed so hard when we made love last night?"

She stared at him, her mouth going dry. What was he suggesting? That his bite had made her climax? No! That was ludicrous.

"A vampire's bite heightens arousal in the vampire as well as the host."

Naomi shook her head, not wanting to hear whatever else he had to say. "No!" Then she stared at the bottle she was still holding in her hand. "You lied to me even after I showed you the bottle I found. After I told you about the story I'm supposed to write. You kept deceiving me."

"I was going to tell you tonight. That's why I brought you here. So we could talk in private, and I could tell you what I am."

"So I'd be alone with you, without anybody hearing me scream," Naomi said, knowing she could never fight him. He was too strong. She was truly at his mercy.

To her surprise he chuckled.

"How's that funny?" she snapped.

"Sorry, *chérie*, it's just that you *will* scream, but not in pain or fear, but in ecstasy, because when we're done here, you'll want me to make love to you and to bite you while I'm inside you."

The arrogance of his words made her slam the half-empty bottle on the shelf in the refrigerator door and brace her hands at her hips. "How dare you, you conceited, self-satisfied jerk, assume what I'm gonna do?"

When the words left her lips, she realized that she wasn't afraid of him. She was pissed off with him. That realization hit her like a punch in the gut. At the same time, she remembered exactly how she'd felt when they'd had sex and he'd bitten her in the neck. She hadn't felt any pain, and afterwards, there'd been no evidence of the bite. And she'd never felt so satisfied in her entire life.

Damian sighed. "Damn it, Naomi, how am I supposed to be able to think clearly, when you're drenched in human blood, and all I can think of is licking it off you?" He ran a trembling hand through his hair. "This wasn't how I was planning to have this conversation."

"Well, that makes two of us, because I wasn't planning on having this conversation at all," she snapped.

"Take the damn top off, Naomi!"

"Make me!" The angry words were out, before she could take them back.

"Fine!"

Before she could even blink, Damian was ripping her top in two, and jerked it off her body. But that didn't get rid of all the blood on her, because some of it had soaked her bra, and clung to her breasts.

"Fuck!" Damian cursed.

Their gazes collided, and in that instant, she knew that she'd never be able to resist him. She was doomed.

The next thing she felt was Damian dipping his head to her breasts. He licked her skin clean of the blood, and all she could do was stand there, paralyzed. Feeling his warm tongue on her skin as he licked her breasts through her bra, catapulted her back to earlier in the night when they'd had sex in her flat… when she'd sucked his cock. The cock of a vampire. Was she so depraved that even now she couldn't find it in her to regret what she'd done? To regret that she'd enjoyed being with him?

"Damian," she murmured, suddenly breathless. "We've gotta stop. We can't just…" But the next words eluded her.

He finally lifted his head from her breasts, and she noticed blood on his lips. Fuck, why did she find that sight so erotic? She should be disgusted.

"Naomi, will you please give me a chance to explain everything? There's so much I need to tell you. About me, my family, the way I live. Can you grant me that? I promise I won't hurt you." His eyes were blue now. And he looked entirely human again.

Slowly, she nodded. "All right. We'll talk." And afterwards? Once she knew everything, what would she do? She had no idea how she would react. Her head was spinning.

"Thank you." He gestured to her bra. "Why don't I give you a T-shirt so you'll feel more comfortable?"

23

After Naomi slipped into one of his T-shirts, Damian felt a moment of relief. He'd been close to biting her again, the smell of human blood mixing with that of her tempting skin was too intoxicating. But he'd managed to restrain himself, and had licked only the bottled blood off her skin, before releasing her.

When he sat down on the large sectional sofa in the living area, Naomi took the armchair that stood the farthest away from him. They were alone. Benjamin was on a 36-hour assignment protecting a client during a business trip to Los Angeles, so they wouldn't be disturbed tonight. He had all the time in the world to tell Naomi about himself.

Actually *showing* her his vampire side hadn't been the first thing on the agenda. He'd hoped to leave that for last, but what was done was done. The cat was out of the bag, and there was no way of shoving it back in. He might as well run with it.

"This wasn't how I was planning to tell you." He shrugged. "But now you know, and it's important that I tell you everything about me, my family, and Scanguards."

"And the bottled blood I found," she added.

"That too. But let me start by telling you about us, about the vampires. I wasn't turned into a vampire. I was born a vampire hybrid. You've seen my father and my mother earlier at the party and commented how young they look. They don't age, just like I won't age anymore either."

Naomi stared at him with wide eyes. "Are you saying your parents are vampires? And vampires can have children?"

"Only my father is a vampire. My mother, Nina, is human."

Naomi instantly shook her head. "That can't be. She looks even younger than your father. And you're what? Thirty?"

"Thirty-one."

"She can't possibly be human."

"Don't tell her that I told you, but she's in her late fifties."

Naomi gasped.

"And the reason she doesn't age is because she's blood-bonded to my father. He shares his immortality with her through his blood. She drinks his blood."

"That's ludicrous. What you're really saying is that he's turned her into a vampire, otherwise why would she drink his blood?"

He understood why Naomi had a hard time understanding what a blood-bond entailed. "You're probably thinking that a human drinking vampire blood turns into a vampire, like the movies suggest. That's not actually the case. Only when a human is on the brink of death, can vampire blood turn the human into a vampire."

"So she's still human, but then why on earth would she drink his blood?"

Damian had to smile. "Because drinking his blood arouses her, and it strengthens the bond they have. Their connection is closer than that of any normal couple. And by blood-bonding with her, my father made himself entirely dependent on her."

"What do you mean?" Curiosity flickered in Naomi's eyes.

"Since blood-bonding, my father can only drink my mother's blood for nourishment." He motioned to the fridge. "If he drank the bottled human blood many of us drink, he'd get sick and eventually die."

There was stunned silence for a moment, then Naomi asked, "But if anything happens to her, if she dies, wouldn't that mean that your father will die too, because he'll starve?"

Damian shook his head. "No. If a blood-bonded mate dies, her surviving mate goes through a change, and he'll be able to drink the blood of any human again. I know two vampires that this happened to. You met one of them tonight: Luther. Katie is his second mate. His first died in childbirth."

"Oh." She contemplated his words, and he didn't press her. "So, because your father is dependent on your mother for his survival, is that why you said that your mother wears the pants in the relationship?"

"That's not the reason. My mother would never deny him her blood. She loves him. But she also has him completely wrapped around her little finger, it's a wonder Dad can breathe. But he's smitten with her, and would give his life for hers if he had to. I've never seen a love so strong than that of my parents."

"How can she love a vampire?" Naomi shook her head.

"I know it's a difficult thing to wrap your head around, but deep down my father is a man with more humanity and deeper emotions than any human. They trust each other completely, and despite of what you might think about a relationship between a human and a vampire, they're equal partners."

~ ~ ~

Equal partners? The spinning in Naomi's head became more intense. How was this even possible? Was she really having this conversation? But when she thought back to the housewarming party and the way Damian's parents had looked at each other, she couldn't deny what she'd seen: love and devotion. But something else too: desire. Even after having been together for over thirty years, they still desired each other.

"And you were born into this? So you're still part human?"

He nodded. "I'm as strong as my father, but I'm not vulnerable to sunlight like he is. I can eat human food, but I also need human blood to stay strong."

She gestured toward the refrigerator. "You drink bottled blood?"

"Most of the time."

A shiver ran down her spine. *Most of the time.* She knew what that meant. When he didn't bite women during sex. But she didn't want to steer the conversation into that direction.

"The blood is bottled by Scanguards. Why? What does a security company have to do with blood? And where do they get it from?"

She noticed Damian take a deep breath of air.

"It's not really my secret to tell, but you're too smart, you would figure it out soon anyway, so I might as well tell you everything."

She nodded.

"Samson, the founder of Scanguards, is a vampire. Over half of his employees are vampires or hybrids. Some are witches. The rest are humans. Most of the people you saw at the housewarming party are vampires or hybrids and their blood-bonded mates."

"Hybrids? That's what the woman was saying."

"Katie. Yes."

"Is she a vampire?"

"No. But she's blood-bonded to one, Luther. And her brother Haven is a vampire. Her brother Wesley is a witch."

Naomi shook her head, trying to take it all in. "So Patrick and Grayson? They're vampires?"

"Hybrids. They were born to a vampire and his human mate. You saw Samson and Delilah. They are just as devoted to each other as my parents."

"And the pregnant woman, Scarlet? She's human, right?"

"Yes, but Ryder is a vampire hybrid like myself. And the babies will be vampire hybrids."

At the mention of babies, Naomi recalled what she'd seen when the toddler had laughed. "Harry, the toddler, he's a vampire hybrid? Those were really fangs, weren't they? And he really tried to bite me."

"He did. I sealed the wound before you could see that he actually drew blood."

"What?" She stared at her finger, but there was no sign of the bite. "That's not possible. I would have seen it."

"Remember that I kissed the spot?" He looked at her, and his eyes suddenly shimmered golden again. "A vampire's saliva can heal small wounds like that instantly, and there won't be any scars either." He pointed to her neck. "Just like there are no scars from me biting you last night."

Her breath caught in her throat. "You licked over it." And there'd been no pain. Just pleasure. "If you really bit me, then why didn't it hurt?"

"Because a vampire's bite doesn't have to be painful. I licked your skin before I bit you. It made sure that you wouldn't feel any pain, only the pleasure that comes with a vampire's bite." He inhaled noticeably. "And the arousal. Just thinking of it now makes me hard."

Naomi gasped. She saw Damian look at her with desire shining from his eyes, and suddenly understood how a human could be drawn to a creature like him, despite knowing what he was. But she couldn't give in to this temptation, because she didn't know what it would do to her. Would she become a mindless creature only driven by lust and other carnal urges? Would she still be herself if she gave herself to a vampire?

Her mind didn't let her surrender, even though her body was weak. But she was a journalist, a person who looked at all sides of a story. That thought reminded her of something.

"Then the allegations of blood sacrifices or a satanic cult at the Mezzanine are somewhat true? Mrs. Zhang really saw vampires."

Damian sighed. "There is no satanic cult and no blood sacrifices. I can assure you of that. But I'm not sure what she saw. The staff and any vampire frequenting the club know that I don't tolerate anybody feeding on a human in public. It's too risky."

"You did it in the club," she reminded him.

"Before you call me a hypocrite, what I did happened in a secret room, away from everybody else's eyes. And it was Halloween. We're somewhat more relaxed during Halloween when everybody is playing dress-up."

"So all the people who were dressed as vampires, they all were real vampires?"

He nodded. "Most of them. It's the only way we can show our fangs in public without anybody getting scared or suspicious."

"How many are there?"

"At the club?"

"No, in San Francisco."

Damian shrugged. "A few thousand. More than in most cities."

"Why's that?"

"Scanguards provides good employment opportunities for vampires, and they also provide free bottled human blood to their employees to encourage them not to drink directly from humans."

"But they still do. I mean, you did."

"There's a reason for that. Most vampires and hybrids that aren't blood-bonded to a human, don't have to bite humans anymore to get blood to survive. They can drink what Scanguards procures from blood banks. They do it for other reasons now. Most of the biting is consensual these days and part of the sex act."

At that she felt herself blush, and it appeared that Damian noticed it, because she caught his gaze dropping down to her breasts, and she now realized that her nipples were hard, and liquid was pooling between her thighs. She was turned on.

"Even vampires bite each other to heighten sexual pleasure, but a vampire biting a human is the most amazing feeling in the world. That's why my father would never dream of turning my mother into a vampire. He values her too much as a human. He would only do it to save her life."

The more she heard about Damian's parents, the less she could conjure up fear at the knowledge that vampires existed and that Damian was one of them.

"There's something else you should know about vampires," Damian added. "When they fall in love, they fall fast, and they fall hard."

He rose from the sofa, and walked toward her armchair. She couldn't move, didn't have the strength to get up, even though she should. Instead, she watched him approach her. In front of her, he crouched down.

"I'm in love with you, Naomi. That's why I brought you here to talk. So I could show you who I really am in the hope that you won't reject me. I was born into this. I've never known any different. And I've never known better people than the ones who're part of Scanguards, because all they do is protect others from monsters, no matter in which form they come: human or preternatural."

His words filled her heart with warmth. She leaned toward him, and of its own volition, her hand moved. She touched his face and rubbed her finger over his lips. His warm breath ghosted over her hand.

"And you won't hurt me?"

"Never, *chérie*."

He placed his hands on her thighs, and she sucked in a breath. Heat surged inside her. Was it crazy to desire a vampire? To crave his touch?

"Show them to me."

Only when the last word was out, did she realize that she'd made a decision. That she would throw caution to the wind. Because she wanted to feel what she'd felt when he'd made love to her in the secret room behind his office. She wanted to feel his bite, this time with the knowledge that those were his real fangs, not fake plastic inserts like she'd assumed, and that this wasn't pretense, but reality.

She wanted to feel this vampire's desire for her.

24

Damian opened his mouth wider and willed his fangs to extend to their full length, while his heart made a somersault. Naomi wasn't afraid of his vampire side. She was curious.

When she looked at his fangs with fascination, he took her hand and led it to his face. "You can touch them. Just keep in mind that for me it will feel as if you touched my cock."

Something lit up in her eyes, and a tiny breath escaped from her throat. Slowly, she moved her hand, and extended her index finger to slide over the outside of his fang.

Damian sucked in a breath and closed his eyes, his heart beating out of control, his cock turning hard in a second.

"You like that?" she asked on a breath.

"Like? I love it." He took her other hand and led it to the front of his pants, pressing it onto the bulge there. "Feel what you're doing to me?"

"Oh." The little minx squeezed his cock, making him jolt in response.

"Fuck, Naomi, you want me to come right here, without even undressing?"

"That's how sensitive your fangs are?" she asked with wonder in her eyes.

"They're even more sensitive when they're piercing a human's skin." He brought his face closer to hers. "I'm dying to kiss you. May I please?"

She moved her lips closer to his. "And if I said no?"

"Then I'd have to take an ice-cold shower."

"That won't be necessary," she murmured and slanted her lips over his.

"Thank God!"

Damian retracted his fangs and captured Naomi's lips. This kiss felt better than any previous kiss he'd shared with her, because she kissed him with the full knowledge of who he was. There was no hiding anymore, no holding back, no secrets. Just the two of them. Alone.

Damian pulled her into his arms, and lifted her up, briefly taking his lips off her. "I wanna make love to you."

"Where's your bedroom?"

He marched toward it, carrying her in his arms, and lowered his lips back onto hers, delving into the sweet caverns of her mouth, tasting her, exploring her. He opened the door to his bedroom, entered, then kicked it shut behind him.

Hungry for Naomi, both for her body and for her blood, he lowered her onto his king-size bed, already tugging at her clothes. Luckily, she wasn't opposed to it, because she undressed him just as impatiently. Still, it took a minute before they were both naked, and both breathing hard, their lips fused, their hands eagerly exploring each other.

Damian kneaded her ample breasts, loving the feel of their weight in his palms and how her nipples turned hard before he even licked over them. He buried his face in her cleavage, loving the feel of her flesh hugging him, her skin perspiring and releasing the sweetest aroma. It made his fangs descend again.

He loved her hands on him, caressing his back, digging into his ass, rocking against him, urging him to thrust into her. But he wanted to get her to the brink of an orgasm before he plunged into her.

"Damian," she murmured, pressing her head into the pillow and thrusting her chest toward him.

"Fuck, I love your tits. They're so full, so heavy." He squeezed them and sucked one nipple into his mouth, licking his tongue over it, before he lifted his head to look at her. "When I bite you tonight, it'll be here." He looked at the nipple he'd just sucked then back at Naomi. "You want that?"

She panted. "Yes, please, yes."

"It turns you on, doesn't it? To know what I'll do?" He slid his hand down her torso to her sex. She was warm and wet already, and he stroked his fingers along her slit.

"Oh God, yes!"

Seeing her eyes dilated with passion, her entire body in full arousal, he couldn't delay any longer. He needed to be inside her. He nudged her thighs apart farther and positioned himself, when Naomi suddenly pressed a hand to his chest.

"You forgot the condom."

"I didn't forget. We won't need it. Vampires don't carry disease."

"But I'm not on the pill. I could get pregnant."

"I can't get you pregnant."

"But you said—"

"Only blood-bonded vampires can impregnate a human. I can't. Not yet."

Her forehead still furrowed. "But you drank my blood before. Doesn't that mean—"

He smiled and shook his head. "No. For a blood-bond we'd have to drink each other's blood while making love. Tonight, I'll be the only one drinking blood. So you have nothing to worry about."

She let out a sigh of relief, then put her hands on his hips, before slanting him a seductive look. "Then what are you waiting for?"

Before her last word had even left her lips, Damian thrust into her pussy and seated himself to the hilt. "Fuck!" This was better than he'd expected. He'd always hated condoms, and from now on he would never have to use one again.

Slowly, he began to move inside her, thrusting in and out of her welcoming body, while he lowered his lips to hers and captured her mouth for a passionate kiss. Their tongues dueled, and their breaths mingled, while their bodies moved as one. He loved the way Naomi's interior muscles squeezed his cock on each withdrawal and welcomed him back on each descent. The pressure was building in his balls, and he knew he wouldn't last much longer.

He severed the kiss and looked into her eyes. "Are you ready for my bite?"

"Yes," she said without hesitating.

"Thank you for trusting me."

He lowered his mouth to her breast and licked over the stiff nipple, and sucked the little rosebud into his mouth. Inhaling deeply, he brushed his fangs over Naomi's skin. The contact sent a shiver down his spine. Unable to wait any longer, he drove his fangs into her breast, lodging them deep in her flesh. When the first drops of blood touched his tongue, the taste sent a spear of fire through his core. Fuck! She tasted even better tonight, because the guilt of biting her without her permission the previous night was gone. All that was left was her sweet blood, her trust, and her acceptance. Together, it made for the most delicious nectar he couldn't get enough of.

Naomi moaned beneath him, and her hips writhed against him, meeting his thrusts, urging him to plunge harder into her. He was happy to comply with her wishes, and slammed his cock more forcefully into her wet cave. Naomi crossed her ankles below his butt, holding on to him for dear life, while he felt her heartbeat accelerate, and knew she was on the cusp. He shifted his angle by a fraction, and on the next thrust, Naomi cried out. He felt her orgasm physically, heard the excited drumming of her pulse, sensed her blood rush faster through her veins, and felt her interior muscles contract and release around his cock. Her climax ignited his own, and he let himself go and shot his seed into the woman he'd entrusted his heart to.

As their orgasms ebbed, Damian pulled his fangs from her breast and licked over the puncture wounds, closing them instantly. When he lifted his head and looked at Naomi, he noticed her look at the spot where he'd bitten her.

"Are you all right?" he asked and braced himself above her.

~ ~ ~

Naomi blew out a breath, her body boneless, her mind blown. "I'm more than all right."

She'd never felt better in her life. And the bite? She had no words for how it had felt. Out of this world amazing.

Damian smiled and rolled off her. He jumped out of bed and walked to the ensuite bathroom, where he disappeared for a moment. When he came back, he brought a washcloth and gently wiped her sex, before joining her in bed and pulling her into the curve of his body.

Damian pressed soft kisses to her neck and shoulder. "Your blood tasted like vanilla and oranges. I had to stop myself from taking too much."

"Is it always like that for you? When you bite a woman during sex?"

He laughed softly in her ear. "Are you trying to figure out how many women I've done this with?"

Was she that transparent? "If you don't want to tell me, that's fine."

"Of course, I wanna tell you. I wanna tell you everything about me." He sighed. "As for other women, I can't pretend that I was a monk before I met you. And I've bitten several women during sex, but not many. I didn't always feel the need for it. But with you, I can't get enough of you."

"And I can't get enough of you," she murmured, feeling insatiable, and not the least bit ashamed that she desired a vampire.

"Even though you know the truth now?"

"Maybe because of it. Last night, I thought you were just intense, but now I understand why. Everything about you turns me on. Even your fangs." Half an hour ago, she could have never imagined that she'd ever say such a thing.

"I'm happy that you feel that way. But I need you to promise me something." He sucked her earlobe between his lips, and licked it gently. "Everything that I told you, about me, my family, Scanguards, it has to stay in these four walls. Promise me that you'll never tell an outsider, not your editor, not your family, not your friends. Or you'll put us in danger. You can never write that story."

She turned halfway so she could look at him. "I can keep a secret."

"Thank you." He kissed her and turned her fully to him.

Naomi took a breath, because she still had questions, only for herself, not for the newspaper. "You said earlier that the thief stole something from the Mezzanine that you were safekeeping for your father. What was it?"

"It wasn't something I kept there for my father. The thief stole an entire crate of bottled blood that we keep for the staff members so they can feed when they need to."

"The bottles with the Scanguards name on it?"

He nodded.

"No wonder you were so furious when you thought I'd taken them." It all made sense now. "Whoever has the bottles can expose you and Scanguards."

"Yeah, and that's why we have to find the thief quickly, before he can put us all in danger."

"So Mrs. Zhang was right that the person she saw was carrying something when he stumbled. He must have broken one of the bottles and then tossed it. But that still doesn't explain the little vial that I found with it. I wish Heather would have been able to analyze what was inside it."

"I know what was inside it," Damian said to her surprise. "I could smell it. It was vampire blood."

Something clicked in her mind. "That's why you wanted me to show you the vial. So you could smell it. What did you do with it?"

"I gave it to my father. I spoke to him and Samson during the housewarming party. They're both very concerned."

"Why would somebody put vampire blood into a vial? What for? To turn a human into a vampire?" she asked, shivering at the thought.

"No. You'd need a lot more blood to turn a human. But it would be sufficient to heal somebody depending on the severity of the injury or illness."

Naomi shot up to sit. "What?"

Damian sat up too. "Vampire blood can heal a human, just like human blood can heal a vampire."

"Wow. That's amazing." She shook her head in wonder. Then she realized something. "So in a way it's a drug. What if what Mrs. Zhang saw during the nights before the Halloween party was a drug deal after all? Just not for coke or heroin, but for vampire blood?"

"That's what I've been suspecting too. I might have a way of confirming who's been dealing out of the back of the Mezzanine." He looked at the clock on the bedside table. "But we have to wait for daytime. Let's sleep a few hours, and then we'll look into it."

Damian pressed her back into the sheets, and she pulled him to her.

"Do we have to sleep?" she murmured and ran her hand down his torso to his groin, where she found his cock hard and heavy.

"Well, since you asked so nicely, maybe you get to stay up a little longer."

Before she could take another breath, he'd rolled her to the side and spooned her. He gripped her thigh and lifted it, and his erection slid between her legs. With one thrust, he was inside her, seated in her still-wet channel.

"Oh," she said on a breathless moan, "that feels good."

Damian kissed her neck and began to move inside her in slow and measured strokes. "Is that what you had in mind?"

"Yes, that's exactly what I was talking about."

"Then let me take care of you, or we'll never get a wink of sleep," Damian said with a chuckle in his voice, and made good on his promise.

25

Damian had slept well with Naomi in his arms. When he woke mid-morning, she was still sleeping peacefully, and he realized how relieved he was that she trusted him enough to allow herself to be vulnerable in his arms. It filled his heart with warmth, and his cock with blood. But there was time for that later.

He had work to do. Nearly thirty hours ago, the case of blood had been stolen, and Mick Solvang hadn't been seen for over forty-eight hours. And as much as he wanted to stay in bed with Naomi, he had responsibilities. The theft of blood and the disappearance of his bartender fell within his domain.

"Time to get up, *chérie*," he whispered to her, and she finally stirred.

They showered quickly, and got dressed. Naomi snatched a piece of fruit and a yogurt from the refrigerator, and ate it.

"Are you not having breakfast?" she asked.

He grinned. "I'm still full from last night." Naomi's blood was still permeating his body, and he didn't feel the need to feed. Besides, the blood from the bottles suddenly had no appeal to him anymore, and soon, he would drink Naomi's blood exclusively—just as soon as she agreed to blood-bond with him.

Naomi's cheeks colored, and she dropped her lids.

"There's nothing to be ashamed of," he said and tipped her chin up with his finger. He pressed a quick kiss to her lips. "It's perfectly natural. Now, let's go, before I drag you back to bed."

They drove to the Mezzanine. Damian parked the Porsche in the parking lot behind the club. As they got out of the car, Damian asked, "Which building does Mrs. Zhang live in?"

"That one," Naomi said and pointed to the tall apartment building across the alley.

Naomi led him to the front entrance of the building and rang Mrs. Zhang's flat.

"Mrs. Zhang, this is Naomi Sutton. I was wondering whether I could speak to you again about your complaint?"

"Yes, come up."

The buzzer sounded, and together, they entered the building, and rode up to the third floor.

"Don't tell her that I'm the manager of the Mezzanine, or she might be hostile."

"How should I introduce you then?"

"Tell her I'm an investigator you work with," he suggested.

When the elevator doors opened, the door to Mrs. Zhang's flat was already open, and she stood there, arms crossed over her chest. When her eyes landed on him, she drew up her eyebrows.

"Mrs. Zhang, thanks for seeing me. I brought my investigator with me," Naomi said immediately, "since I think this case warrants a much closer look than I'd thought at first."

Damian suppressed a smile. Naomi sure knew how to butter up the old woman and make her feel important.

"Mrs. Zhang," he said, "may we come in? I'd like to show you photos of a few suspects."

Her eyes lit up, and she stepped aside. "Of course, please, come in."

Inside the flat, Damian glanced around and noticed the impeccable cleanliness.

"May I have a look from where you were able to see that something strange was going on at the club?"

"I saw everything from my bedroom."

She walked ahead, and he and Naomi followed. When she pointed to the window, Damian stepped closer and looked outside. Mrs. Zhang definitely had a direct line of sight to the back exit of the club, as well as the parking lot and the dumpsters. But could she really see that clearly?

Damian turned around, and pulled out his cell phone, navigating to the photo app, where he'd loaded photos of all his male staff at the club.

"Would you please have a look at these men, Mrs. Zhang, and tell me if you recognize any of them as the man you saw with blood on him, the one who was meeting with another person several times a week?"

He held the phone in front of her, and scrolled through the lineup.

"This one. That's the man," she said in a firm voice.

Damian looked at the photo. It was Mick, the missing bartender. He nodded. "Thank you very much, Mrs. Zhang. You've helped me a lot."

"What will you do now?" she asked.

"I'm going to look into this person, and if there's anything nefarious to find, I'll find it. We'll be in touch. Thank you for your time, Mrs. Zhang," he said, and turned to leave.

"Thank you, Mrs. Zhang," Naomi added, before they both left the flat.

Once outside the building, Naomi turned to him. "Who was the man she recognized?"

"Mick Solvang."

"The missing bartender? So there is something to her story. Do you think Mick was trading vampire blood?"

"It looks like it. I never thought that Mick would sink so low, and put us all at risk." Damian shook his head. "But then I didn't think he was cheating on Angelica either."

"What? How do you know that?"

"Patrick called me last night, remember? Just when we got to my place? He said that one of the other bartenders, Andrew, thought that Mick was seeing somebody else other than Angelica."

"Then maybe that woman knows where he is. Perhaps he's staying with her," Naomi suggested.

"It's possible, but we don't know who she is, or if she even exists. It was just a suspicion Andrew has, though he's often right. Apparently, he overheard Mick speaking on the phone to her."

"Then maybe your IT guy can find something on Mick's cell phone."

"I already called Eddie last night, right after I spoke to Patrick. He's looking for any recent calls Mick made to a woman other than Angelica. If he used his cell phone, we'll find out who she is." He pulled his cell phone from his pocket once more. "Let me call him to see if he was able to get anything done after the housewarming party, or if he and Thomas went straight home to sleep."

Naomi put her hand on his forearm. "Eddie sleeps during the day, right? Isn't he gonna be pissed off if you wake him?"

"Don't worry, when there's a crisis at Scanguards that affects us all, nobody sleeps much until it's all taken care of."

Damian dialed Eddie's cell phone, and his uncle picked up the call instantly. Judging by his voice, he was fully awake.

"Hey, Damian, I was about to call you."

"Hey, Eddie, did you get anything interesting from Mick's cell phone?"

"Actually, yeah. You were right that Mick was seeing somebody besides Angelica. He's been talking to another girl for the last three months or so, and they seem pretty lovey-dovey in their text messages. The phone number is registered to a Tracy Horng. I was just about to log into the DMV to see where she lives. Give me a sec."

While he heard Eddie tapping away on his keyboard, Damian addressed Naomi, "Mick's been texting with another woman. Eddie is getting me the address."

"Good, that's a lead," Naomi said.

"Who are you with?" Eddie asked through the phone.

"Naomi."

"So I take it she took it well? Or did you chicken out and not tell her?"

"I told her, and she's good with it." Better than good. He locked eyes with her, and a smile formed on his lips. "Right, *chérie?*"

"Good for you," Eddie said. "Got Tracy Horng's info. She has a license. I'll text it to you so you have a photo too. She's Asian, and… wow, only twenty-one. Mick's definitely been robbing the cradle."

"Thanks for that, Eddie. We'll go check her out. Maybe she knows something, or maybe Mick's holed up at her place."

"Oh, before I forget it: the last call Mick got was from Tracy. She called him the night before Halloween."

"Thanks, Eddie."

"Talk later."

Damian disconnected the call. A moment later, his cell phone pinged, and he looked at the display. Eddie had sent him a photo of Tracy's driver's license. "This is her."

Naomi looked at the picture on the license. "She's young, and pretty too."

"Let's pay her a visit."

26

Tracy Horng's flat was located in a run-down apartment building in the Tenderloin. There were plenty of drug addicts and homeless men and women, many clearly mentally ill, that roamed the streets, and every corner smelled of urine and feces. Naomi tried to hold her breath.

The entrance door to the building was unlocked. Damian pushed it open, and they entered. The elevator was out of order, so they took the stairs to the fifth floor. On Tracy's floor were six flats. They knocked at Tracy's door, and waited. Nothing happened.

"Maybe she's at work?" Naomi said, looking at Damian.

"I can't hear any sounds coming from inside. Let's check it out."

He pulled out something from his jacket pocket and stepped closer to the door.

"Are you gonna break in?" she asked under her breath and looked over her shoulder, worried that somebody would see them.

Damian cast her a sideways glance. "It's not like I'm gonna steal anything. I just want to see if there's evidence that Mick was here."

She watched in fascination as he made quick work of the lock like a professional burglar and turned the door knob a moment later to let them inside. Quickly, Damian shut the door behind them.

"Did you learn that at Scanguards?"

He winked at her. "Beats kicking in the door."

Naomi rolled her eyes, but secretly she wished she had skills like that too. Though she'd probably be too scared to do something like that as part of her job. Had she been alone, and not in Damian's company, she would have never even attempted to break into the flat. But she felt safe with Damian. She knew instinctively that he would protect her. And as a vampire, he was stronger than any human.

The flat was small, the rooms tiny. There was a miniscule kitchen consisting of a two-burner stove, a small oven, a sink, and a small refrigerator. The bathroom was equally tiny, with a pedestal sink, a toilet and an old bathtub that had seen better days.

The living room doubled as a dining area, and the furniture was old and worn and a mish-mash of styles. The bedroom was dark, the curtains in front of the window heavy, covering it fully. Damian switched on the light upon entering.

Naomi let her eyes roam. The bed was unmade, and there was only one nightstand. The door to the built-in closet was open. An array of clothes hung on hangers, and on the bottom of the closet there were stacks of haphazardly folded sweaters and pants.

"This place is depressing," Naomi said.

Damian looked over his shoulder. "Yeah, and the landlord here doesn't want to fix anything either. The place is a health hazard."

"You know the landlord?" she asked, surprised.

"No, but my father does. He's been trying to get him to sell the place to him. But the owner is stubborn and wants more than what the building is worth."

"What would your father do with it? Turn it into condos?"

To her surprise, Damian shook his head. "Where would the tenants go if he did that? Already there isn't enough affordable housing available in this city. He would like to bring the place up to code, modernize it so it's actually livable."

"And have the same tenants stay?"

Damian nodded.

"But he'll never get his money back on his investment. With rent control, he won't be able to raise the rents sufficiently to cover his costs."

He shrugged. "Doesn't matter. He's not doing it to make money. He's got enough. But he loves this city, and he wants to clean it up to make it more livable for the next generations."

"That's quite noble. I wasn't expecting that from a—"

"A vampire?"

"Not just a vampire, but any investor."

"As I said last night, my father's a big softy." Damian crouched down to the bed and sniffed. "Mick was definitely here. But it's been a few days. His scent is very faint."

"You can smell him?"

"A vampire's sense of smell is as good as that of a bloodhound. And Mick and Tracy clearly had sex here. That makes the scent even more intense. That's why I can still smell him, even after a few days."

"That's pretty handy." That reminded her of something. "The vial. You said you smelled that it was vampire blood. Was it Mick's?"

"Not sure. The little that was left in the vial was at least a week old, and had already deteriorated too much for me to make a positive identification. But I'm assuming it was Mick's." He gestured to the closet. "Why don't you check in the closet to see if you can find any bottles of blood? I'll check the kitchen."

"You think that Mick came back during the Halloween party to steal the case of bottled blood?"

"It's possible," he said, "though he wouldn't need the blood, if he feeds from Tracy."

"You think she knows he's a vampire?"

Damian pointed to the dark drapes. "Looks like she made sure that no sunlight shines into the bedroom."

He had a point. While Damian went into the kitchen, where she heard him opening and closing cupboards, Naomi searched the closet. She found no bottled blood.

"Anything?" she asked when she saw Damian move from the kitchen to the living room.

"Nothing. And there aren't really any places to hide anything in this flat." He motioned to the kitchen. "There's a partially eaten sandwich on the counter. And by the looks of it, it's a couple of days old. It doesn't look like anybody's been here in a few days."

Naomi met Damian's gaze. "Do you think Mick and Tracy left together? Maybe he wanted to break it off with Angelica, and thought it was easier if he just left town with his new girlfriend? Maybe he didn't get kidnapped after all."

Damian shook his head. "Mick has a good job at the Mezzanine. And Scanguards' protection. He wouldn't simply run away from this life for something unknown. It's not easy for a vampire on his own. We're reliant on each other."

Before Naomi could answer, her cell phone rang. She pulled it from her pocket and looked at Caller ID.

"Damn, that's my editor. He probably wants to know whether I've found anything yet. What should I say?"

"Stall him. Just say you're following a promising lead."

Naomi answered the call. "Hey, Wei."

"Naomi, how are you coming along with the story? What have you found so far?"

"I'm following up on a really promising lead at the moment."

"What is it?"

"Uhm, I can't really say yet. I don't want to jinx it. But I should know more soon."

"When?"

"Uh, tomorrow. I should have a better idea tomorrow. Gotta go. Talk soon."

She quickly disconnected the call, and looked at Damian. "What am I gonna tell him tomorrow?"

"We'll cross that bridge when we get to it."

"Easy for you to say."

"Don't fret. I always have good ideas." He pulled her closer, and instantly her body was on fire again. He pressed a soft kiss to her lips, then released her again. "The bottles of blood aren't here. Let's go to Mick's flat. I was planning to go there last night, but that was when I realized that I was being tailed."

She caught his pointed look. "Sorry. I guess I'm not very good at tailing people."

He chuckled. "Well, let's go there now. Angelica was already at his place. That's where she found his phone, but maybe she overlooked something. Besides, she doesn't know that a crate of bottled blood went missing. So even if she saw it at Mick's place, she wouldn't have thought it odd."

"Where does he live?"

"In the Inner Sunset."

As they left the flat, Naomi pulled the door shut behind her, but she didn't hear the lock click. She turned around. "It's not locking."

Damian looked over his shoulder. "Can't do anything about that. It's another thing that sucks in this building. Most of the doors in here only lock if you have the key. Just pull it shut. Most burglars around here won't bother walking all the way up to the fifth floor."

Naomi shrugged. While she didn't like the idea that Tracy's flat didn't lock, there wasn't really anything worth stealing inside. And perhaps Damian was right. A thief would first try to break into flats on the lower floors, rather than getting trapped in a narrow stairwell when trying to escape.

To Naomi's surprise, Mick's flat was much nicer and bigger than she'd expected. It was a two-bedroom flat on the first floor of a triplex, and was nicely furnished.

"So we're looking for bottles of blood?" Naomi asked.

"Yes, and if you see anything that looks like grey dust or ash, let me know."

At his words, an odd shudder went through her. "Does ash mean what I think it means?"

"I'm afraid so. Vampires and hybrids can be killed with a stake through the heart, and all that's left will be ash—and any metal items like jewelry or phones."

She stared at him. "There wouldn't be anything left for a vampire's loved ones to mourn. That must be terrible."

Damian smiled at her unexpectedly and stroked his knuckles over her cheek. "You understand us now. You know that we love and we mourn, we have the same emotions as humans."

"Because you showed me that you don't have to be human to have humanity in you." She put her hand over his, clasping it, and turned her face to press a kiss into his palm. His eyes started to shimmer golden, and the sight turned her insides to molten lava. "How do you do that?"

"Do what?"

"Make your eyes look like liquid gold?"

"I don't do anything. It's simply a reaction to what I feel and what I'm thinking." He leaned in. "Do you want me to tell you what I'm thinking right now?"

A pleasant shiver slithered down her spine. "No." She dropped her gaze. "It's pretty obvious from where I'm standing." The bulge in his pants was hard to ignore. She lifted her lids. "How come you're always hard?"

A soft chuckle rolled over Damian's lips. "How come you're always sexy?"

He stepped back. "We'd better get on with this search, before we do something we shouldn't be doing here."

"Good point."

They divided their efforts, and went through the flat. In the bathroom, Naomi found something of interest.

"Damian?" she called out, and he joined her.

"What did you find?"

She opened the box she'd found underneath the sink. "A whole box of empty glass vials. The same as the one I found underneath the dumpster. It was hidden in a larger box, and had cleaning materials on top of it. I almost didn't see it."

"Hmm." Damian contemplated the find for a moment. "He didn't want Angelica to find them, hence the cleaning materials. She doesn't like cleaning, and she would certainly not do it at her boyfriend's place. Mick knew that."

Twenty minutes later, Damian found something else.

Naomi walked into the bedroom he'd been searching. "What did you find?"

Damian turned around. He held bundles of cash in both hands. "Mostly twenties and fifties. Used bills. I think this pretty much confirms that he sold his blood. Maybe for fifty or a hundred bucks a vial. It's definitely worth that. And finding the money here with him gone means he didn't leave voluntarily."

Naomi nodded. "You're right. Nobody would leave money behind, not if he's going on the run."

"Exactly. Somebody took him." Damian tipped his chin up. "When you spoke to Mrs. Zhang yesterday, are you sure she didn't recognize the person Mick was meeting with or where the thief on Halloween disappeared to?"

"She said she couldn't see the face of the person Mick met with, but she saw where the thief disappeared to, but she couldn't tell what type of car it was. She said she knows nothing about cars."

"But she saw it?" Damian asked, suddenly sounding excited.

"Yes, but that doesn't help us if she can't remember or describe it. And she didn't write the license plate down either."

"Don't worry. I think I have an idea how we can make her remember."

Naomi swallowed hard. "You're not gonna torture her, are you?"

"Torture? Of course not, but I know how we can figure out what she saw. And if I'm right, we might be able to catch two birds with one stone: find whom Mick sold vampire blood to, and find the thief who stole the bottled blood. Come."

27

The sun had already set when a black BMW M760i pulled into the alley behind Mrs. Zhang's apartment building, and stopped where Damian and Naomi were waiting. A man got out of the car, dressed in black pants, and a white shirt, his long leather coat open in the front. His hair was tied into a low ponytail, and his brown eyes were vigilant. He was an imposing figure not just because of his size, but because the scar that reached from his eye to his chin made him look like a hitman for the Mafia.

Naomi sucked in a nervous breath as the vampire walked toward them, and Damian squeezed her hand in reassurance. "A teddy bear, just like my dad," he murmured. Then, louder, he addressed the vampire, "Thanks for coming, Gabriel."

"Of course. This is serious. We've gotta get a handle on it quickly." He stopped in front of them and looked at her. "I'm Gabriel Giles. You must be Naomi. Nice to meet you." He stretched his hand out, and she had no choice but to shake it if she didn't want to come across as impolite.

"Nice to meet you too," she managed to reply, though her throat was still dry. "Damian said you could help us find out what else Mrs. Zhang remembers?"

Gabriel cast a look at Damian. "You haven't told her what I do?"

At the question, a cold shiver ran down Naomi's back. So it was torture after all.

"It's your gift," Damian said cryptically. "I didn't know how much you wanted her to know."

Gabriel nodded. "I had a word with Amaury earlier. He filled me in. So, it's all right." He turned his face to her. "I have a psychic gift. I can delve into people's memories, see what they've seen. So even though Mrs. Zhang doesn't *remember* the make and model or the license plate of the thief's car, I'll be able to see it, as long as she did."

She'd never heard of such a skill. It stunned her, but at the same time, concern rose up inside her. "Does it hurt?"

"No. She won't even know what I'm doing."

"What are we gonna say why we're there? I mean, she'll get suspicious…" She hated having to point this out, but it was true. And she couldn't even blame the woman. If Damian didn't vouch for Gabriel, Naomi wouldn't let him into her home either. "And… no offense… uhm, I'm not sure she'll want to invite you into her flat."

"None taken. That's why she'll never remember that we were there. I'll wipe her memory when it's over."

Naomi's chin dropped. "You can do that?"

Gabriel nodded. "Every vampire can."

Her gaze shot to Damian. "Hybrids too?"

"Sure, why?" Damian replied.

Something struck her immediately. Damian could have easily wiped her memory so she wouldn't even remember that she'd found the broken bottle of blood and the vial, yet he'd chosen not to. He'd chosen to allow her to keep her memories.

"Nothing," she said, and they walked around to the entrance of the building. At the door, Naomi pressed the doorbell and waited.

"Yes, who is this?"

"Mrs. Zhang, it's Naomi Sutton again from the Chronicle. I have news, and I thought you might want to hear it right away."

"Yes, yes, come up, please."

The buzzer sounded, and Damian opened the door. She heard Damian and Gabriel exchange a few words she couldn't hear. When they stood in front of the apartment door, which Mrs. Zhang had already opened, she noticed that Gabriel was staying back on the staircase where he couldn't be seen by Mrs. Zhang.

"Mrs. Zhang," Naomi started, but realized that the woman wasn't looking at her. She stared at a fixed point in the distance. Was she having a stroke?

"She's all right," Damian said. "Gabriel, you can come out now. She's under mind control."

"Mind control?" Naomi echoed. What else was there that vampires could do?

"I'll explain later," Damian promised as he guided Mrs. Zhang back into the flat.

Naomi followed, and Gabriel entered behind her and closed the door.

"Take a seat, Mrs. Zhang," Gabriel ordered gently, and the woman sat down on an armchair. Gabriel stepped behind her, and held his hands above her head.

Naomi watched in fascination as he closed his eyes.

"I'm going back to Halloween night," Gabriel said in an even voice.

For a few seconds there was silence. Then he added, "She's getting up and looking outside the window toward the club. There's a person dressed in a Harlequin costume with a Venetian facemask, gold and red, maybe five foot seven or eight, weight is hard to make out under the costume, but rather on the skinny side. He, or she, is carrying something. Looks like a small crate. He looks over his shoulder, but there's nobody. He crosses the parking lot and walks toward the end of the alley. Write this down, Damian: he gets into a white Toyota Corolla. The license plate is dirty. I can only make out a few of the letters. K, then a 5 or an S, then dirt, and the last digit could be a C or an O, but I can't be sure because of the dirt on the plate. It's a California license plate."

"That's something," Damian said.

"The car has a bumper sticker to the left of the license plate."

"What's it say?"

"Stop global warming."

"Did you see where the thief stumbled and tossed the broken bottle toward the dumpster?" Naomi asked, surprised that Gabriel had left out that detail, even though he'd described the thief in more detail than Mrs. Zhang had.

"He didn't stumble. And he didn't toss anything away," Gabriel said, his eyes still closed.

Surprised, she exchanged a look with Damian. "She told me he stumbled and something broke, and that's why he tossed something toward the dumpster."

"She lied," Gabriel said. "That didn't happen. Let me go back further now to see when she saw Mick meeting with somebody."

"She said he met with somebody at least four or five times a week," she added for Gabriel's benefit, hoping it would help him find the right place in the woman's memories.

"She recognized Mick from the photos I showed her," Damian said.

"I know what he looks like. I see him. Hmm."

Naomi noticed frown lines appear on Gabriel's forehead. "What?"

"Mick is clearly meeting with somebody back there. But it's definitely not a drug deal. He's making out with a young woman."

"Angelica, his girlfriend?" Damian asked.

"Petite, long black hair, Asian?" Gabriel asked.

"No," she and Damian said in unison.

"Yeah, then it's not Angelica."

"Can you go further back?" Damian asked. "Maybe he sold the vial with his blood at another time?"

For a while, Gabriel was silent, and Naomi held her breath.

"No, sorry, it doesn't look like he ever met with anyone and exchanged anything."

Gabriel opened his eyes again and looked at Damian. "She's been lying."

"But why?" Naomi asked.

"Let's discuss it outside," Gabriel said. "Wipe her memory. I'll be outside."

~ ~ ~

Gabriel left the flat, leaving him and Naomi to deal with Mrs. Zhang. Damian looked at the old woman and sent his thoughts into her mind.

You were alone all evening. Nobody visited you. You spoke to nobody. You never saw me, or Gabriel, or Naomi. Now sleep.

He turned his head to Naomi and noticed her watch him with a confused look on her face.

"Okay, it's done, let's go." He took her hand, and they quickly left the flat and shut the door behind them.

"That's how easy it is to wipe somebody's memory? Just by staring at them?"

It was a little more than that, but to Naomi it would have looked like he wasn't doing anything. "Kinda. I basically sent my thoughts into her mind. Sometimes it's necessary. I prefer not to do it if I don't have to."

Outside, Gabriel was waiting for them.

"You're sure you saw Mick with an Asian girl?" Damian asked and pulled out his cell phone. He scrolled through his messages and clicked on the last message he'd received from Eddie. "Did she look anything like the girl on this driver's license?"

Gabriel looked at it, then nodded. "That's her. No doubt."

"Mick never met anybody to sell his blood to," Damian said. "Mrs. Zhang lied about everything. If the thief didn't stumble and toss a bottle toward the dumpster like she told Naomi, then how did it get there?" He had a suspicion, but he wanted to make sure that his mind wasn't the only one going into that direction.

"It must have been planted," Naomi said with wide eyes.

"That's the most likely explanation," Gabriel agreed. "Well, at least we have a partial license plate and the make and model of the car the thief used to get away. Send that to Thomas and Eddie, and they'll find him. As for why Mrs. Zhang lied…" Gabriel shrugged. "Your guess is as good as mine. You might want to look into her a bit more."

"Thanks, Gabriel," Damian said. "Really appreciate your help."

Gabriel nodded. "Good luck, guys, and once you have some hits on the license plate, and I assume there'll be multiple hits given that it's just a partial, find out from Quinn what staff's available and track down the thief. Work in teams. We don't know whether we're dealing with humans or other preternatural creatures."

Gabriel jumped into his car and drove off.

"What now?" Naomi asked, while Damian already composed a text message to Eddie.

"I'm sending the partial license plate over to Eddie and Thomas to start working on it," he explained. "I've gotta go to Scanguards, check on a few things, and then I need to be ready to follow up on any hits they get from the license plate search. I can drop you off at your place. It's not far from the office." And once he was done for the night, he could pick her up to take her back to his place, or just stay at hers.

"Can't I come with you? Maybe I can help?"

"Absolutely not. It's too dangerous." He didn't want her anywhere near the thief, particularly since he didn't know yet whether the thief was human or vampire. This was his job, not hers. She'd helped already more than he'd expected. "I'll call you later when I know what we have, I promise."

Disappointed, she sighed. "Fine. But I'm not going home. I'll swing by my office."

"Aren't you worried that you might run into your editor?"

She shook her head. "He hates working late. He won't be there. And I want to see if I can find out more about Tracy Horng. Maybe I can find some of her friends. They might know where she disappeared to."

"How?"

"Have you already forgotten that I'm a reporter? I have ways of getting information."

He had to smile. "You sure do. But be careful. And if you find anything, call me right away."

"I will."

She kissed him on the lips, before she turned in the other direction, and Damian hopped into his Porsche. Eddie would need a little while before he got any hits from the DMV, which meant he could take care of something else before he had to be at Scanguards.

28

It didn't take Naomi long to find out where Tracy Horng worked. And she was in luck: the nail and waxing studio was open until nine p.m. just like the surrounding stores on Union Square. She entered the salon and looked around. Several young women in pink lab coats with white leggings helped customers at their various stations. One girl was waxing a woman's eyebrows, while another employee was applying makeup for an older woman with blotchy skin.

Tracy wasn't among the employees. Naomi walked to the counter in the back of the store where a middle-aged woman was ringing up a customer's purchases. She waited patiently, until the woman left, before smiling at the cashier.

"Hi, I'm looking for—"

"An eyebrow wax, right?" She gestured to Naomi's face. "And maybe a little coloring too, make them a little darker? You have such a light complexion."

"Uhm, actually, I was looking for Tracy."

"Tracy?" the woman asked, and her voice took on a displeased tone. "I'm afraid she's not working today."

"It's just, I'm worried about her," Naomi lied. "I haven't seen her in a few days, and she hasn't answered her phone. So I thought I'd check."

"Oh," the woman replied. "Well, she's not here. She didn't show up for her shift. And she didn't call either, so if you do speak to her, let her know if she doesn't show up tomorrow, she won't have a job to come back to." She tipped her chin up and looked past Naomi. "Now if you will excuse me, I have paying customers to take care of."

Naomi turned away and walked toward the exit, when she caught the gaze of a young woman who was just finishing with a customer and handing her a tube of foundation. Naomi stopped not far away from her, and pretended to be interested in the various lotions displayed on a table. A few seconds later, the woman joined her.

"I'm Cynthia," she said. "I overheard you asking for Tracy."

"Hi, Cynthia, I'm Naomi. Do you know where she is?"

Cynthia shook her head. "No, but I'm worried about her too. It's not like her not to call. Are you a friend of hers?"

Naomi cleared her throat, stalling for a second. "I know her because of her boyfriend. And I haven't seen either of them in the last few days. I'm really getting worried about them."

"Mick? You know Mick?"

"Yes. Do you know him too?"

She shook her head. "No, I've never met him, but she talks about him all the time."

"Yeah, he's a great guy," Naomi said, hoping to draw more information out of Tracy's colleague.

Cynthia sighed. "It's a shame her family doesn't think so."

"What do you mean?"

"You don't know about her grandmother? She calls her the dragon lady."

"Oh, her," Naomi said quickly as if she knew the woman. "Have you actually met her? 'Cause I haven't."

"I haven't either, but she makes Tracy's life hell. That's why she moved out. She couldn't stand being under that woman's thumb any longer. And ever since she started dating Mick, it's been even worse. Her grandmother thinks he's a bad influence. Just because he's a bartender."

"Yeah, people judge others really quickly," Naomi commented. "It's not fair."

"Exactly. And her uncle isn't any better."

"She never talks much about him, or about her parents," Naomi fished.

"He's her mother's brother. So tragic that her parents died so young. I wouldn't wanna be raised by a neat-freak grandmother." Cynthia leaned in, and quickly looked over her shoulder, then took a lotion as if to try to sell it to her.

Naomi played along.

"If I had to guess, she and Mick probably left town. She was always talking about leaving with him as soon as they had enough money saved up. Because as long as she's in San Francisco, her grandmother and her uncle will always try to control her."

"You're right, Cynthia. I just wish she or Mick would call me back so I know they're okay. Did Tracy say anything to you about where they would go?"

Cynthia shook her head. "No, she never mentioned a place."

Naomi gave her a grateful smile. "Thanks so much for talking to me. I'll leave another message for her on her cell, and hope she'll call me soon."

"Tell her I said hi."

"I'll do that. Thanks, Cynthia."

Outside the salon, Naomi took a deep breath, and contemplated what to do next. If Tracy was planning to get away from her family, then maybe there was some evidence in her flat about where she would go. When she and Damian had searched Tracy's flat earlier, they'd looked for Mick and the stolen bottles of blood, but had found nothing. They hadn't looked at paperwork or anything else that might reveal what Tracy and Mick had been planning.

Her cell phone rang, and Naomi pulled it from her handbag and looked at the display.

"Hey, Heather."

"Weren't you supposed to drop off another sample of that blood you found so I can run a second test?"

Damn it. She'd forgotten that she'd told Heather she would give her another sample to analyze. But she couldn't do that now. Not after everything that Damian had told her. She had to keep his secret.

"Ah, yeah, I know I was supposed to, but it turns out there was nothing left. I just couldn't get another sample. Sorry. And it looks like the story is fizzling out anyway," she lied. "False alarm. Sorry. Happens."

"Are you sure?"

"I am. It's all been cleared up, and unfortunately there's no story. I shouldn't even have asked you to run the test. It was such a long shot to begin with."

"If you say so. So, when are you gonna tell me about that guy of yours?"

"Soon," she promised. Just as soon as she'd discussed with Damian what she could tell her friend. "Listen, gotta go. Talk soon."

"Later," Heather said, and Naomi disconnected the call.

She sighed, hating that she had to lie to her friend, but it couldn't be helped. Getting back to her earlier thoughts, Naomi hailed a cab to drive her back to Tracy's flat in the Tenderloin.

"You sure that's the right address, Miss?" the cab driver asked with a glance at the drug addicts and homeless people loitering near the entrance.

"Yes, that's it, thank you." She paid him and got out of the cab.

Naomi shivered uncomfortably as she walked to the entrance of the apartment building, feeling the eyes of several people on her. For a second, she wondered whether she should have called Damian to accompany her to Tracy's flat, but she knew he was busy with following up on leads regarding the partial license plate.

Inside the building, she quickly walked up to the fifth floor, feeling winded when she reached it. She was totally out of shape. Grateful now that the door to Tracy's flat hadn't locked, she quickly let herself into the apartment and closed the door behind her. She flipped the deadbolt, and let out a sigh of relief.

Naomi switched on the light, and started searching the bedroom. The closet she'd searched earlier revealed nothing new. Under the bed were several boxes with shoes, and in the nightstand were tissues, earplugs, a book, and allergy pills.

She skipped the bathroom, because she'd searched it earlier and found no papers, money, or any other items of interest. The kitchen cabinets were rather bare, so was the fridge. The half-eaten sandwich was still on the counter and attracting flies. Naomi took it and tossed it in the trash. She even checked the freezer, because she figured it would make for a good spot to hide something, but except for an old bag of frozen peas, it was empty.

In the living room with the dining area, a small TV stood on a rickety TV stand. Below it were a few newspapers, two Manila folders, and a shoebox. The newspapers were old. One folder contained bills, the other coupons from supermarkets. Naomi reached for the shoebox and lifted the lid.

Inside it were photos. Curious, she sat down on the sofa, the shoebox on her lap, and went through it. There was no particular order to the photos. Many of them were older, from when Tracy was a young girl. Several showed her with a young Asian couple. On the back of it, she'd written who the people were.

With Mom and Dad, Universal Studios, 2011.

Naomi sighed, and looked at the photo again. The girl in the photo beamed at the camera. How long after this photo had been taken had her parents died?

The next photo was turned over, and she read the description first: *High School Graduation with Grandma and Uncle Wei, 2019.*

She turned the photo around and almost choked on her own saliva. She knew the people in the photo. The woman, Tracy's grandmother, was Mrs. Zhang. The same woman who'd claimed to have seen Mick with blood on him, when in reality she'd seen her own granddaughter making out with Mick. But that wasn't the only reason Naomi was in shock. The person on the other side of Tracy was Wei Guo, her editor. He was Tracy's uncle.

"Fuck!"

This couldn't be a coincidence. Wei hadn't mentioned that Mrs. Zhang was his mother. In fact, he's said *a Mrs. Zhang* as if he had no idea who she was. They didn't have the same last name, which she knew wasn't unusual since Chinese women often kept their maiden name. Why would Wei send her to his own mother to investigate allegations of a satanic cult or blood sacrifices in the club when his mother was the witness? And Naomi used the word witness very loosely now, because after Gabriel had delved into the woman's memories, it was clear that she hadn't witnessed anything of the sort.

Wei Guo had set her up. He was fabricating the entire story. But to what end? She could come up with a few theories. But before she got lost in a rabbit hole, she had to get out of here and talk to Damian.

Naomi put the photo with Wei Guo and Mrs. Zhang into her handbag and pulled out her cell. She called Damian's number, but it went straight to voicemail.

"Damian, I found something in Tracy's flat. I think somebody is trying to frame the club. Call me as soon as you get this message."

She disconnected the call and hurried out of the flat. When she left the building, it felt as if even more drug addicts and homeless people were loitering, and her earlier unease grew even more. She looked up and down the street, but there were no available cabs.

Damn it, she didn't want to wait around here for an Uber that might take twenty minutes to come. When a young junkie made a beeline for her, she quickly turned on her heel and headed in the other direction. At the next side street, she turned right to get away. She looked around and read the street name, realizing that she was only three or four blocks away from Damian's flat. She knew he wouldn't be there, but perhaps she could see if his parents answered the door so she could get off the street until she could reach Damian by phone.

Looking over her shoulder to make sure the junkie hadn't followed her, Naomi hurried toward Damian's building. When she reached it, she looked at the intercom, but hesitated. What would his parents think if she just showed up unannounced? Perhaps it was better if she went home and waited for Damian to call her back. But the thought that Wei Guo, her own editor, was clearly doing something that was wrong, or illegal, or both, made her nervous. Wei Guo knew where she lived. He'd sounded impatient when he'd asked her about her progress with the story. What if he suspected that she had no intention of writing the story and was simply stalling?

"Excuse me."

Naomi spun around and found herself face-to-face with a woman she recognized immediately: Damian's mother. She carried a take-out bag in one hand, a set of keys in the other.

"You must be Naomi," she said. "I'm Damian's mother."

"Hi, Mrs. LeSang, it's so nice to meet you."

"Nina, please."

"Uhm, you're probably wondering what I'm doing here. It's just I was trying to reach Damian, but he's not picking up his phone, and I have some information for him—"

"Maybe he didn't hear it ringing." She looked up at the building. "I saw light in his flat. He's probably got the music on." Nina unlocked the door. "Come on up. I'll let you in."

Naomi entered behind Nina, but wondered why Damian would be at home. Had he already finished what he needed to do for Scanguards? Hadn't Gabriel said that most likely there would be several hits from the partial license plate that would need to be investigated?

"Thank you, Mrs... uhm, Nina. That's very kind of you."

Nina ushered her into the elevator, then inserted her key into a slot, before pressing the top floor and the one beneath, and the doors closed.

"Amaury and I didn't get a chance to meet you yesterday," she said with a smile.

"Yeah, sorry, there were so many people, and I didn't really know anybody, and I wasn't invited..." She was babbling, nervous about being alone with her boyfriend's mother. Boyfriend, how odd that sounded. She wasn't used to saying that. And she definitely wasn't used to making small talk with his mother.

"Don't worry, you'll get used to us all. The whole gang can be quite overwhelming at first."

"I didn't mean to offend—"

"You're not offending anybody."

The elevator suddenly stopped, but the door didn't open. Naomi remembered why: when she'd entered Damian's flat via the elevator the night before, he'd had to unlock the door, because it led directly into his flat.

"I can already hear the music," Nina said, and Naomi heard it too. She unlocked the door. "I hope I'll see you again soon, Naomi."

"Me too. Thank you."

Naomi pushed the door open and entered the flat. The living room was ablaze, and music was coming from one of the rooms. Naomi walked toward Damian's bedroom, but it was quiet there, so she turned toward the doors on the other side of the kitchen. That's where the music seemed to be coming from.

"Damian?"

She knocked, but didn't get a reply. Nina was probably right. The music was too loud for Damian to hear her. She turned the doorknob and pushed the door open.

Her breath got caught in her throat, and her heart stopped beating. The room was another bedroom, and on the king-size bed, Damian's naked body was bathed in sweat. As was that of the skinny bitch he was fucking from behind.

How could he do this to her after all the things he'd said to her? After telling her he was in love with her? A sob tore from her throat.

Damian whirled his head in her direction, his eyes glaring red. "What the fuck!"

The skinny dark-haired girl looked in her direction too. Naomi recognized her now. She was the same young woman who'd flirted with Damian at the Halloween party.

"How could you?" Naomi choked out, barely able to hold the tears in. "After everything we did last night?"

"You told me you were out of town last night," the naked girl said in a shrill voice.

"I hate you! I hate you!" Naomi spat.

Damian stared at her, looking utterly confused now. "Hey, who the—"

Naomi spun around and slammed the door shut behind her. She ran to the elevator, but the door wasn't opening. She punched the call button, but she couldn't wait for it. She had to get out of here. Agitated, she ripped the door next to the elevator open and ran into the stairwell. She raced down until she reached the foyer of the building. Tears were streaming down her face now, and her vision blurred.

How could Damian do this to her? And with a girl with a model figure and model looks. Apparently fucking a fat chick had gotten old very quickly. Her heart clenched painfully, and in that moment, she realized with horror that she was in love with Damian. And he'd betrayed her.

She charged out of the building without looking back. She wished she'd never met him, because then her heart would still be intact. Not shattered into a thousand pieces like it was now.

29

Damian got into his Porsche, and Cooper got in on the passenger side.

"That was a bust," he said and started the engine.

"Wish Gabriel had been able to read more of that license plate so we wouldn't have to waste our time," Cooper commented.

"Can't be helped. At least we've got something to chase down. Without him and without Naomi leading us to Mrs. Zhang, we wouldn't have any leads at all. Where to next?"

Cooper looked at his cell phone. "Lower Pacific Heights."

"Okay," Damian said when his cell phone suddenly rang over the car's speakers. He looked at the dashboard, where he saw who was calling, and pressed the answer button on his steering wheel. "Hey, Bro. You still in L.A.?"

"Nope, I got back a few hours ago," Benjamin replied.

"Hey, Benjamin," Cooper said.

"Hi, Coop."

"We could use your help," Damian said. "We're chasing down some leads on the thief who stole the crate of bottled blood."

"Yeah, I heard about that, but that's not why I'm calling." He cleared his throat. "You wouldn't by any chance be fucking a blond chick with boobs like Dolly Parton's?"

"That's my girlfriend you're talking about. So be careful what you say," Damian replied.

"Well, then you've got a little problem. I've been trying to call you for the last hour."

"Had to go stealth. Phone was on silent. What's the problem?"

"She showed up here."

"Naomi? That's not a problem. She knows what we are. Just tell her to make herself comfortable. But I'll still be a few hours."

"Yeah, can't do that. She ran off, crying."

"What?" Damian's heart beat into his throat. "What the fuck did you do to her? I swear if you touched her—"

"I didn't," Benjamin interrupted. "I was too busy fucking a girl I met at the Halloween party. And Naomi barged in and saw us. By the time I realized she was thinking I was you, she was already gone."

"Ah, fuck!" Damian slammed his hands on the steering wheel. "Fuck, fuck, fuck!"

"Yeah, and the girl I was fucking wanted to hightail it outta here when she thought I lied to her about being out of town last night. She thought I was fucking Naomi last night, until I explained to her that I have a twin. She's taking a shower now, but we've gotta fix this, or neither you nor I are getting laid. And I wasn't done."

That was the least of Damian's problems. He made an illegal U-turn. "Tell her to calm down. I'm on my way to Naomi's. When I get there, I'll call you."

"Yeah, hurry."

Damian disconnected the call, then looked at Cooper. "I'll drop you off at HQ. Call Quinn and see who can take over for me for the next few hours."

Cooper nodded and made the call, while Damian wanted to whip himself for not having told Naomi that he had an identical twin brother. The question had never come up. There was only so much he could cover in the less than forty-eight hours that they'd known each other. And since Benjamin had been accompanying a client to Los Angeles, there had been no occasion to introduce him to Naomi.

"Quinn said that Grayson is available right now. I'll check out the next leads with him," Cooper said and put his cell phone away. "You and Benjamin being mistaken for each other can't be new, right?"

"It's not. But right now it's the worst thing that could have happened." Naomi was probably pissed off, and he wouldn't be surprised if she hurled heavy items at him the moment he entered her flat. At least he hoped she'd be home, but considering that it was almost eleven o'clock at night, where else would she go after leaving his flat?

"I'm sure you can fix it."

Damian sighed. "I hope so." He pulled up in front of Scanguards HQ. "I'll check in later, once I've taken care of this, okay?"

"No problem. Good luck, bro," Cooper said and hopped out of the car.

Damian drove off. There was no parking available on Naomi's block, so he circled the block and parked in the alley behind it. He rushed to the entrance door and rang the doorbell. He waited, but nobody replied. He stepped back and looked up at the windows. There was light in Naomi's flat, but she was clearly ignoring him. He pulled out his cell phone to call her and saw that he'd a missed call from her and a voicemail. He listened to the voicemail.

"Damian, I found something in Tracy's flat. I think somebody is trying to frame the club. Call me as soon as you get this message."

Stunned at the message, he realized now why she'd come to his flat in the first place. She needed to talk to him about the case, and he'd missed her call. He tapped her phone number and let it ring, but after the fourth ring, it went to voicemail. He didn't bother leaving a message. Instead, he pulled out his lockpick and made quick work of the entrance door.

Moments later, he stood outside her apartment door and knocked. "Naomi, it's me. We need to talk. Please let me in."

First there was silence, then he heard the creaking of the old wooden floorboards.

"Naomi, please."

"Get lost! I never want to see you again."

"I'm sorry, Naomi, but the person you saw in my flat wasn't me. It was my twin brother."

"Bullshit. Leave, or I'll call the police and have you arrested for trespassing."

Yeah, that wasn't gonna happen. He used his tools to pick the lock and let himself in. Naomi stood in the living room, glaring at him. She wore a nightgown, and held a tub of ice cream in her hand. Her eyes were puffy and red. Rather than looking furious, she looked heartbroken. His heart clenched in response.

"Naomi, I'm so sorry for this misunderstanding. I should have told you about my twin." He pulled his cell out and navigated to the video call app, then tapped on Benjamin's number. "I can prove it to you. I'm calling Benjamin now."

"Probably some trick," she choked out. "Why don't you just leave? You've had your fun fucking the fat girl."

"You're not fat!" he shot back. "And I'm not done with you."

Before he could say more, the video call connected. "Benjamin, I'm with Naomi. Can we please clear this up now?"

"Yeah, about time. Tiffany was about to run out on me."

Damian looked at the display and saw that a pretty dark-haired woman stood next to his brother. "Hey, Tiffany, I'm Damian. And that idiot next to you is my brother."

He looked up and walked closer to Naomi, then turned the phone so that she could see the screen.

"Naomi, meet my twin, Benjamin."

Naomi stared into the screen, and he noticed her eyes widening.

"Hey, Naomi, sorry about earlier. I didn't realize Damian hadn't mentioned me before." With a slightly louder voice he added, "As if my idiot brother forgot that I existed."

Damian stepped next to Naomi so he could see the screen. "Yeah, well, a lot of things happened since the Halloween party. I was a little busy, okay?"

"All cleared up now?" Benjamin asked. "Naomi, can you please tell Tiffany that I wasn't with you last night, and that you were with my brother?"

Finally, Naomi seemed to find her voice again. "I'm so sorry. I really didn't know. I should have never barged into your bedroom. Sorry, Tiffany."

"That's okay, Naomi," the girl replied. "It's all their fault. Take care."

"Night, guys," Benjamin said and disconnected the call.

Damian shoved his cell phone back into his pocket. "Are we good now?"

Naomi nodded and set the ice cream tub down on the coffee table. "When I saw him and thought it was you..." She shook her head. "I guess I got a bit hysterical." She dropped her lids in apparent shame.

Damian put one arm around her waist and pulled her to him, then put his finger under her chin and tipped her face up so she had to look at him. "It's my fault. I should have told you that I have a twin brother, and that we share the flat. It just never came up. Forgive me."

"There's nothing to forgive."

"Good. But now I have a bone to pick with you."

"What?" Her gaze snapped to his.

"After I told you last night that I'm in love with you, did you really think I'd be capable of sleeping with another woman? Didn't you trust me?" He noticed her hesitate.

"I did, but we barely know each other, and no guy really means it when he says after a couple of days of meeting someone that he's in love."

He sighed. "Oh, Naomi, didn't I tell you that vampires fall hard and fast? That it hits us like a freight train, and we have no power to resist that feeling? That's what happened to me. *Chérie*, the thought of touching another woman ever again disgusts me. All I want is you. And I'm happy to demonstrate that for as long as is necessary so that you'll never again have any doubts about my feelings for you."

"Demonstrate?" she echoed, her forehead furrowing.

"Uh huh," he grunted and backed her against the wall.

"What are you—?"

He smothered her protest with his lips, kissing her hard. The thought that such a stupid misunderstanding had caused her pain, made him want to whip himself. This could never happen again. It was bad enough that she still had insecurities about her body, and only with time would he be able to convince her that she was perfect for him. But for her to think that he would fuck another woman, that was a thought he had to eradicate once and for all. He would pound it into her.

Damian held her pressed against the wall, while he undid the button of his pants, and lowered the zipper. Then he pushed his pants and his boxer briefs down to mid-thigh. His cock sprang free, hard and heavy, and ready for Naomi.

Impatient, he shoved her nightgown up to her waist, hooked his arms under her thighs, and lifted her, spreading them wide. With one thrust, he seated himself in her pussy, warmth and wetness welcoming him.

Naomi gasped into his mouth, and he released her lips.

"See? I only want you." He looked into her blue eyes, and saw her looking back at him with lust and passion. "I love you, Naomi, and that's never gonna change."

She lifted her hand to his face. "Damian, when I thought you'd betrayed me, it broke my heart."

"I'm so sorry."

"It hurt so much. That's how I realized that I love you."

"I love you too." Her declaration made him want to howl with satisfaction, and he thrust deep and hard into her, while he held her suspended against the wall.

"Do me a favor: unbutton your gown, and take your tits out." If he had a free hand, he'd do it himself.

"Yes," she replied breathlessly and opened the three buttons on the front of her gown, then shoved the material to the sides, and pulled her breasts out. They were topped with hard nipples ripe for the taking.

"Fuck, you're gorgeous." He lifted his eyes to meet hers. "You make me so hungry."

Her lips parted on a shallow breath. "Please, bite me. Drink from me." She put her hands on either side of her breasts and guided them to his face like an offering. He'd never seen anything more erotic. Her tantalizing scent wrapped around him, and her heartbeat and the excited drumming of her pulse confirmed that she yearned for his fangs.

A violent shudder raced through his body, and he realized that the mere thought of drinking from her was making him climax. He licked over one nipple, before sinking his fangs into her tit. When Naomi's rich blood coated his tongue and ran down his parched throat, he felt her moan. Farther below, she was trying to rub her groin against his, and he shifted his angle just a little bit so his pelvic bone rubbed against her clit with each descent into her delicious cave. His seed and her juices mingled, and permeated the room, and the scent made him even more lust-drugged than he already was.

His fangs deep in her breast, he licked over the nipple in his mouth, and felt Naomi's pussy spasm. Yes, he could do that to her because the bite rendered her even more sensitive to his touch, driving her arousal to its peak again and again. Naomi moaned out loud, her head pressed against the wall, her hands still on her breasts, still offering them to him. While she climaxed, he slowed his thrusts to an easier tempo, allowing her to catch her breath, before he fell into a faster rhythm, and pounded into her just as hard as before.

"Damian, oh God! That's good, oh, oh… Don't stop."

Slowly, he withdrew his fangs and closed the puncture wounds with his saliva. "Believe me now that you're all I want?"

"Yes!" she cried out. "Please, Damian, please… more…"

Deep satisfaction spread within him at seeing Naomi let go of all her inhibitions and only live for the moment, the moment of sheer and utter bliss.

"I love every inch of you," he professed. "Every gorgeous inch."

"And my tits? You love my tits?"

"I wish I could eat them. They feel ripe and heavy, just how I like them." He licked over one nipple, then the other, and felt Naomi shudder again.

"I love your cock inside me," she said on a breathless moan. "So hard, so big."

"You can have my cock anytime you want. You just have to tell me. I'll never refuse you." Because he wanted her just as much as she wanted him. He would never get tired of her, of driving her from one orgasm to the next, of making sure she was always satisfied.

"Fuck! I'm coming again," he cried out. Moments later, semen shot through his cock and exploded from the tip, making Naomi's pussy even wetter.

"Wow." Breathing hard, Naomi put one hand on his nape and dipped her forehead to his. "You got me so hot."

"*I* got you hot? *Chérie*, you're already so hot I'm surprised I'm not being incinerated when I touch you." He stopped moving inside her, and pressed a soft kiss to her lips, then took a few deep breaths. "I'm sorry I didn't even take you to bed. You must think I'm a savage."

"I like a bit of savage in my man."

He chuckled. "That was the wrong thing to admit. Now you're not safe from me anywhere. Who knows where and how I'll take you next?"

"Surprise me," she murmured and kissed him.

30

After cleaning up in the bathroom, Naomi went back into the living room, where Damian pulled her onto his lap on the couch. He nuzzled his face in the crook of her neck and pressed open-mouthed kisses to her skin.

"That was amazing," he said and looked up. "I love it when you show me what you want." He laid one hand on her breast and squeezed it gently. "I've never been with a sexier woman than you. I wish I could spend the rest of the night making love to you." He sighed. "But I've gotta get back soon."

"I understand." And this time, she really did. But she couldn't let him leave before she'd told him what she'd found out about Tracy. "I left you a message earlier."

"Sorry, I only saw it when I got here. You went back to Tracy's flat? Alone?" He tsked. "Not a great area at night."

"I know. But I knew you were busy, and I wanted to check on something."

"But we already searched her place."

"Yeah, for the blood, and for Mick. But I went there because of what I found out from a girl Tracy works with."

"You found out where she works?"

"Yeah, it's a little beauty salon, you know, waxing and stuff. Just off Union Square. Her colleague Cynthia told me that Tracy was scheduled to work but didn't show up and didn't call in sick either. And Cynthia knew about Mick, and that Tracy's family didn't like him. They thought he was a bad influence on her. They wanted to control her life. Because of that, apparently Tracy and Mick wanted to leave together just as soon as they'd saved up enough money."

"So you think they really left of their own free will? But then why would Mick leave the money behind? The cell phone I get: it would mean that he couldn't be tracked, but the money?" Damian shook his head.

"My thoughts exactly. So I went back to Tracy's flat, and did a more thorough search. I hoped to find papers that would tell us where they were planning to go. Instead, I found photos." She jumped up and snatched her purse from the armchair where she'd dropped it after coming home in tears.

As she pulled the photo from her bag and walked back to Damian, she continued, "Cynthia said that Tracy grew up with her grandmother and her uncle. And that they were both very strict."

She handed Damian the photo and sat down next to him.

"Oh my God!" In disbelief, Damian stared at the photo. "Mrs. Zhang is her grandmother?"

Naomi nodded.

Damian ran a hand through his hair. "According to Gabriel, she saw her granddaughter make out with Mick. And she lied about it. She didn't want her to be with Mick. That's her motive for stirring up trouble for the club."

"That's not all." Naomi pointed to the man in the photo. "This guy is her son, Tracy's uncle. And my editor at the San Francisco Chronicle, Wei Guo."

"You're shitting me!"

"No, it's him. He was the one who told me to check out the story. He set it all up. It's all fabricated. He and his mother probably concocted the story so they could pin something on Mick, and when the police didn't listen to Mrs. Zhang's allegations, they figured they'd use the newspaper to bring down Mick and the Mezzanine. And somehow it must have gotten out of hand." Naomi felt her heart beat out of control. "Maybe Wei Guo kidnapped or killed Mick. And all this is a cover-up. And who knows where Tracy is. Perhaps they locked her up somewhere until they can break her."

Naomi shuddered at the thought.

"It's possible. When it comes to family, people are capable of doing just about anything. And you're right, we have to assume that Wei Guo somehow got to Mick and managed to capture or kill him, though I can't imagine how." Damian gestured to the photo. "He doesn't look that strong. And Mick is a vampire. He could easily overpower a human even if he's as big as Dwayne Johnson or Arnold Schwarzenegger."

"What if he tricked Mick and lured him somewhere? Didn't Eddie tell you that the last person calling Mick was Tracy? What if Wei Guo forced Tracy to make that phone call to lead Mick into a trap? And then he planted the broken bottle and the vial and told his mother to tell me so that I'd find it?"

"That's a distinct possibility." Damian took a deep breath. "We already know that Mrs. Zhang didn't plant the evidence, otherwise Gabriel would have seen it in her memories."

"Exactly. So it was probably Wei Guo. Do you think Mick is dead?"

"I'm not sure. But one thing gives me hope that he's still alive: the stolen bottles of blood. And the fact that the thief was about Wei Guo's size. Because why would he steal an entire crate of blood other than to keep Mick alive?"

"Let's hope you're right."

"Get dressed. We're going to Scanguards. I'll need to discuss this with my father and Samson, before we decide how to approach your editor. He can't know that we suspect him."

"You think he might hurt Tracy if he realizes that we're on his tail?"

"Or Mick."

Naomi went into her bedroom, and quickly dressed in jeans, a T-shirt, and a cardigan. Ten minutes later, Damian drove into the parking garage underneath Scanguards' headquarters, and parked his Porsche.

Before he opened the car door, he put his hand on Naomi's forearm. "One rule, once we're inside."

She raised her eyebrows.

"This time of night, the place will be crawling with vampires. So please stay by my side at all times. I'm breaking about a hundred rules by taking you in there."

"Trust me, I have no intention of wandering off." At the thought of entering a building where a bunch of vampires worked, she shivered, even though she knew that Damian would protect her.

They got out of the car, and Damian led her to an elevator, pressed his thumb onto a scanner inside, then pressed the button for the top floor. As they rode up, Naomi slipped her hand into Damian's.

He smiled at her, and lifted their joined hands to his lips, then pressed a kiss to her knuckles.

When the elevator stopped, they exited. Naomi didn't know what she'd expected, but the top floor of the building looked just like the interior of any other office building. Nothing indicated that Scanguards was run by vampires.

At one of the doors, Damian knocked, before opening the door. "Dad?"

But the office was empty.

From the corridor, a man looked at them. "He's with Samson."

Damian turned around. "Thanks, Quinn."

Quinn cast her a curious look, then looked back at Damian. "I really don't know why we still have this stupid rule of no humans on the executive floor when everybody breaks it anyway."

"Beats me," Damian said with a shrug.

With a shake of his head, Quinn disappeared into an office.

"How did he know that I'm human?" Naomi asked with a lowered voice.

"Vampires can see auras. And yours is human."

"Auras? Wow. There's so much I don't know about vampires."

"Don't worry. I'll tell you everything, just as soon as this mess is taken care of. Promise."

They stopped in front of a door, and Naomi read the name indicating whose office this was: Samson Woodford's. She took a deep breath, nervous about meeting the Scanguards boss in person.

Damian opened the door, and they entered the large office. Samson and Amaury stood near Samson's desk and looked at them. Damian closed the door behind them.

"Hey, Samson, Dad."

For a moment, there was silence in the room, and all Naomi could hear was the sound of everybody breathing. Then suddenly, Samson took a step toward her.

"Given that Damian is bringing you here, I'm assuming he's told you what we are."

Naomi swallowed hard. "Yes, and I'm sorry I'm on a floor where no humans are allowed."

Samson chuckled unexpectedly. "Yeah, like anybody's ever followed that rule. It's good to meet you, Naomi. I'm Samson."

"Nice to meet you too."

Amaury walked past Samson and stretched out his hand in greeting. "I'm Amaury, Damian's father."

Naomi shook his hand. "Hi, I ran into your wife earlier tonight."

"Yeah, she mentioned it, and you're just as beautiful as she described you," he replied.

Naomi felt herself blush, and she noticed Damian and Amaury exchange a look.

"Welcome to the family," Amaury said, and released her hand.

Samson motioned to Damian. "I thought you were out following up on the leads from the partial license plate. That's our top priority."

"I know," Damian replied. "And I was, but then Naomi found something that might lead us to Mick's kidnapper."

"Let us hear it," Samson said and made an inviting gesture to the sitting area.

After Damian filled Samson and Amaury in on what Naomi had found out about Mick's girlfriend and her family, he laid out a plan that he'd come up with.

"Since we don't know where Wei Guo and his mother are keeping Mick, we have to make sure neither of them can warn the other. We'll have to go in with two teams simultaneously."

"You're gonna scare the living daylights out of Mrs. Zhang," Naomi said.

"Can't be helped," Damian said. "After all, she's taken part in the deception. Now she has to pay the price."

"He's right," Samson agreed. "Wei Guo can't be allowed to contact anybody. He mustn't see us coming."

"Let's do it," Amaury said, nodding. "Is Wei Guo married?"

Naomi nodded. "Yes, and he has two kids. I think, they're around ten or eleven."

Damian exchanged a look with Amaury and Samson. "I don't wanna go in and scare the children, or his wife. They've got nothing to do with this."

"Then we'll have to make sure he leaves the house, and we grab him outside," Samson said.

"I think I know how," Naomi offered. "But we'll have to wait till about seven o'clock. He leaves his house early every day to go to the office."

Damian glanced at his watch. "That's in three hours. But there will be too many people in his office. It's not a good place to snatch him."

"I can make sure that he won't go to the office," Naomi said.

"How?"

"I'll give him what he wants: the story." She looked at him, then at Samson and Amaury.

"Okay," Samson said with a nod. Then he gestured to Damian. "Put the teams together. Check with Quinn who's available."

"And Mrs. Zhang?" Naomi asked.

"We'll make sure she stays put in her flat and doesn't contact anybody," Samson said. "Damian, have Eddie or Thomas disconnect her landline and her cell phone, and then—"

"She has no cell phone," Naomi interrupted.

"Even better," Damian said. "I'll have Eddie cut the landline, and I'll station one of the hybrids outside her flat."

"Let's get this show on the road," Samson said.

31

It was still dark, when Damian got into the passenger seat of Naomi's car, which was parked at the top of Twin Peaks. The view from here into the city was stunning. And since it was November, there was no fog, only a clear sky with millions of stars.

"Make the call."

Naomi pressed the button on her cell phone and put the call on speaker. It rang twice, before the call was connected.

Wei Guo answered the phone. "Naomi? It's early."

"I know, I know, but this is urgent. I found something. And it's gonna blow this story wide open."

"Excellent. Meet me in the office. I'm heading in now."

"No, not the office," Naomi said quickly. "We can't be overheard. This is huge. I mean, real huge. Meet me at the top of Twin Peaks. Nobody will see us there."

Wei Guo hesitated. "Uhm, okay then. I'll be up there in less than fifteen minutes."

"Thank you." Naomi disconnected the call.

"Well done," Damian praised. Then he lifted his own cell phone to his ear. "Eddie, disconnect the phones."

"On it," Eddie replied. "Oh, and I checked the two cars registered to Wei Guo. None of them match the partial license plate of the thief's getaway car."

"That means he has an accomplice."

"Most likely, because Mrs. Zhang doesn't have a car. Nor does Tracy."

"Are Grayson and Cooper still following up on the leads from the partial license plate?"

"Yes, and Ryder and Vanessa are doing the same. Nothing so far."

"Thanks, Eddie."

Damian shoved his cell phone back into his pocket and leaned across to Naomi. "The moment you hear his car drive up, get out of your car. I'll have you in my sight at all times."

"Okay."

He kissed her, then exited the car and walked to the bushes his colleagues were hiding behind. They'd parked the blackout van on the far side of the little hill, hiding it from view. Damian joined Sebastian and Ethan. Since the sun would rise soon, none of the full-blooded vampires were on the mission to capture Wei Guo. They were waiting at Scanguards HQ.

"He should be here in less than fifteen minutes," Damian announced. "He lives in the Outer Sunset."

They didn't have to wait long until a red Lexus pulled up and parked next to Naomi's Mini. Naomi already stood next to her car, waiting for Wei Guo. The short Chinese man exited his car and shut the door. He wore a windbreaker over his dress shirt and dark pants, and it was impossible for Damian to see if he was armed.

The way Naomi had positioned herself, Wei had to face away from the hill, looking out toward the city, which meant that Damian and his two fellow hybrids could approach him without being seen.

"So, what did you find?" he asked eagerly.

"Hi, Wei, you're not gonna believe this, but this is way bigger than a satanic cult. Way bigger."

"Well? What is it? Come on, don't keep me on tenterhooks."

Damian stopped right behind Wei. "Yeah, way bigger," Damian repeated.

Wei whirled around, his eyes widening in shock. "What the—"

Damian flashed his fangs at the man, while Sebastian and Ethan grabbed his arms so he couldn't reach for a weapon.

"What the fuck is this? Help!"

"Shut up!" Damian snapped, and patted him down. "He's unarmed."

"Who the hell are you? Let go of me! Naomi?" He looked over his shoulder.

Naomi stood there, her arms folded over her chest.

"Who are these people?" He glared at her, while he tried to fight against Sebastian's and Ethan's hold, without any success. "You set me up!"

"Yeah, and you set me up earlier. I'd call that even," Naomi replied calmly.

"Let's go, we'll take him back to HQ," Damian ordered. "Naomi, follow us in your car."

"Let go of me!" Wei Guo screamed. "Help! Somebody help me!"

"Nobody's gonna hear you up here," Ethan said and rolled his eyes. "So shut up, or I'm gonna gag you."

Damian watched Naomi get back into her car and start the engine, while Sebastian and Ethan dragged a thrashing Wei Guo back to the blackout van and put him in the back, where they restrained him.

"Jesus, I can't hear myself think," Ethan ground out.

When Wei still didn't stop screaming for help, Ethan put a gag in his mouth to silence him.

Damian jumped in on the driver's side and put the van in gear. It was only a fifteen-minute ride from the top of Twin Peaks to HQ.

When they reached Scanguards, Damian drove the van into the underground garage, and made sure that Naomi's Mini entered behind him, before he closed the electronic gate behind her.

"Take him down to the interrogation room." Damian got out of the van and walked to Naomi's car, while the two hybrids dragged the still defiant Wei Guo toward the elevator.

Naomi got out of the car. She looked pale.

"You did well," Damian praised her, and pulled her into his arms. "You okay?"

"Just a little shaken. I'm not used to cloak and dagger operations like you and your colleagues."

"You think that was cloak and dagger?" He chuckled. "For us, that's just a regular Thursday."

"That's 'cause you're Superman, and I'm just regular Lois Lane."

"I thought you were Little Red Riding Hood." He would always see her like that, no matter what she wore, or what she did. But he couldn't indulge in that kind of thinking right now. "Let's go. You can't be in the interrogation room, so—"

"No! I brought him in. I need to—"

"I'll bring you to the observation room. You'll be able to see and hear everything that goes on in the interrogation room."

When Naomi's face lit up, he added, "Did you really think I'd shut you out, when you were the one who tipped us off to Wei Guo and his mother? We're a team, you and I." And soon they'd be much more than that.

They rode the elevator down to where the observation room was located. It was a booth similar to the kind of room sportscasters used during live sports events, only that this room wasn't overlooking a football field but a large interrogation room. With his access card, Damian opened the door to the observation room and ushered Naomi inside.

The room wasn't empty.

"Nicholas, hey," Damian said. "What are you doing here?"

Zane's twenty-seven-year-old son sat on a chair in front of the two-way mirror and turned his head. "I'm gonna watch my dad interrogate a suspect. Should be interesting."

"What suspect?"

"They just brought him in."

Damian stepped closer to the window to look down into the room. "Ah, fuck!"

Zane stood in the room, several tools on a table next to him. Wei Guo already sat on the only chair in the room.

Damian pushed the button on the microphone. "Zane, get the fuck away from the suspect!"

Zane looked over his shoulder. "Just doing you a favor. It'll be faster." Then he turned back to the prisoner.

"Fuck!" Damian hissed and rushed to the door, where he looked over his shoulder at Zane's son.

"Nicholas, she's mine. You touch her, you're dust."

He didn't wait for the hybrid's reply and rushed down the stairs instead of waiting for the elevator. When he reached the door to the interrogation room, he pushed it open and charged at Zane who was about to set a pair of pliers to Wei Guo's right thumb.

Damian jerked Zane's arm back. "I said: get the fuck away from the suspect! Sometimes, you're such an asshole."

Zane huffed. "I get results. And we don't have time to waste."

"I can handle this." He pointed to Wei Guo. "Torture won't be necessary. Or haven't you noticed that he's already peed his pants?" The smell of urine and the wet stain on Wei's pants were hard to miss.

Zane glanced at Wei then back at him. "As I said, I get results. He's all yours." He snatched his tools from the table and walked to the door. "You're welcome."

"Your mate must be a saint," Damian growled. "How else can she bear your insufferable arrogance?"

The bald vampire with the violent temper looked over his shoulder, his mouth twisting into a half-smile. "Portia can bear a lot more than that. Maybe one day you'll find a woman who'll overlook all your faults too and love you anyway."

"I already have."

Zane raised an eyebrow, then chuckled to himself and left the room. The door was about to close behind him, when Samson and Amaury marched into the room.

Damian looked at them. "Whose idea was it to have Zane have a crack at my suspect?"

Samson scoffed. "Zane's. 'Cause it sure wasn't mine or Amaury's."

"I can handle this guy myself."

"We know," Samson said, while he and Amaury remained standing near the door.

"We won't interfere," Amaury assured him.

"Good." Damian turned to Wei Guo. "Let's have a little chat. This can go one of two ways: you tell us the truth, and I won't hurt you. You lie, and you'll learn very quickly that I have a short fuse."

Wei Guo looked thoroughly intimidated, though there was still defiance in his tone. "I don't know what you want from me."

"Where is Mick? And where is the crate of blood you stole?"

Wei shook his head. "I don't know what you're talking about."

Damian stepped closer and leaned in, towering over the seated prisoner. "Maybe you didn't understand the question, so I'll repeat it: You kidnapped Mick Solvang, a bartender from my nightclub, and your niece's boyfriend. Where are you keeping him? Is that question clear enough for you now?"

Wei's lips quivered. "I didn't kidnap anybody."

Annoyed with Wei's refusal to answer the question, Damian allowed his fangs to descend and parted his lips so his prisoner got a good look at his deadly canines. He growled to underscore his displeasure and leaned in, bringing his face to within inches of Wei's. The Chinese man shrank back in his chair, but couldn't get away, since the metal chair was bolted to the floor, and his arms and legs were shackled to it.

"Fuck!" His voice shook, and the stench of fear permeated the air. "What the fuck are you?"

"You know what I am. And you know what Mick is, or you wouldn't have stolen the crate of human blood to keep him alive. You want me to spell it out for you?" Damian paused and willed his eyes to turn red.

A strangled gasp burst from Wei's lips.

"I'm a vampire. And I'm gonna take a bite out of you if you don't tell me the truth."

"Please don't hurt me! I didn't do anything. I didn't. I never touched Tracy's boyfriend. You have to believe me." His voice broke.

Damian let another growl roll over his lips. "Try again. This time I want the truth."

~ ~ ~

Tears welled up in Wei's eyes, and from the observation booth above the interrogation room, Naomi could see him break. All fight went out of him. It would surprise her if it were otherwise. Damian looked intimidating, and if she didn't know how gentle and loving he could be, she would be afraid of him too.

A pleasant shiver went down her spine at the knowledge that this powerful vampire was in love with her. It hadn't escaped her what he'd said to Nicholas. That she was his and that if he touched her, he'd die. And if that wasn't enough to stake his claim, he'd told Zane that he'd found the woman who loved him no matter his faults. The tone in Damian's voice had been one of possessiveness. He hadn't backed down from the scary looking bald vampire who looked like he loved inflicting pain. The strength and power Damian exhibited when he stood up to Zane were even more of a turn-on than his good looks and charm.

Feeling herself get hot, Naomi concentrated on the interrogation again.

Wei looked like a weak and scared man now. "I'm sorry, all I wanted was for Tracy to break up with him. She changed when she met him." He sniffled, and a sob tore from his chest. "But I didn't hurt him. I just planted the evidence to get him and the club in trouble... so the city would shut down the club, and he'd leave. He was controlling my niece."

"Bullshit. You figured out he's a vampire, and you kidnapped him. Why else would you steal the bottles of blood, other than to keep him alive while you locked him up. Where the fuck is he?"

Tears now streamed down Wei's face. "I don't know. I didn't steal any bottles of blood."

"You just admitted that you planted the evidence. We found the broken bottle and the vial. It proves you stole the whole crate."

"I found the bottle in Tracy's flat. In the trash. I could tell it was blood. And I saw the label on it." He swallowed away some of the tears, and cleared his voice. "I suspected that he was pulling Tracy into some satanic cult. I had to stop it. So I took the bottle from her flat."

Naomi saw Damian glance at Samson and Amaury, who were listening with interest.

"Are you saying you didn't know that Mick was a vampire?"

"No, I had no idea. Vampires... they don't exist... they can't exist." Wei stared at Damian's fangs. Naomi realized that he kept them extended to intimidate Wei into compliance. "They can't... it's not possible. It makes it so much worse. Tracy... I can't believe she would do that... date a creature like that... No." He shook his head, still in denial.

Was it possible that Wei Guo really didn't know that Mick was a vampire?

"Both Mick and Tracy have disappeared. Where are they?" Damian asked.

Wei shook his head, his shoulders dropping. "Why don't you ask Mick? He should know where she is. I haven't spoken to Tracy in days.

When she didn't return my calls, I went to her flat. I found the bottle and that little vial, but Tracy wasn't there. I wanted to flush that guy out by exposing what he's doing… so Tracy would realize how wrong he is for her. I only want her best."

Naomi snorted involuntarily. More like he wanted to control his niece.

The door to the observation booth suddenly opened, and Naomi looked over her shoulder. Zane, the bald vampire, entered.

"Hey, Dad."

When Zane's eyes fell on her, he cocked his eyebrows. "And you are?"

Before Naomi could find her voice, Nicholas answered, "She's Damian's woman. He said if I touched her—"

"Let me guess," Zane interrupted. "He threatened to stake you? Figures." He ran a long look over Naomi that made her feel as if she was being inspected and didn't pass muster.

"I'm Naomi," she said, annoyed by how uncomfortable the intimidating vampire made her feel. "The guy down there is my boss."

"You keep crappy company." One side of his mouth tilted up, then he gestured to Nicholas. "Nikki, go see Eddie."

"Don't call me Nikki," Nicholas ground out and glared at his father. "Not in front of others."

Zane grunted. "Touchy. Now go to Eddie's office. They've got another lead on the partial license plate, and need another team to check it out. You might have to take Lydia with you. I don't think anybody else is available."

Grumbling something unintelligible, Nicholas left the room.

"I'll keep you company," Zane said and sat down in the chair Nicholas had occupied earlier.

"I don't need—"

"Let me rephrase that: I'll watch you."

Yeah, that was more like it. But she refused to admit that his presence intimidated her. "Suit yourself. We done with the chitchat? 'Cause I'd like to listen to the interrogation."

"Guess the kitty has claws."

Naomi ignored his comment and looked back down into the room to concentrate on the interrogation.

Damian turned away from the prisoner, and approached Samson and Amaury. "I think he's telling the truth."

Samson nodded, while Amaury replied, "It looks that way. He's clearly afraid of us. He wouldn't continue lying."

"Then he's a dead end. All we've got is the partial license plate of the thief's car." He ran a hand through his hair. "Damn it. If he really doesn't know that Mick is a vampire, and he didn't kidnap him, then all he and his mother were trying to do is stir up trouble in the hope of Tracy leaving Mick. It's despicable, and not very smart either. As if stirring up shit for the club and for Mick would have made Tracy leave him."

Naomi knew Damian was right. If Tracy really loved him, the knowledge of what her family had tried to do would drive her even further into Mick's arms.

"But that doesn't get us any closer to finding Mick or the girl," Damian added.

"Back to square one," Amaury said. "Let's concentrate on finding the person who stole the crate of blood."

Samson nodded. "I'm with both of you. Wei Guo doesn't have the guts to continue lying to us. He's telling the truth. We can have Gabriel confirm, just in case he's a better liar than we think, though I don't believe Gabriel will come to a different conclusion than the three of us," Samson said and pulled out his cell phone, when it suddenly rang. He looked at the display, then hit the accept button. "Grayson?"

Samson listened, then addressed Amaury and Damian, "I think we found the thief."

32

After locking up Wei Guo in a cell on the same level as the interrogation room, Damian went to the observation booth to pick up Naomi, when to his surprise, Zane stepped out of the room.

"What the fuck, Zane? Where is she? If you hurt her, I swear—"

"Just keeping her company," Zane interrupted.

Behind him, Naomi emerged.

"Naomi, you okay?"

Naomi nodded. Damian knew that as a blood-bonded vampire, Zane would never touch another woman in a sexual way, but he was absolutely capable of inflicting pain, whether on a woman or a man.

Zane snorted. "You're just like your father. Lighten up a little."

"Says the man who has no sense of humor," Damian retorted.

Zane shrugged. "Didn't want her to wander off, particularly without a visitor's badge."

"Like you're one for following the rules." Zane had broken plenty of them in the decades he'd been with Scanguards.

Naomi rolled her eyes. "When you're both done whipping out your dicks to compare who's got the bigger one, maybe we can go and snatch the thief?"

Damian turned his gaze to her, surprised that she didn't seem to be the least bit intimidated by Zane, and—admittedly—by their excessive display of testosterone.

"Gotta say," Zane said with something that looked almost like a smirk. "She's got *cojones*."

Despite his annoyance with Zane, Damian grinned. "Yep, she does." He reached his arm out to take her hand. "We're meeting everybody upstairs."

As they walked down the corridor to the elevator, and Zane went in the other direction, Naomi leaned closer to him. "That guy scares the shit out of me."

"Yeah, he has that effect on people. Zane's not known for his congeniality."

"No joke," Naomi said. "So, what's gonna happen to Wei Guo now?"

"We haven't decided yet. Gabriel is gonna make sure he's not in cahoots with the thief, and while we're trying to find Mick and Tracy, we'll keep him locked up here so he can't interfere in any way."

"You have a prison here?"

"Not a real prison, no. The vampire prison is in Grass Valley, and only vampires are incarcerated there. But we have holding cells in this building."

"Are you kidding me? There's a vampire prison?"

They stepped into the elevator, and Damian pressed the button for the top floor. "Yep. Just like humans have their bad apples, our society does too." He pulled her closer to him. "You must be tired. But I hope all this will be over soon. And then you and I will spend twenty-four hours in bed without any interruptions."

"That's no guarantee for sleep." She winked.

"I can guarantee you it'll be better than sleep."

"Promise?"

"Promise."

Before he could sink his lips on hers, the elevator doors opened on the top floor.

In the small conference room, several vampires and hybrids were already assembled. The monitor on the wall showed a live feed of the front entrance of a small house.

"Now that everybody is here," Samson started, "Grayson, bring us up to speed."

The video on the screen moved, and Damian realized that it was coming from Grayson's cell phone. He and Cooper were outside the suspect's home.

"Okay, this is what we found," Grayson said. "The thief's car is parked right outside the house and fits the description Gabriel gave us, right down to the bumper sticker. From the info we got from Eddie, the car is registered to a Ralph Lassiter, and the yellow house you see here is the address on the registration. We got here about an hour ago, and so far, we haven't seen anybody enter or leave. There is an attached garage, but I don't think this place has a basement where he could keep a vampire out of sunlight. It's possible he's using the garage, but when I did a walkaround, I couldn't smell anything that would lead me to believe that Mick is inside."

"What neighborhood are you in?" Damian asked.

"Outer Richmond."

"Yeah, most houses there don't have a basement," Damian said.

Grayson continued, "Eddie, do you have more details on this Ralph Lassiter?"

Eddie sat at the conference table, his laptop in front of him. "Couldn't find much. The house is a rental. He's the only one on the lease. Couldn't find any W-2 or any other source of income for him. At least not for the last two years. Before that, he worked as an auto mechanic. The garage he worked for, Ken's Motors in Hunter's Point, went out of business a while ago. Ralph seems to be unemployed right now." He clicked a remote control, and the screen split. Grayson's live feed was pushed to one side, and a driver's license appeared on the other. "That's Ralph Lassiter. He's twenty-nine. I can't find anything on social media about him. I'll dig deeper, but so far, that's all I have on him."

"Grayson, is there evidence that the house is occupied?" Damian asked.

"Yes, I could hear water running a little earlier. He probably took a shower. Not sure how much longer Cooper and I can wait around here. People are starting to leave their houses to get to work. We have to make a decision. Go in or wait?"

Damian exchanged a look with Samson.

"It's your call, Damian," Samson said.

That was all he needed to hear. "All right. Quinn, call the other teams off their targets, and have Ryder and Vanessa meet me at the suspect's house. Grayson, you and Cooper wait for my arrival." Damian rose. "I'll be there in twenty-five minutes. Nobody goes in there before I get there, understood?"

"If you say so," Grayson replied.

"Hold it," Cooper suddenly said. "The entrance door is opening."

Grayson zoomed in with his cell phone camera, revealing a young woman, dressed in a Parka and jeans, leaving the house.

"Do you guys see that?" Cooper asked.

"It's not his wife," Eddie reported. "He's not married. Perhaps his girlfriend, or a roommate. The house is a two-bedroom."

"Oh my God, I know her," Naomi said with a gasp.

Damian whipped his head to her. "You do? Who is she?"

"That's Cynthia, the woman who works at Louisa's Salon with Tracy. She's the one who told me about her family, you know, about the fact that her grandmother and her uncle don't like Mick and are trying to control Tracy's life."

"Shit!" Damian cursed. "This can't be a coincidence."

"She's approaching Lassiter's car," Cooper reported, and everybody could see it on the monitor. "What do you want us to do?"

As Cynthia unlocked the old Toyota Corolla and got in, Damian ordered, "Grayson, you'll follow her with the car. Cooper, stay watching the house. I'll be there as soon as I can."

"Ryder and Vanessa are only ten minutes out," Quinn said, and put down his cell phone.

"Good," Damian said. "Eddie, track Grayson's GPS and send it to Sebastian's cell. Sebastian, you'll join Grayson."

"Hold on," Eddie said. "I've got something on the girl. The only Cynthia working at Louisa's Salon is Cynthia Lassiter. Same last name as our suspect."

"So she *is* his wife?"

"No. They were born on the same day. She's his twin sister."

Damian nodded. "Okay, let's get them. Eddie, disconnect their cell phones so that if either of them spots that they're being watched, they can't warn the other."

He looked at Naomi and was already making a move to get up. "You'll stay here." He glanced at his father. "Dad?"

Amaury nodded. "Don't worry, son, Naomi will be safe with me."

Then Damian dashed out of the conference room.

33

Grayson followed the rust-bucket Cynthia Lassiter was driving. Traffic was starting to pick up in the city with people heading into work early. He was driving one of Scanguards' blackout vans rather than his sportscar and for once, was glad for it because it was less conspicuous. Still, he was pissed that Damian had asked him to follow the woman, rather than stay at the house to take down Ralph Lassiter.

He knew why Damian had sent him on this fool's errand to shadow the suspect's sister: he was still pissed that he'd called Naomi fat. Well, he was paying for opening his mouth now. He would have gladly apologized to Damian when he'd realized that Naomi was the woman he loved, had his father not interfered and tossed him out of the study. But whenever his father treated him more harshly than he treated anybody else, Grayson saw red. Unfortunately, it appeared that he and his father were cut from the same cloth, not that he'd ever admit that to anybody.

Well, he'd do his job, and follow the woman, and be the obedient soldier his father wanted, rather than the leader Grayson craved to be. His day would come. Now, if he could only muster a little patience, then things would be easier. But patience wasn't exactly his middle name. That was another trait he shared with Samson.

As he followed Cynthia clear across town, Sebastian called him, and Grayson was able to pick him up on a corner without losing his target.

"Where do you think she's going?" Sebastian said as he hopped into the passenger seat.

"Not to the best neighborhood, that's for sure." They were already in the Bayview district, in the southeastern part of San Francisco and heading farther south and closer to the San Francisco Bay.

"Hunter's Point?" Sebastian asked.

The moment Sebastian said the words, something clicked inside of Grayson's mind. "The garage." He exchanged a look with his fellow hybrid. "If it went out of business, it's probably empty."

Sebastian nodded in agreement. "Let me check with Eddie." He pulled out his cell and called HQ. "Hey, Eddie. Cynthia Lassiter is heading toward Hunter's Point. We suspect she's going to the garage where her brother worked. Can you see if the business was sold?"

There was silence, and Grayson continued navigating the van through traffic, staying close to his target.

"Thanks, Eddie, appreciate it." Sebastian disconnected the call. "The place is empty. Nobody bought it."

"Makes a good hiding place, I bet," Grayson commented. "Perhaps Lassiter even kept a key. They could be keeping Mick and Tracy captive there."

"Good place for that. But don't you find it odd that she's the one driving there alone, without her brother?"

He'd been wondering the same ever since he'd suspected that she was driving to the garage. "Something isn't right. I can feel it."

"Maybe she's the one doing his dirty work?" Sebastian guessed. "And he's the brains behind it?"

Grayson shrugged. "Possible."

Cynthia's car slowed, until she finally pulled into one of the parking spots in front of the defunct garage. Not wanting to attract attention, Grayson drove past it, then turned right at the next corner and stopped.

"As soon as she's inside, we're following her."

Sebastian nodded, and kept looking out the passenger side window. "Okay, she's inside."

Grayson jumped out of the van and shut the door quietly. Sebastian did the same. They approached the rickety building, and looked around, making sure nobody was watching them. This wasn't a residential area, but consisted mostly of industrial buildings, many of them abandoned and ready for redevelopment. Many *for lease* and *for sale* signs lined the street. This was the perfect area to hide somebody away without having to worry that anybody would discover them. The garage itself had few windows, and all of them were either boarded up or painted black, making it virtually vampire-proof inside. Yes, if he needed to lock somebody up, he would have chosen this place too.

"Follow my lead," Grayson advised. "She might be armed. Let's do this as quietly as possible, so she won't have a chance to harm the hostages."

Sebastian nodded. "Shouldn't we call for backup?"

"Two hybrids against one human? Please!" Grayson shook his head. "We've got this."

"Okay then."

They walked to the door. The glass insert had been covered up with plywood. Grayson tested the doorknob. It turned in his hand. He looked over his shoulder, giving Sebastian a sign, then pulled on the door, opening it a couple of inches so he could peer into the interior. As expected, it was dark inside, and musty. The smell of blood was in the air. Not just human blood. Vampire blood too. He'd come to the right place.

Grayson allowed his eyes to adjust to the dark interior. The workshop wasn't entirely empty. The owner had left behind tools, tires, and various auto parts. In one corner of the large two-story high garage was the only room, an office. The walls of the large office weren't simply plywood like Grayson had expected, but made of brick and mortar, perhaps because the previous owner wanted a more secure location to store valuable parts and money. Even the door was reinforced with bars, so thieves would have a harder time raiding the place.

On the outside of the office door was a heavy iron rod, and at its end, Grayson noticed a large padlock. It was open.

He looked over his shoulder to Sebastian. "Large office in the left far corner," he whispered.

Sebastian nodded, understanding, his gun ready.

Grayson opened the door wider and snuck inside, looking left and right, before stalking toward the office, his senses on high alert. When he reached the door, he noticed that it was ajar. There was light inside, but a filing cabinet blocked his view. However, he could clearly smell vampire blood, as well as the fragrant perfume of a woman.

He kicked the door open and charged inside. Sitting on the floor, chained to a radiator, was Mick Solvang, while Cynthia crouched before him. Mick's eyes instantly shot toward Grayson, and Sebastian, who was rushing in as well. But Cynthia didn't immediately turn her head—as if she hadn't heard the door open.

It took him only a second to realize why: she was wearing headphones that covered her ears completely, while she held Mick's bleeding wrist over a plastic container to collect the blood. With one swift move, Grayson snatched her from behind and tossed her on her back. A surprised shriek burst from her lips. That's when he noticed something else: she was wearing sunglasses.

"Mick, you okay?" he asked, and cast a quick look at the chained vampire. "Sebastian, untie him!"

Mick sagged back against the radiator. "Thank God, you found me." He looked drained, but relieved. "Tracy, is she safe?"

"Let go of me!" Cynthia yelled, but Grayson pinned her down without much effort.

The human's strength was no match for his. He pulled the earphones off her head and separated her from her sunglasses.

"Shut up, bitch! I'll deal with you later!" Then he turned his head back to Mick. "Tracy's not here?"

"No. You have to find her," Mick pressed out.

"He needs human blood," Sebastian said, as he looked at the chain. "And I need a bolt cutter."

"Check in the garage," Grayson ordered. Then he grabbed Cynthia by the front of her parka and jerked her closer to his face. "Where's the blood? And don't you lie to me, or I'm gonna have him drink from you!"

With wide eyes, Cynthia stared at him. Grayson allowed his fangs to descend and his eyes to turn red to underscore his demand.

"In the filing cabinet," she stammered.

He looked at it and saw that it was locked with a padlock. "Key?"

When she didn't answer fast enough, he gave her a violent shake and growled in displeasure.

"My, my keys are in my r…r…right pocket."

He let go of her parka so she fell back onto the ground so quickly that she had no time to brace herself. But he had no pity for her. She was draining a vampire of his blood, most likely to make a profit from it, and a crime like that wouldn't go unpunished. He dug his hand into the parka's pocket and found a keyring with several keys, just as Sebastian came back with a bolt cutter.

"Sebastian, open that filing cabinet. The blood's in there." Grayson tossed him the keys, before turning back to Mick, but he appeared too exhausted to be of use. He looked at Cynthia again. "Where are you keeping Tracy?"

"Not here," Mick said with a weak voice. "Or I would have…tried…"

"Here's the blood," Sebastian announced and crouched down next to Mick, holding the open bottle to his lips. Mick drank greedily and gulped down the entire bottle.

When Sebastian set the empty bottle down, and picked up the bolt cutters to cut the iron chains around Mick, Grayson looked at the old radiator. It was rusted, and shouldn't have been too much of an obstacle for a vampire, though getting out of the room would have been harder, since it was brick and mortar.

"I don't see any silver," Grayson said. "You didn't try to escape? You could have ripped the radiator out."

Mick lifted his head, already looking better. "I couldn't, or she would have hurt Tracy."

Grayson nodded, understanding. "That's why they split you guys up." Then his gaze fell onto the headphones and the sunglasses. From the headphones music droned as if to drown out everything else. He narrowed his eyes at Cynthia. "You knew that Mick could employ mind control, and you managed to block him out."

"I tried, Grayson, but it didn't work," Mick added.

Grayson nodded. Cynthia had busied her senses with other stimuli so she wouldn't be susceptible to mind control. "Clever little bitch. I suppose your brother is watching Tracy. Don't worry, we'll get him."

"No!" Cynthia screamed and tried to sit up, but Grayson pinned her down. "My brother has nothing to do with this! You leave him alone!"

Grayson scoffed. "Yeah, not bloody likely!" He shifted his position and used his knees to keep her pinned to the ground, while he reached for his cellphone, and called Damian's number.

"Grayson?" Damian answered the call.

"Mick is secure. And we've got Cynthia."

"Is Mick okay?" Damian asked.

"She drained quite a bit of blood from him, but he'll be okay. We're heading back to HQ with them in a few minutes."

"And Tracy?"

"They're keeping Tracy locked up at a different location. My guess is her brother is watching her."

"Okay, we're going in now."

Grayson disconnected the call and looked at Mick. "Don't worry, Damian will free Tracy. And then we'll dole out punishment."

He glared at Cynthia. If it were up to him, he'd make sure that the punishment was very painful and lasted very long.

34

Everybody was pacing in the conference room, which didn't make Naomi feel any better. She hated waiting for word about how the mission was going. Why was it taking so long to hear back from them?

Every five minutes, she looked at the large clock on the wall, only to realize that time was passing at a snail's pace.

"Damian's very well trained," Amaury said from behind her. "Don't worry. He's been on much more dangerous missions before. He can handle this."

She turned to him and forced a smile. "I'm still nervous."

"It's normal. You care about him."

She met Amaury's gaze and realized for the first time how much Damian had inherited from his father, not just his blue eyes, his dark hair and chiseled face, but also his confidence and his charm.

"I do."

"Don't worry, he's pretty indestructible." Then he suddenly looked past her toward the door, and his gentle expression turned to one of adoration.

Naomi looked over her shoulder and saw Nina breeze into the room. She was dressed in tight jeans, and a figure-hugging top and cardigan, her blond hair short, her eyes already seeking those of her husband.

Naomi's heart skipped a beat. The way Amaury looked at Nina reminded her of how Damian had looked at her when they'd made love.

"*Chérie*," Amaury said, as he pulled Nina into his arms.

"Hey, baby, I came as soon as I heard. Any news yet?"

"It's too early."

"Hi, Naomi," Nina said with a smile.

"Good morning, Nina. It's nice to see you again."

"How about you and I go to the lounge for some breakfast?" Nina asked.

"I should stay here to wait for news from Damian," Naomi said, while her stomach betrayed her and growled.

"You two go," Amaury said in an encouraging tone. "I'll let you know the moment we hear anything."

"You sure?"

Nina took her arm and whisked her away, and Naomi allowed it. Perhaps some food would calm her nerves. Nina took her to a lounge on the first floor, which looked more like the first-class lounge at an airport complete with complimentary food and drinks than a cafeteria. Not that she'd ever been in a first-class lounge.

"I'm not sure I can eat anything."

"You need to," Nina said with a smile. "It'll be a long day. You need to keep up your strength."

As they filled their plates with pastries, fruit, and other breakfast items, Naomi had to admire how calm Nina was.

They sat down at one of the comfortable sectionals, and Naomi noticed that there were only a few other people in the large room, and they kept to themselves.

"Aren't you afraid when your husband or your sons are out there trying to take down criminals?"

"Of course, I'm always afraid of what could happen," Nina said with a soft smile. "But Amaury, Damian, and Benjamin are strong, and they're well-trained. They can take care of themselves."

Naomi bit into a Danish, pacing herself so she wouldn't eat too much, though the food was very tempting, and the previous night she'd emptied an entire pint of Ben & Jerry's ice cream instead of eating dinner. Nina ate with great appetite, and Naomi was surprised at how she managed to keep her slim figure if she always ate like that.

"Aren't you hungry?" Nina asked and pointed to Naomi's plate.

"Oh, I am, but I can't eat that much, or my weight will just balloon." She made a gesture to Nina's figure. "You must tell me how you stay so slim."

Nina chuckled, and there was a sparkle in her eyes. She leaned in and dropped her voice to a whisper. "I'm eating for two."

Naomi gasped. "You're pregnant?"

She laughed, and shook her head. "No. But I have to eat enough for me and Amaury."

Finally, it clicked. "Oh, sorry, sometimes I'm so dense."

"It's all new for you. Just go ahead and have another Danish. You won't gain any weight."

"But I always do."

Nina put her hand on her forearm. "Has Damian bitten you yet?"

Heat shot into her cheeks, and she was lost for words.

"Just like I thought. I haven't seen you with him yet, but Amaury told me how Damian looks at you. It would have surprised me if he wasn't drinking your blood."

"I'm… it's…" Goddamn it, she was as flustered as if her boyfriend's mother had just walked in on them having sex. No, worse, having sex and Damian sinking his fangs into her breasts.

"No need to blush, Naomi. Damian didn't just inherit Amaury's good looks. Even as a little boy, his appetite for blood was quite insatiable." She smirked. "So have another Danish. You'll need it. Because whenever the boys come back from a rescue mission, they're quite hungry. And not just for blood."

Naomi couldn't believe how openly Nina talked about sex. She'd never met a mother who was as easygoing as her. Nina was talking more like a girlfriend than a woman who was at least thirty years her senior. She didn't just look young, she *behaved* young.

"You're so nice."

"I like you too, Naomi." She was about to say something else, when her cell phone chimed. She looked at the display. "That's Amaury." She picked it up and pressed it to her ear. She listened for a while, then said, "Thanks, baby."

Nina disconnected the call. "They've freed Mick. He's alive, just a bit drained. Literally. Grayson and Sebastian are bringing him in, together with Cynthia. They should be here in about fifteen minutes."

"And Tracy?" Naomi held her breath.

"No word from Damian yet."

Her heart began to beat faster, and again she experienced the same nervousness as before. Warm hands on hers startled her.

"Damian will be fine. Besides, he's got three hybrids as backup. Now eat, and we'll join Amaury and the others when they bring in Mick. They'll probably take him down to the medical center."

"The medical center. Damian mentioned the other day that Scanguards has its own little hospital, and its own emergency response unit."

"We do, because we can't send people with certain injuries to a regular hospital. There would be too many questions."

"You mean you don't just treat vampires there? Humans too?"

Nina nodded. "If they were attacked by a vampire, or if they are associated with Scanguards, then yes, we treat humans there."

"All the things I've seen and heard about in the last few days, they're amazing. This is like a separate world. I still can't believe that I'm seeing all this. I want to pinch myself to see if I'm dreaming."

"And do you like that dream?" she asked unexpectedly.

Naomi met Nina's gaze. "Yes, I do. Because Damian is in it."

35

Damian shoved his cell phone back into his pocket. "Mick is safe, but Tracy wasn't held at the same location. She's most likely here." He gestured to the house on the other side of the street.

He, Ryder, Cooper, and Vanessa were sitting in Ryder's SUV.

"Ryder, you and Vanessa go around the back, and make sure Ralph doesn't escape out that way while Cooper and I enter in the front." Damian motioned to Cooper. "How are your lockpicking skills coming along?"

Cooper smirked. "Quinn says I'm the best he's ever taught."

"Time to apply those skills," Damian said, and they all got out of the car. He was glad that Ryder was part of the backup team, because he was experienced and cool-headed, not like Grayson, who was a hothead and stubborn as hell. Though he had to admit, he was glad that Grayson had freed Mick so quickly, and apprehended Cynthia.

Ryder and Vanessa walked along the tradesman's entrance on the left side of the house, and quietly made their way into the back. There wasn't much vegetation to hide them, but with some luck nobody would bother asking what they were doing.

Damian headed for the front entrance, Cooper by his side, while he kept an eye out for any movement behind the windows facing the street. The curtains were drawn.

At the entrance door, Damian shielded Cooper from view by any nosy neighbors, while the young hybrid used his lockpicks. He hadn't lied when he said he was good. In fact, Damian had never seen anybody picking a lock that quickly.

"It's open," Cooper whispered and stepped aside.

Damian turned the doorknob and eased the door open a tiny sliver, just sufficient so he could listen to the sounds from inside the house. He heard somebody breathing hard and tried to isolate the sound. It seemed to come from somewhere in the middle of the house. There were no other sounds, no creaking floorboards, no water running, only the low humming of an old refrigerator from the back of the house.

Making a sign to Cooper, Damian opened the door wider and entered. Within a second, he assessed his surroundings: a living room to his left, its door ajar, another door on the same side that probably led to an adjoining dining room, and a kitchen in the back of the house. Along the corridor were also three doors on the right. Two bedrooms and a bathroom if he had to guess.

When he stepped farther into the hallway, Cooper on his heels, a floorboard creaked, and Damian instantly froze.

There was a sudden change in the breathing pattern he heard. Then a male voice. "Cynthia? You back?"

Damian exchanged a look with Cooper, and motioned him to walk to the next door on the left. Since many of the houses in this neighborhood were constructed in the same way, he figured that the first door led into the living room, the second into the connecting dining room. They would enter simultaneously to disorient their suspect and cut off his escape route.

Damian used his fingers to count down. Three, two. On one, both he and Cooper opened their respective doors and charged in. The scene wasn't at all what Damian had expected. There was little furniture in the combined living and dining room, an old couch, a coffee table, and a table with four chairs, no decorations other than a standing lamp and a mirror over the fireplace.

At the dining table sat a young man bent over a bowl of cereal, his figure gaunt, his posture sunk in. He was dressed in pajamas and a bathrobe. Damian could barely recognize him as Ralph Lassiter, the man whose car the thief had driven. It was clear that Ralph couldn't have been the driver. A walker stood next to his chair, because Ralph was too weak to walk without it.

Ralph shrieked, but even his shriek was weak. "Who are you?" His voice trembled. "What do you want? I have nothing worth stealing."

Damian walked closer. "We're not here to steal anything."

"Who let you in?" He tried to rise from his chair, but faltered and fell back onto it.

Seeing that this man was no danger to any of them, Damian addressed Cooper, "Let Ryder and Vanessa in."

Cooper left the room.

"What do you want from me?" Ralph asked again.

"Where is Tracy?"

"I don't know any Tracy. You have the wrong address."

"Let me give you a hint: she works with your sister, Cynthia. And she was kidnapped, together with her boyfriend. And my people just found where you locked him up. Your sister led them right to him."

"What?" Genuine confusion spread on the young man's face. "You hurt my sister? You hurt Cynthia?"

"We didn't hurt her, but we arrested her. Now tell us where you're keeping Tracy."

Ralph shook his head. "Arrested? My sister would never hurt anybody. Why would she kidnap somebody? You must be wrong."

"Are you saying you know nothing of what your sister has done?" Could it be that Ralph really didn't know that Cynthia had kept Mick locked away so she could tap him for his blood? Damian glanced around the room. If she was selling Mick's blood, she wasn't using the money she was making to help her brother. Something didn't add up.

"Where's Tracy?"

"I don't know anybody with that name. I swear. Do you really think I could lock somebody up? I can barely make it to the bathroom on my own." A bitter laugh ripped from Ralph's throat. "Look at me!" His voice was suddenly more forceful, and tears shot to his eyes. "The doctor said I have a month left at best. That was five weeks ago. I'm already living on borrowed time. So you can do whatever you want to me, but don't hurt my sister. She's never done anything wrong in her life."

Ryder popped his head into the room. "No sign of Tracy in the house."

"I'm checking the garage," Vanessa called from behind her brother.

Damian pulled a chair out from under the table and sat down opposite Ralph. "Tell me something Ralph. What do you suffer from?"

He shrugged. "What does it matter?"

"It matters."

"Pancreatic cancer, stage four."

Fuck! That was a death sentence.

"And you said the doctor told you that you only had a month left?"

"Tops. He sent me home to die. Can't afford hospice care. No insurance."

Damian nodded. When Ralph had lost his job, he'd lost his health insurance too. It was so clear now what was happening here. Everything made sense now. "Tell me, your sister, has she given up like you have?"

An unexpected smile curled Ralph's lips upward. "She'll never give up on me. I told her she should. But she's trying all kinds of snake oil to heal me. Experimental drugs and all, but I don't believe in it."

"Has she actually given you something, a brew, or a tincture, or something similar?"

Ralph gave him a strange look. "How did you know? She puts something in a glass of water for me. Tastes awful. But it does make me feel better when I drink it." He shook his head. "But all this is doing is just dragging out the inevitable."

"Did she tell you what it is?"

"Some tincture from a new age wellness store or something. I told her not to waste her money, but she wouldn't listen."

From the door, Cooper called out, "We've got Tracy. She's unconscious and tied up in the garage."

Damian jumped up. "Cooper, watch him."

"The garage?" Ralph asked. "But why would a stranger be in our garage?"

Damian looked over his shoulder. "When did you last set foot in the garage?"

"I've haven't been in there in months." He motioned to the walker.

Damian rushed into the garage, joining Vanessa and Ryder who bent over a young Asian woman: Tracy. Her hands and feet were bound and the rope was tied around the pipes of a water heater. A gag lay next to her on a filthy mattress.

It was obvious now: Cynthia was behind the kidnapping and the theft of the blood, and she'd kept it all from her sick brother. And because

Ralph was too sick to walk anywhere without his walker, he would have never noticed that his sister was keeping a hostage in the garage. Another thing was clear too: Cynthia wasn't selling the blood she'd taken from Mick. She was giving it to her brother in the hopes of healing him.

"How is she?" Damian asked.

Vanessa, who often helped her mother in Scanguards' mini medical center on one of the lower levels of the headquarters building, looked up. "Her breathing is very shallow, and her heartbeat is slow."

"I already sent for the ambulance," Ryder added.

"I think she was given an opioid to knock her out. And she might have gotten too high a dose. She needs medical attention immediately."

"Fuck!" Damian cursed. "How far out is our ambulance?"

"Ten minutes," Ryder replied.

"I can give her my blood," Vanessa suggested. "It'll help her fight off the drugs. I'm not sure I want to wait for the ambulance with the Naloxone."

"Do it!" Damian ordered. They couldn't risk for Tracy to die. Mick would seek revenge on Cynthia and Ralph Lassiter. And he didn't have to be a mind reader to guess that it would be a bloody massacre.

As Vanessa extended her fangs and bit her own wrist, Ryder addressed him, "What's with the brother? Ralph?"

"I'm pretty sure that Cynthia kept him in the dark about what she was doing to save his life."

Ryder raised an eyebrow.

"Pancreatic cancer," Damian said.

"Shit!" Ryder sighed. "This isn't gonna be an easy case to judge. How do we punish her for what she's done to Mick and Tracy? It's not all black and white."

"No, it's not. I hope I won't have to make that decision."

"Then who? The vampire council?" Vanessa asked, while she let her blood drip into Tracy's mouth.

"If it comes to that." Damian motioned to Tracy. "She and Mick will have a say in it. But for right now, we have to bring everybody to HQ, including Ralph. We can't take the chance of him talking to anybody about what's going on here." He turned to the door. "Cooper and I will get him ready, and once the ambulance arrives, we'll transport them both back to Scanguards."

36

The ambulance pulled into Scanguards' parking garage, and Naomi watched it stop right in front of the elevators, two dark SUVs entering behind it. The driver jumped out of the ambulance, and with relief, Naomi saw that Damian was uninjured. Without looking at her or at Nina and Amaury, with whom she'd been waiting for their arrival, he ran to the back of the ambulance, and opened the doors.

Damian helped lift out the gurney, and Maya, who Amaury had explained was the vampire physician who ran the medical center, jumped out. Together, they rolled the gurney toward the elevators. On it lay Tracy. She was unconscious.

"Damian," Naomi said, and walked toward him. "I'm so glad you're okay."

He cast her a quick look, but she didn't see the warmth in his eyes with which he normally looked at her.

"I'm Benjamin." He jerked his thumb over his shoulder. "Damian is behind me."

"Oh, sorry." She whirled around, and saw Damian help a frail young man out of the SUV. She looked at the stranger's face, and could barely recognize him as Ralph Lassiter, the man whose driver's license Eddie had projected on the monitor in the conference room. His cheeks were hollow, and his eyes had sunken in, his skin had an ashen quality to it. He looked gravely ill. This man, who by the looks of it couldn't walk on his own, and was now helped by both Damian and Sebastian, was the thief who'd kidnapped Mick and his girlfriend? Impossible.

She caught Damian's gaze, and their eyes locked for a moment. Yes, this was Damian. How could she have ever mistaken Benjamin for him? Though they were identical twins, there was something in Damian's eyes that made him look so very different from his bother. She saw that now, and she realized that she would never again mix the two brothers up.

"Hey," he murmured softly as he and Sebastian passed her with Ralph.

"Hey," she replied, then looked back toward the elevator where Maya and Benjamin were waiting with the gurney.

Nina stepped closer to Maya and Benjamin. "How is she?"

"Morphine overdose, but I gave her Naloxone in the ambulance," Maya, a beautiful dark-haired woman who looked like she was in her thirties replied. But just like Nina, she was much older than she looked. "She'll pull through, but she has a few rough hours ahead of her."

The elevator doors opened, and a young woman exited, pushing an empty wheelchair. While Benjamin and Maya wheeled the gurney into the elevator, Damian and Cooper helped Ralph into the wheelchair.

"Jenny," Damian ordered the young woman, "take him down into the med center. Maya will check him out after she's taken care of Tracy. Cooper, go with her. And send the elevator back up for us."

When the elevator doors closed behind them, Damian walked back to Naomi and hugged her for a short moment. "Everything went well."

She sighed with relief. "I was worried that something would go wrong."

Damian released her and kissed her on the forehead. "It's all over now. But it wasn't exactly what we expected."

"What's wrong with Ralph?" she asked. "He looks sick."

"Pancreatic cancer. Final stage."

Shocked, a gasp issued from her throat.

Damian turned to his parents, and Naomi's gaze fell onto a woman and a man who'd gotten out of the second SUV. They had to be Ryder and Vanessa, who'd helped with Tracy's rescue.

"Have Grayson and Sebastian gotten back yet with Cynthia Lassiter and Mick?" Damian asked, addressing his father.

"They got here fifteen minutes ago. Cynthia is locked up downstairs for now. Mick is upstairs in the conference room. We were waiting for you. Didn't want him to have to tell us everything twice," Amaury replied.

Damian nodded. "Good. Let's talk to him." He put his arm around Naomi's waist, and together, they all packed into the elevator.

Feeling Damian's arm around her, made her finally relax a little.

"Well done, son," Amaury said and patted Damian on the shoulder. Naomi saw pride shine from Amaury's eyes.

"Well, we couldn't have done it without Naomi's help," Damian said. "If she hadn't alerted us to Mrs. Zhang, we wouldn't have found the thief so easily."

"That was a stroke of luck," Amaury said. "Ryder, Vanessa, I really appreciate you guys helping out with this."

Vanessa chuckled. "It was easy."

"Totally," Ryder added.

"Why don't you guys head home? Get some rest. You were out all night," Amaury said.

"We want to see it through to the end," Ryder said, and Vanessa nodded in agreement.

"I'm kind of curious how a human managed to trap a vampire and lock him up," Vanessa admitted.

At Vanessa's words, Naomi suddenly remembered Wei Guo. "Amaury, what about Wei Guo? Is he still locked up here?"

Amaury nodded. "Yes, but we're planning to release him soon. Gabriel confirmed that he had nothing to do with the kidnapping or the theft of the blood. We've already pulled off the guard outside Mrs. Zhang's flat, and restored her phone line."

"What are you gonna do with Wei Guo? I mean, he's seen that you guys are vampires." She looked at Amaury and Damian.

"We'll have to wipe his memory and that of his mother too," Damian said. "And not just of us, but also of the plot he hatched with his mother to get back at Mick. Neither of them can be allowed to know anything about the bottled blood."

"But doesn't that mean you have to go back at least a week or so? I mean, Wei Guo and his mother might have been thinking about this for a while," Naomi wondered.

"Gabriel will help us with what we need to erase," Damian replied. "Wei Guo won't remember that he ever gave you the assignment to investigate the Mezzanine."

Naomi nodded. "Good. Nevertheless, I'm not gonna continue working there."

Damian gave her a quizzical look.

"I can't work for somebody who has no qualms about using the power of the press to destroy somebody because of a personal vendetta. That's unethical."

"Good for you," Damian said.

"Damian told me that you're a good investigator," Amaury said.

"Thank you. I enjoy that kind of work."

"You make a good team," Nina added. Her husband drew her closer to him, and they exchanged a loving look.

~ ~ ~

Damian understood what his parents were trying to tell him: they approved of Naomi. Not that he would give her up if they didn't, of course. But it was good to know that they accepted her. She would fit perfectly into his family.

In the conference room, everybody involved in the rescue who wasn't in the medical center taking care of Tracy and Ralph, was assembled. Plus a few others, chief amongst them Samson.

Mick sat at one end of the large table, a half-full bottle of blood in front of him. He continued to drink from it. Damian released Naomi and walked toward Mick, who instantly rose.

Damian hugged him. "Fuck, man, you gave us a fright."

"Thanks, Damian. I knew you guys would come." Then he looked toward the door. "And Tracy? Is she okay?"

Damian nodded. "Maya is taking care of her. She'll be fine. You can go see her a little later."

Mick exhaled a sigh of relief. "Thank you."

"But first, we've gotta talk. Take a seat." Damian turned around to look at the assembled, and the quiet murmurs died down. "Okay, first the good news: Tracy, Mick's human girlfriend, is in the medical center downstairs. She'll be fine. And we have the perpetrator in custody." He looked at Grayson. "Grayson, did you guys recover the stolen bottles of blood?"

"Yes, they were all in the abandoned garage where we found Mick. We brought them all back, including the empty bottles, as well as the blood Cynthia drained from Mick."

"Thanks, Grayson, great job," Damian praised. Grayson was both reliable and surprisingly thorough. Maybe he hadn't given the guy enough credit in the past, just because he could be arrogant and a hothead. But Grayson was capable when it counted.

"Here's the bad news: the case isn't quite as clear-cut as we'd expected at first."

"Elaborate, please," Samson demanded.

"We'll have to do a lot of damage control," Damian explained. "And the villain isn't your usual bad guy. And not just because the villain is a woman: Cynthia Lassiter. Her twin brother had no idea what she was doing. Being a twin myself, I understand why she did what she did. If I had to choose between committing a crime to save the life of my twin brother or letting him die, I might have chosen the former too." He met Benjamin's gaze, and knew his brother felt the same.

"Are you saying her brother will die?" Samson asked.

"Pancreatic cancer, stage four. According to him, he's already outlived his doctor's prediction by a week, most likely because Cynthia was giving him Mick's blood."

Samson raised his eyebrows, and several of the other vampires and hybrids let out surprised gasps. Samson motioned to Mick. "Tell us what happened. And start at the beginning. Damian and Naomi found the empty vials in your flat, so Mick, do us a favor, and don't lie to us. You got this mess started, now own it."

Damian sat down next to Naomi and took her hand in his.

Mick nodded, a guilty look on his face now. "I'm sorry, you're right, it was my fault that all this happened. But when I met Tracy, I just lost my head. I... uhm, I couldn't think straight anymore." He sighed. "She was being assaulted by a couple of guys one night, and I rescued her. We fell in love, but her family didn't want her to date me... I guess a bartender wasn't good enough for them. Her grandmother and her uncle made life hell for her. She wanted to leave San Francisco."

It was consistent with what Wei Guo had revealed during his interrogation, and what Cynthia had told Naomi.

"I told her that we could leave together, but we didn't have any money, so I decided to sell my blood." Mick dropped his lids in shame.

"Who to?" Damian asked.

Mick shrugged. "Just some ordinary people. We were discreet. Tracy knew that my blood could heal a human, because the night I rescued her, I gave her some to heal her." He looked up. "Those two assholes had beaten her and broken her wrist."

"Go on," Damian demanded. "Who did you sell it to?"

"Tracy knew a lot of people who were sick, you know, people who didn't have health insurance. She told them she could get them something that would help with their ailments. She never told them what it actually was. And when it worked, I guess those people told others, and we were able to sell more, and save some money."

Damian shook his head, and he saw Samson and some of the others do the same. "How much did you charge per vial?"

"We weren't greedy. I charged a hundred dollars a pop," Mick said quickly. "We just needed enough to make a new start somewhere else, away from Tracy's family. We wanted to leave the day after Halloween, and Tracy was saying goodbye to the few friends she has. I guess she got a little tipsy when she went out with her colleague, Cynthia. I didn't know at the time that Cynthia had bought a vial of my blood a couple of days earlier."

Damian immediately realized where this story was heading.

"Somehow Tracy must have let it slip that what she was selling Cynthia was vampire blood, and she put two and two together, and figured out that I'm the vampire it came from. She'd already given her brother one of the vials, and she must have seen an improvement in his condition, so when she heard that Tracy and I were leaving, and there wouldn't be any more vampire blood for her to buy, she got desperate."

"She couldn't let you leave, because she wanted to save her twin's life," Damian guessed.

Mick nodded. "I got a call from Tracy's cell phone, but it wasn't Tracy. Cynthia said that she had Tracy, and she would hurt her if I didn't meet with her. I had no choice. I figured I could easily overpower her, but I guess Cynthia knew more about vampires than I thought. She probably threatened Tracy so she would tell her more about my vulnerabilities. And she was smart. She said if I didn't do as she said, and if I even tried to escape, I would never find Tracy, and she would die, because she was drugged and tied up somewhere."

"You believed her?" Damian asked.

"She showed me a video of Tracy, tied-up, gagged, and unconscious. I couldn't risk her life. I couldn't even use mind control on Cynthia."

When Samson furrowed his brow, Grayson interjected, "The bitch wore sunglasses and headphones with loud music."

Mick nodded. "I guess it drowned out my efforts to use mind control on her. Besides, I was weak, because the first thirty-six hours she didn't give me any blood. I begged her to go to the Mezzanine to steal the bottled blood, and told her that I would die if she drained me of more blood and didn't feed me human blood right away. She believed it, and I gave her my keys for the storage room. I knew that she'd be caught on camera." Mick looked directly at Damian. "I knew that either you or Patrick would realize that something was off. I was counting on you trying to find the thief. I knew sooner or later you'd figure out that the blood was for me, and that I was locked up."

"Good thinking," Damian said. "Unfortunately, it took us a while, because Cynthia used the Halloween party as cover, and was wearing a costume with a facemask."

Mick nodded. "She brought the blood, but she only gave me half of what I would normally drink in one night. That's why she locked up the blood and chained me to a radiator, and I remained weak."

"No silver?" Samson asked.

"No," Mick admitted. "Maybe I could have freed myself from the chains, and attacked her the next time she opened the door to my prison, but what would have happened to Tracy then? I had no idea in what state her brother was. What if he would have hurt her if Cynthia didn't come back within a certain time?"

Damian couldn't fault Mick for his thinking. He wouldn't risk Naomi's life either, even if that meant he had to suffer in her stead. He would do anything to keep her safe, just like Mick had complied with his captor's demands so she couldn't hurt the woman he loved.

"Besides, Cynthia said she'd let us both go once her brother was cured," Mick added.

Samson rose from his chair. "Mick, you do realize that by selling your blood, you've put us in a precarious situation."

"I understand that."

"If you really understood it, then you wouldn't have done it in the first place. It was irresponsible." He let out a breath. "You'll be a guest of Scanguards until we've decided what to do about this mess." He gestured to Quinn. "Quinn, take him down to the holding cell for now."

Mick rose. "But I need to see Tracy."

"You'll get to see her after we've spoken to her and heard her side of the story," Samson said firmly.

When the door closed behind Quinn and Mick, Samson added, "Now, anybody with suggestions regarding damage control, deterrence, and punishment, we'll meet in my office in fifteen minutes."

People started to get up from their seats.

Naomi put her hand on Damian's forearm. "What I don't understand about Cynthia is why she even told me that she knew about Tracy and Mick."

"It's simple," Damian said. "When you came sniffing around the salon, she probably wanted to find out how much you knew about their disappearance. And if you'd told her about your suspicions, she would have used that knowledge to evade us."

"You're right."

Damian rose. "I've gotta be in that meeting with Samson. It'll take a while. You okay?"

"Don't worry about me," Naomi replied. "Go, do what you need to do. I should probably go home and take a shower. I'll just get an Uber downstairs."

"I can give you a ride," Nina said from across the table. "I'm going home anyway."

"But it's in the opposite direction," Naomi said.

"It's no trouble. Honestly."

"Thank you, that's so nice of you."

"Thanks, Mom." Damian said, before squeezing Naomi's hand. "Come back here in a few hours. I'll leave your name at the reception so that they'll let you in. Or I can pick you up from your flat when I'm done here."

"I'll meet you back here."

Damian pressed a kiss to her lips, then left the conference room.

37

"This is a royal mess," Samson said and leaned against the desk in his office, hands clamped around the edge of the desk. "To be honest, I'm not quite sure who the victim really is. Mick brought this on himself."

"Which doesn't excuse what Cynthia and her brother did," Grayson commented.

"Her brother had no idea," Damian interrupted.

"You believe him?" Grayson asked, surprised. "You can't tell me that he didn't know she was giving him vampire blood."

"That's exactly what I'm telling you. You didn't see him." Damian shook his head. "Ralph has resigned himself to his fate. He knows he's dying. He has nothing to gain by lying to me. Cynthia told him that it was some new-age wellness elixir. She diluted it in water. Trust me, he's probably the only innocent party in this."

"Damian is right, Grayson," Samson said. "But the rest of them all bear responsibility, even Tracy. And she's probably the one suffering the most right now." He looked straight at Damian. "How is she really? Will she pull through?"

"Vanessa gave her her blood when we found her, because she recognized the signs of a drug overdose. And Maya administered Naloxone to counteract the opioid Cynthia used to keep her sedated. Maya thinks she'll pull through, but because she's been given high doses over several days, she might go through withdrawal."

"Do we know where she got the opioid from?" Amaury asked.

"I haven't had a chance to question Cynthia yet, but my best guess is that it was prescribed for Ralph to make his last days painless." Damian looked at Grayson. "Have you interrogated her yet?"

"No, I figured I'd let her stew in her cell for a while first."

"She can wait," Samson said. "First, we've gotta figure out how to proceed. We have several main issues to address: damage control, punishment, and deterrence. Suggestions?"

"I say Mick's gotta do a stint at Grass Valley," Grayson said immediately.

Damian wasn't sure whether vampire prison was such a great idea. The prison in Grass Valley housed mostly violent vampires who'd committed unspeakable crimes. "Mick isn't a violent offender. You throw him in there, and he'll turn violent just to survive."

Amaury cast him a sideways look. "Damian isn't wrong. I'm thinking more of community service."

"Community service?" Grayson repeated. "Doing what?"

"Hmm." Samson didn't comment, instead he asked a question. "What about the punishment of the human offender, Cynthia?"

Grayson shrugged. "Wipe her memory, and turn her over to SFPD."

Damian shook his head. "Never gonna fly. Don't you think she's being punished enough by her brother dying? And you want to separate them in the last few days he's got left?"

"Well, how would you punish her then?" Grayson snapped. "She knows too much."

"I agree," Damian said.

"Are you condoning what she did?" Grayson retorted, his eyes narrowing. "What if it had been you she'd been bleeding dry?"

"I wouldn't have been stupid enough in the first place to sell my blood and open myself up to being used like a vending machine," Damian growled.

"So you're blaming Mick for everything?"

"I'm not. But both parties bear responsibility. That's why we can't just toss them both into a cell and throw away the key. That's not a solution."

"Then what is the solution?" Samson suddenly asked, drawing all eyes onto him. "Let's start with damage control, because that's more urgent than punishment. What are our steps?"

"Find out how many vials Mick and Tracy sold and to whom," Damian said immediately.

Grayson nodded eagerly. "And since Mick says that Tracy was the one dealing with the buyers, we'll have to wait until she's conscious and can give us their names."

"Good," Samson said. "What else?"

"Mick can at least tell us how many vials he sold," Damian suggested, "so we'll know how many people we're dealing with."

"And once you have the names?" Samson prompted.

"Wipe their memories," Grayson said.

Samson exchanged a look with Amaury. "We could be dealing with hundreds of people."

Damian shook his head. "Probably not. I found the cash Mick hid in his flat. It couldn't have been more than seven or eight thousand dollars. So we're talking seventy to eighty people. Still quite a bunch, but there could be repeat customers, which would bring the number down."

"True," Samson admitted. "You'll need to question Tracy to find out what she really told these people about what she was selling them. We might not have to erase everybody's memory. At least I hope not."

Damian hoped that too, because erasing a person's memories was draining for a vampire, and time consuming. "That leaves what to do with Mick, Cynthia, and Tracy. And frankly, I'm torn about if and how to punish them all. We need a compromise."

"I agree," Samson said. "A compromise that will satisfy all parties."

"A compromise is all good and well," Grayson said, "but what about Ralph Lassiter? Are we just gonna let him die?"

Surprised to hear compassion in Grayson's voice, Damian looked at him and contemplated his fellow hybrid's words. "You said you brought back the blood that Cynthia drained from Mick?"

"Yeah, I did. Couldn't leave it there for somebody to find."

"Where is it now?"

"Refrigerated in the med center. I figured Maya will give Mick a transfusion later."

"Good. I may have an idea that might make all parties happy, and harm nobody."

"Let's hear it," Samson demanded.

38

When Naomi returned to Scanguards, the sun had set, and the building was buzzing like a beehive. She felt a little better after having taken a shower at home, and gotten changed into fresh clothes. Vanessa met her at the reception.

"Hey, Naomi," Vanessa greeted her. "Damian is downstairs in the med center. I'll bring you to him."

"Oh thanks." They walked toward the elevators together. "How is Tracy? Is she pulling through?"

Vanessa smiled. "Yes, she woke up a little while ago, and Mom says she'll be fine once she's fully detoxed."

"Oh, thank God."

They stepped into the elevator, and Vanessa pressed a button for a lower floor. "Boy, am I glad that drugs have no effect on vampires and hybrids."

"I didn't know that." There were still so many things she didn't know. "I guess that's good."

"Mostly, yes, but that means we can't get drunk either."

"Trust me, you're not missing anything," Naomi said chuckling. "Hangovers are no fun."

The elevator stopped, and the doors opened.

"Come," Vanessa said, and ushered her toward the end of the corridor.

Two double doors led into the clinic. Inside, it looked like an emergency room of a large hospital. It was well-equipped and modern. She spotted Damian immediately. He stood in one of the patient rooms, the door open. The girl sitting up in bed was Tracy. Mick sat on the edge of the bed, holding Tracy's hand, while they both looked at Damian, listening to him.

"Go right in," Vanessa said to her. "I'll see if my mother needs help."

"Thanks, Vanessa," Naomi said quickly and approached Tracy's room. As she stepped closer, she saw that a fourth person was in the room. Grayson stood next to Damian at the foot of the bed.

Before she reached the room, Damian suddenly looked over his shoulder. He motioned her to come in.

"You're back," he said and took her hand. Then he addressed Mick and Tracy. "This is Naomi. Without her we might not have found you both as quickly as we did."

Tracy looked at her. "Thank you so much." She was teary-eyed, and although she was conscious, she still looked exhausted.

"Thank you, Naomi," Mick said with a nod. "Damian told us how much you helped. We're grateful."

"You're welcome. But it was these guys who found you." Naomi motioned to Damian and Grayson. Then she looked at Damian. "So, is everything sorted out now?"

"Almost." He turned his head back to Mick and Tracy. "So, here's the deal. Mick, what you did put all of us in danger of exposure. And that is something we have the right to punish with imprisonment. The same rule goes for Tracy. Therefore—"

"Please don't punish Tracy," Mick begged. "I'll take the punishment. I'm responsible. I'll do her time on top of mine."

Damian lifted his hand. "Hear me out. We have a proposal. We'll wave the sentence if you agree to the following: Tracy, you'll be giving us every single name of your buyers, including how many vials they purchased, and what exactly you told them they were buying."

Tracy nodded eagerly. "I can do that."

"Good. Mick, we have the blood that Cynthia drained from you earlier today. If you agree to let us use the blood to heal Cynthia's twin brother, Ralph, we won't turn you over to the vampire council for punishment. Should we need more blood to heal Ralph, you'll be providing more. Another infraction that puts our entire society in danger, and you'll be turned over to the council. Don't expect any leniency if that happens."

Naomi saw that Mick swallowed hard.

"Yeah," Grayson added, "and guess who'll be pouncing when you slip up? And I'm not as nice as Damian."

Naomi had no trouble believing Grayson's words. He was definitely not as nice as Damian.

"And what will happen to Cynthia?" Tracy asked.

"We'll be erasing her memory," Damian replied. "She won't remember that she ever bought any vampire blood, or that she figured out that Mick is a vampire."

"You're not punishing her?" Mick asked, surprise evident in his voice. "She kidnapped us."

"She won't be imprisoned if that's what you mean. Since she's human, and her crime didn't result in anybody's death, we have no reason to kill her. She's not a danger to society, and despite what she did to you, she's not violent. If it makes you feel better, we'll be watching her once she's released. Should she ever commit another crime against us or anybody else, I assure you we'll take action."

Naomi's heart suddenly pounded. She believed Damian. He wasn't making empty threats.

"Make a decision," Damian demanded. "It's a package deal. All or nothing."

Mick exchanged a look with Tracy. "We agree."

"Good choice," Grayson said. He looked at Damian and gestured to the door. "I can get started with the names of the buyers, if you take care of Ralph."

"No problem," Damian agreed and turned to the door.

Together they left the room, and Damian shut the door behind him. He pulled her into an embrace, and Naomi pressed herself to his chest.

"Just a little while longer," he said, "and we can get out of here. Let's check in on Ralph."

"Will Mick's blood really cure him?" she asked.

"At least it gives him a chance." He released her from his arms and took her hand. Then he let his gaze sweep over the circular room with its treatment bays that were separated by long curtains, just like in a real hospital. "Maya?"

The female physician Naomi had seen earlier when the ambulance had arrived, stepped out of one of the treatment bays. She approached them.

"What's the verdict?" she asked, then cast a quick look at Naomi.

"It's a go."

"All right. Then let's do this before it's too late." She walked toward a large refrigerator and opened it. Naomi watched as she took out a bag filled with blood, then pulled more medical supplies from a drawer. "I already prepared everything. Come. We put him in the long-term patient room."

Maya swung a door open, and Naomi and Damian followed her into another corridor. There she stopped in front of a door. Next to it, a large window afforded a view into the room. To Naomi's surprise this didn't look like a normal hospital room. It was much larger, and was furnished like an expensive hotel suite. Ralph lay on a bed, hooked up to a machine that monitored his vital signs.

When they entered, Ralph turned his head slightly to look at them, but he didn't sit up.

"I want to see my sister," he murmured, his voice weak, his eyes pleading. "I don't have much time left."

Damian stepped closer, and Naomi stood back. "You'll get to see her soon. But first, we have an experimental treatment that can cure the cancer. All we need is your permission to treat you."

"More snake oil? More pain?"

Naomi heard the hopelessness in his voice, and her heart ached for him.

"No pain," Damian promised. "Your sister risked a lot for this. Do you really want her efforts to be in vain?"

Tears welled up in Ralph's eyes, before he closed them. "All right. Do it, but if it doesn't work, just let me die in peace."

"You have my word." Damian stepped aside, and allowed Maya to approach her patient.

"It's a transfusion," Maya explained and hung the bag with Mick's blood onto the IV stand.

Damian took Naomi's hand and led her outside, closing the door behind them. In the corridor, he turned to the window to look back into the room.

"When will we know if it works?" Naomi asked into the silence while they watched Maya set up the IV.

"Soon." Damian let out a sigh. "But there's nothing you and I can do right now. It's in Maya's hands."

She squeezed his hand in reassurance. "I'm glad you're not punishing Ralph for what his sister did."

Damian smiled at her, then stared back into the room. "Samson agreed to it. But Ralph won't remember why his cancer is going into remission. Once he's healthy again, we'll have to wipe his memory. Nobody outside our community can know that vampire blood can heal humans."

"Or they'll hunt you for your blood," Naomi concluded. "No wonder you were so concerned when you realized what was in that little vial I found."

"Yes. And it's not that we don't want to help humans, but when would it stop?"

"It wouldn't. But you're making an exception for Ralph."

"And for the people who work for us, or those who are harmed by a vampire. But that's where our charity has to end. There's only so much blood we can donate without endangering ourselves."

She put her arms around him. "You're a good man, Damian."

"I'm glad you think that." He lowered his face to her and kissed her. "How about we go home? It's been a long day for both of us. We can check on Ralph in the morning."

She yawned. "I think that's a good idea."

39

Damian carried the sleeping Naomi into his flat, and kicked the door shut behind him. She'd fallen asleep in the car on the ride home, and he wasn't surprised. The last twenty-four hours had been draining for him too. Without switching on the light in the living room, he walked to his bedroom and laid her down on the bed. He took her shoes off, then began to undress. He emptied his pockets and placed the items in the drawer in his nightstand. As exhausted as he was, he needed to wash the grime, sweat, and dust off his body.

Naked, he walked into his ensuite bathroom, shut the door behind him, and stepped into the oversized shower. Bracing his hands on the tiles, he let the spray of the warm water run over his head and face and down his body. It washed away some of the tension of the last hours. The water massaged his muscles, and he began to relax.

He wasn't sure how long he'd stood there, when he suddenly heard the creaking hinges of the bathroom door. A smile spread on his face. It appeared that Sleeping Beauty was awake. Slowly, he turned away from the tile wall. When his eyes fell on Naomi, he nearly choked. In the span of two seconds, his cock rose from its sleep, pumping full of blood quicker than ever before.

Naomi stood in front of the shower, dressed in her Little Red Riding Hood costume—minus the cape. Her boobs were nearly spilling out over the top, and she was barefoot.

"When did you—"

"—bring more clothes?" she asked with a coquettish smile. "Your mom suggested I bring a few things from home. She said if you're anything like your father, I wouldn't get a chance to go to my place for a while. She came to my flat with me, and then she dropped the bag off here. I hope that's all right."

"All right? Remind me to buy my mother an enormous bunch of flowers." Then he stepped out of the shower and pulled her to him. He slid his arms down to her ass and pushed up the ultra-short skirt, realizing immediately that she wore no panties. "I think you forgot to pack underwear."

She lifted her face up to his. "I didn't think I'd need it. Or do I?"

"No, you don't," he murmured and captured her lips.

He invaded her mouth and danced with her tongue, his need for sleep suddenly gone. Naomi kissed him back with the same enthusiasm, her hands traveling over his wet skin, igniting a fire inside him that threatened to incinerate him. He ripped his lips from hers and turned her in his arms so she faced the mirror over the vanity, and he stood behind her.

He didn't need to tell her what he wanted, because the little vixen in his arms had planned this, knowing exactly what turned him on, and made him as randy as a sailor, and half as refined.

She leaned over the marble countertop, her perfect ass pointing at him. Damian gripped her hips, and met her gaze in the mirror. She looked at him with passion-clouded eyes, then tugged on her bustier and pulled it down sufficiently so her tits popped out over the top, her nipples stiff.

"Ah, fuck!" he cursed. "This is gonna be over really fast."

"Fuck me already."

He didn't need to be told twice, and slid his cock between her thighs. When its tip touched her pussy, warmth and wetness welcomed him, and he thrust into her without preamble.

Naomi gasped at the forceful invasion and gripped the countertop for balance. She was slick and tight. Perfect for him. While he fucked her from behind, sliding in and out of her, his tempo increasing with every second, he looked in the mirror and watched her breasts as they bounced up and down. He'd never seen a more erotic sight. He lifted his gaze and met Naomi's eyes as she watched him, her lips parted, her face a tableau of passion. She panted, her breaths uneven, her heartbeat accelerated, the scent of her blood intensifying as her body heated.

He released one hand from her hip and reached for the zipper of her bustier, pulling it down. Her breasts spilled out fully, and she moaned.

"Touch them," she begged.

He slowed his thrusts, and cupped one breast, squeezing it in his palm. He loved the feel of her responsive flesh filling his palm, the hard nipple brushing against his skin. On his next thrust, he released her other hip too and captured her left breast, kneading it in the same way he touched the right, before he continued pounding into her.

"Oh, yes, baby." She moaned. "Just like that." Her eyelids fluttered. "Oh, I love your cock. I love how you take me."

"'Cause you're mine, all mine." Their gazes collided in the mirror. "I'll make you mine tonight."

Her eyes sparkled. "Yes."

He pulled himself from her sheath and whirled her around. "Yes? You want to blood-bond with me? Now? For all eternity?"

Naomi ran her hands over his chest and slid them to his nape. "Yes, forever. I want you to be mine. My vampire, my mate. I want you to drink only from me."

He pushed the costume down over her hips until it pooled at her feet, then lifted her into his arms. "Only from you. From your neck, your breasts, your thighs." He carried her into the bedroom, and laid her on the bed, the light from the open bathroom door shining on her hair. It was fanned out around her head like a halo. "I love you."

~ ~ ~

Naomi looked up at Damian as he stood next to the bed looking down at her. His cock was hard and coated in her juices, his eyes were shimmering golden, and his fangs were fully extended. Oh God, how she loved this man, this vampire. She'd never seen a more beautiful creature or a sexier one. He embodied everything she'd ever dreamed of. She could see it in his eyes now, and hear it in his voice: the love he felt for her, the certainty with which he pledged his eternal devotion to her. She understood the risk he was taking by asking her to blood-bond with him. He was making himself vulnerable for her.

"Your heart will always be safe with me," she promised and reached for him. "Make me yours, because I can't imagine living life without you."

Damian joined her on the bed, and braced himself above her. She spread her legs wider, making space for him, and she pulled his face to hers. "I want to lick them."

Damian plunged into her, and moaned. "Go easy on me. I'm already on the edge."

She chuckled softly "Why's that?"

"You little minx. As if you didn't know."

He withdrew and thrust back into her, and the feeling of his cock stretching her pussy made a contented sigh roll over her lips.

"Next time you play dress-up, pick a time when I'm well-rested so I can take my time to play." He smirked. "Now, didn't you want to lick my fangs?"

Damian opened his mouth and showed her his deadly canines. She'd never imagined that she would find this sight erotic, but she did. To know what she could do to him by licking them, made her feel powerful. Slowly, she drew him closer until their lips were almost touching. Gently, she swiped her tongue over one fang then ran it along his teeth to the other side to lick his other fang. She noticed Damian's eyes close as he sucked in a breath.

All of a sudden, he pulled back his head. "That's all I can take right now." He began to thrust in and out of her, first in a steady, slow rhythm while he kissed her deeply, taking his time to explore her mouth the same way she explored him.

Beneath her hands, Damian's skin was soft and warm, the muscles beneath it firm and strong. She would never have the kind of sculpted body he had, but it didn't matter anymore, because the way Damian looked at her, the way he touched her and made love to her, made her feel beautiful inside and out. His cock inside her made her feel desirable, and his lips on hers made her feel adored.

With every thrust, she felt her arousal rise. Her skin tingled pleasantly, and her clit throbbed every time their bodies came together. When Damian severed the kiss, she knew instinctively that it was time.

He looked at her as he lifted one hand, and she watched his fingers turn into sharp claws like those of a beast. He used one claw to slice into the perfect skin on his shoulder. Blood oozed from the wound.

"Drink from me. Make me yours, and I'll make you mine."

Damian lowered himself, and she licked over the incision, lapping up the blood. She closed her eyes, letting the taste spread in her mouth. A jolt went through her. Damian's blood didn't taste metallic like she'd expected. No, it was rich and sweet, and it made her suddenly feel more aware of her own body—and of his.

"Oh my God," she murmured and put her mouth over the incision.

As she began to suck and drink more of Damian's blood, he lowered his face to the crook of her neck. "This is better than I ever thought it would be," he murmured. "I love you."

He licked over the spot where she could now feel her vein drum against her skin as if to signal to him what she wanted. Then she felt his sharp fangs pierce her skin and lodge in her neck, while his cock plunged deep and hard.

Her entire body felt as if she were floating on a bed of cotton balls, and out of nowhere, she climaxed. Every cell in her body seemed to explode like little fireworks in the night sky. And every time she thought she would pass out from the intense pleasure, more waves of pure bliss crashed over her. Damian's cock spasmed inside her, and she felt the warm spray of his semen fill her.

I'm yours now, Naomi. Forever yours.

She heard the voice in her head, and knew it was Damian's, even though he couldn't have spoken because he was still drinking from her neck, just as she was drinking from him.

Damian? What is this?

Damian lifted his head from her neck and licked over the puncture wounds, while he slowed his thrusts.

"It's a way for a blood-bonded couple to communicate," he said with a smile. "Forgot to mention that earlier. But you seduced me, and I didn't get a chance to tell you all the other things you don't know yet."

Naomi laughed softly. "Telepathy, huh? I can't believe it."

"Believe it. And there's something else I didn't get a chance to do."

"What's that?"

"There's a party at Scanguards this weekend. And there's something I want you to wear for it."

"Another costume?"

Damian reached toward the nightstand and opened the top drawer. When she saw him retrieve a small jewelry box from it, she gasped in surprise.

"I'd planned to get down on one knee tomorrow to ask you to be my wife and my blood-bonded mate, but then you dressed up as Little Red Riding Hood, and all my good intentions went out the window."

He grinned and opened the box. Amidst a cushion of black velvet sat a platinum ring with a center diamond framed by two blue sapphires.

"Oh my God, Damian..." She'd never seen anything more beautiful.

"Will you wear it to show everybody that you're mine?"

Tears rose to her eyes, and she nodded, choking up. "I didn't need a ring. Having you is all I want."

His eyes sparkled. "I know that." He paused for a moment, then added, "I can always return it."

"Don't! I love it."

Damian threw his head back and laughed. "Then let me put it on your finger." He slid the ring onto her finger, and it fit perfectly. "How about a kiss for your mate?"

"I can do better than that." She brought her hands to her breasts and pushed them up, making her nipples brush Damian's chest. "I don't think you're done with your dinner yet. How about dessert?"

"You're spoiling me," he murmured. He gazed at her breasts and licked his lips. "But I'm not one to turn down such an enticing offer. You're too generous."

"I do have an ulterior motive," she admitted.

He raised an eyebrow. "Which is?"

"If I give you more blood, you might make love to me again, despite you being tired."

Damian chuckled softly. "Can't argue with that."

He sank his mouth onto one nipple, and licked over it, making her moan out loud. When she felt the sharp tip of his fangs on either side of her nipple, her heart began to beat excitedly. The moment she felt the sharp canines lodge in her breast, her entire body felt as if she was floating on a cloud of bliss.

I love your bite.

And I love your blood, he replied, *my insatiable temptress.*

40

"What's the reason for the party anyway?" Naomi asked as the elevator opened on the first floor of Scanguards HQ.

Damian let his eyes roam over her lovely body. She wore an azure-blue cocktail dress with a wide, flowing skirt and a tight bustier that accentuated her ample breasts. In the last forty-eight hours they'd barely left the bed, and he'd bitten her on every conceivable spot on her body, greedily drinking her delicious blood. Naomi hadn't turned him down a single time. On the contrary, she'd seduced him at every turn, demanding he make love to her every waking moment.

Earlier today, he'd woken from an erotic dream, only to realize that it wasn't a dream. No, Naomi was really sucking his rock-hard cock with such skill that he'd woken just when he was climaxing and shooting his seed into her mouth. Fuck, just remembering that moment made him want to drag her back into the elevator and drive back home so they could continue where they'd left off.

"Uh, the party." He cleared his throat. Did she know what he was imagining right now?

"You're naughty," Naomi murmured and cast him a sinful sideways glance. "I guess I have to do that more often."

"Fuck, *chérie*," he cursed, realizing how easily Naomi could read him, and not just because they had a telepathic bond. "You can do that anytime you want. But we have to attend this damn party right now. Just for a little while anyway." For the first time he truly understood his parents, and the fact that they couldn't keep their hands off each other even in public—because he felt the same with Naomi.

She smirked. "Okay. So, what's the occasion for this party?"

"One of our former employees is visiting with his wife from New Orleans. We haven't seen him in a while, so Samson decided to throw a party." He smiled at her. "It's perfect timing, because I want to show you off and introduce you to everybody."

"Do they all know that we're blood-bonded now?"

"My parents know, and they're so happy about it that I'm sure the news has spread like wildfire. Or why do you think Benjamin has made himself scarce the last two days? He wanted to give us some privacy."

Naomi's cheeks turned rosy. "That's very considerate of him. But you can't expect him to stay away from his flat forever."

He winked, and leaned in. "I know. That's why you'll have to let me know where in San Francisco you'd like to live, so I can buy us a house or a condo, whatever you want."

"Are you serious?"

"Of course, I am." Had she really thought they'd be sharing a flat with his twin? As much as he loved his brother, he wanted to live alone with Naomi. Well, until they had kids, though he didn't want to start a family as quickly as Ryder. He wanted time alone with Naomi first. "Now, let's party."

He swiped his access card at the card reader outside the V lounge and opened the door. Inside the large room, vampires, hybrids, and their mates and children were already assembled. The lights were festive, and jazz music was coming from the speakers in the ceiling. The seating areas had been rearranged so that there was space to dance later. The bar in the middle of the room that normally served only blood on tap, offered wine and other spirits tonight, as well as finger food.

"Scanguards really likes their parties, don't they?" Naomi said from next to him.

Most women were dressed in pretty cocktail dresses, most men in elegant suits just like Damian. He caught Eddie's eye, and ushered Naomi in his direction.

"This is my uncle, Eddie," Damian said. "This is Naomi, my—"

"Mate," Eddie finished his sentence and grinned. "I heard." He pulled Naomi into his arms and hugged her. "Sorry we didn't get a chance to talk the other day in the conference room. Welcome to the family."

"Thank you, Eddie," Naomi replied.

When he released her, Thomas emerged from the crowd, and made a beeline for them.

"This is my mate, Thomas," Eddie said.

Thomas slapped his hand on Damian's shoulder, before he hugged Naomi briefly. "Damian sure has an eye for beautiful women."

Pride filled Damian's chest.

"And jewelry," Eddie added and took Naomi's hand to look more closely at her ring. "A perfect match to your eyes. It looks great on you, Naomi."

Naomi beamed. "Thank you."

Damian met her loving gaze. *I love you.*

"Do you have the feeling we're the third wheel?" Thomas asked with a look at Eddie.

"Reminds me of how my sister and Amaury look at each other," Eddie said with a smirk. "Like father like son."

Damian rolled his eyes. "Trust me, you two aren't any better at hiding your feelings."

"Fair point," Thomas said dryly. Then he changed the subject. "Have you spoken to Maya yet?"

"No." A sense of dread surfaced. "Don't tell me Ralph isn't doing well."

"Relax, he's actually doing great. Maya did a CT scan, and the cancer cells are dying off. She thinks another three or four days of transfusions, and he'll be free of cancer."

"Thank God!" Damian let out a sigh of relief, and he saw Naomi let out the breath she'd been holding.

"I'm so happy for him," Naomi said, and a wet sheen appeared in her eyes.

Damian pulled her to him. "See? It'll all turn out fine. We can go visit him later, if you want."

Naomi sniffled. "I'd like that."

All of a sudden, the music died down, and Damian's attention was drawn to the area in front of the fireplace, where Samson stood with Delilah by his side. Next to them were Cain and his mate Faye.

"Time for the obligatory speech," Eddie murmured under his breath.

Samson raised his hand, and all conversations died down. "Thank you all for coming. When I started planning this party a short while ago, I could have never imagined, how timely it would turn out to be. Thanks to all your efforts, we were able to avert another threat that could have exposed our secrets. For that I'm grateful to all of you."

He smiled, and his gaze searched the crowd until it rested on Damian and Naomi.

"As a result of the events of the last week, one of our own has found true love. Please join me in congratulating Damian and Naomi on their blood-bond. Damian, you couldn't have made a better choice."

The crowd clapped, and several people whistled.

"Thank you, all," Damian said and pulled Naomi close to his side. "I'm just lucky that Naomi picked me."

"And not me," Benjamin called out from across the room. "No offence, Naomi, but I'm not ready to be shackled yet."

Laughter erupted in the room. As it died down, Samson continued, "But the reason I planned this party in the first place was to celebrate something else." He looked at Cain and Faye. "Many of you know Cain Montague, the vampire king of Louisiana from the time when he was a bodyguard for Scanguards."

Next to Damian, Naomi whispered, "Is he serious? He's a king?"

Damian brought his mouth to her ear. "Yes, he is. I'll tell you the story later."

"We've been talking about this for a few months now, and finally, we're ready to make the announcement. Cain?"

Cain grinned. "Scanguards will be opening a branch in New Orleans. Thank you, Samson, and also a big thank you to Brandon King for not only making the suggestion, but also for funding the expansion."

The audience clapped and cheered.

"Okay, speeches are over," Samson announced. "Let's dance!"

"Who's Brandon King?" Naomi asked.

"Remember the housewarming party? He's Scarlet's father."

"Oh."

"Now, how about a dance?" Damian asked, and already pulled Naomi toward the dance floor.

She chuckled. "But you have to behave."

"Don't I always behave?"

Before Naomi could reply, Damian's gaze fell on Orlando, who stood at the edge of the dance floor, looking serious as always.

"Hey, Damian," he said and nodded. "Congratulations." He offered his hand, and Damian shook it. Then he shook Naomi's hand too, not making any attempt at a hug, which Damian appreciated. "Congratulations to you too, Naomi. I wish you all the best."

"Thank you, Orlando."

Damian pulled Naomi into his arms, and they started dancing. On the next turn, his gaze fell on Orlando again. His facial expression suddenly changed from one of indifference and seriousness to one of hunger and lust. He'd never seen Orlando like that.

Curious to find out who elicited such a reaction in the stoic bodyguard and bouncer, Damian followed his gaze. It landed on Isabelle, Samson's daughter. She was dancing with Brandon King and laughing at something he said.

~ ~ ~

"How long are you guys staying?" Samson asked with a look at Cain and Faye, while he snaked his arm around Delilah's waist.

"At least a week," Cain replied. "We need the break, right, baby?"

Faye rolled her eyes. "It's not that bad."

Samson furrowed his forehead. "What's going on?"

"The triplets," Faye said. "They can be a bit much at times."

"But they're grown up," Delilah interjected.

"They just turned thirty-one, didn't they?" Samson added.

"And your point is?" Cain asked with a deadpan look. He ran a hand through his short dark hair. "I swear, they're taking years off my life."

"You're immortal," Faye said with a smirk.

Cain grimaced. "So are they."

"You're having trouble with the boys?" Delilah asked softly. "It's normal. That's what boys are like."

"Oh, it's not Zach and David I'm complaining about. It's Monique."

"Monique?" Delilah asked.

"She's headstrong, opinionated, rebellious, and—"

Faye put a hand on her mate's forearm. "Monique is just trying to find her place in life. It's not easy growing up as a princess."

"A princess who picks a fight with anybody about anything every single day." Cain shook his head and met Samson's eyes. "It's exhausting. Frankly, I don't know where she gets the energy from."

Samson chuckled. "We all have a problem child."

"Are you saying Isabelle is the same?" Cain asked with interest.

"God, no!" Samson replied immediately. "She's the best daughter a father could imagine. Smart, sweet, loving." He exchanged a smile with Delilah. "Right, sweetness?"

"We're so proud of her."

"Now Grayson, on the other hand…" Samson added. "Show him a wall, and he'll ram his head into it."

"And guess from whom he inherited that stubbornness," Delilah said.

"Ouch," Samson said in mock-pain, before he looked at Cain again. "And he goes through women as if they were going out of fashion."

"Sounds like somebody I know," Cain said with a grin. "Monique leaves broken hearts in her wake like beads during Mardi Gras. Sometimes I wish that she'd meet a guy who treats her the same, just so she'll learn that she can't just run roughshod over everybody."

Samson nodded in agreement. "Yeah, I hear you. And I wish Grayson would finally meet a woman who gives as good as she gets. My son needs a firm hand, or he'll never grow up."

For a moment, nobody said anything, when he noticed Cain cast a look at Faye.

She shook her head. "You wouldn't…"

But Cain looked back at Samson. "Maybe there is a solution to both our problems."

"You know what?" Samson said, the wheels in his head turning, latching on to Cain's unspoken idea. "It might not be such a bad idea."

"You can't," Delilah said with a gasp and looked at him and Cain. "It'll never work. The moment they realize that you're setting them up, they'll refuse to even talk to each other, just to spite you."

"Then we'll just have to make sure they don't know that they're being set up," Samson said with a grin, liking the idea more and more by the second.

"How hard could it be?" Cain commented.

"This'll blow up in your faces," Faye warned, and Delilah nodded.

Samson grinned. "We'll see about that." Then he changed the subject. "Now, how about a dance, sweetness?"

~ ~ ~

Reading Order Scanguards Vampires & Stealth Guardians

Scanguards Vampires

Prequel Novella: Mortal Wish
Book 1: Samson's Lovely Mortal
Book 2: Amaury's Hellion
Book 3: Gabriel's Mate
Book 4: Yvette's Haven
Book 5: Zane's Redemption
Book 6: Quinn's Undying Rose
Book 7: Oliver's Hunger
Book 8: Thomas's Choice
Novella 8 ½: Silent Bite
Book 9: Cain's Identity

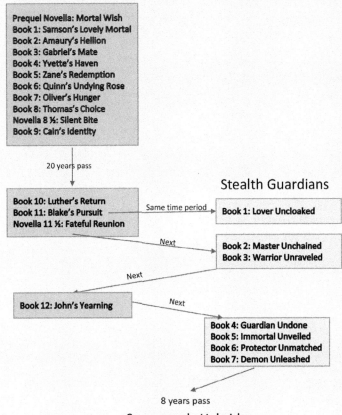

20 years pass

Book 10: Luther's Return
Book 11: Blake's Pursuit
Novella 11 ½: Fateful Reunion

Same time period →

Stealth Guardians

Book 1: Lover Uncloaked

Next

Book 2: Master Unchained
Book 3: Warrior Unraveled

Next

Book 12: John's Yearning

Next

Book 4: Guardian Undone
Book 5: Immortal Unveiled
Book 6: Protector Unmatched
Book 7: Demon Unleashed

8 years pass

Scanguards Hybrids

The Scanguards Hybrids will also be numbered within the Scanguards
Vampires series (SV 13 = SH 1) to preserve continuity.

Book 1 (SV 13): Ryder's Storm
Book 2 (SV 14): Damian's Conquest

More to come...

ABOUT THE AUTHOR

Tina Folsom was born in Germany and has been living in English speaking countries for over 25 years, since 2001 in California, where she married an American.

Tina has always been a bit of a globe trotter. She lived in Munich (Germany), Lausanne (Switzerland), London (England), New York City, Los Angeles, San Francisco, and Sacramento. She has now made a beach town in Southern California her permanent home with her husband and her dog.

She's written 47 romance novels in English most of which are translated into German, French, and Spanish. Under her pen name T.R. Folsom, she also writes thrillers.

For more about Tina Folsom:
http://www.tinawritesromance.com
http://trfolsom.com
http://www.instagram.com/authortinafolsom
http://www.facebook.com/TinaFolsomFans
https://www.youtube.com/c/TinaFolsomAuthor
tina@tinawritesromance.com

Printed in Great Britain
by Amazon